THE MEASURE
OF A MASTER

"This volume can only hint at Dickson's diversity, his continuous development, his lifelong striving toward higher peaks. . . . He is among the best storytellers we have ever had. Yet Dickson is far more than a spinner of yarns with which we can pass an agreeable hour. These are damn good narratives. You can read them for their action, invention, people, way with words, and enormously enjoy them. But if you read them over again, or just sit and think about them for a while, you'll realize they have shown you something that at the time you were not aware you were seeing. . . ."

—Poul Anderson, from his *Introduction*

Look for all these TOR books by Gordon R. Dickson

BEYOND THE DAR AL-HARB
HOKA! (with Poul Anderson)
THE LAST MASTER
THE MAN FROM EARTH
THE OUTPOSTER
PLANET RUN (with Keith Laumer)
THE PRITCHER MASS
SLEEPWALKERS' WORLD
STEEL BROTHER

GORDON R. DICKSON

STEEL BROTHER

A TOM DOHERTY ASSOCIATES BOOK

STEEL BROTHER

Copyright © 1985 by Gordon R. Dickson

First printing: December 1985

A TOR Book

Published by Tom Doherty Associates
49 West 24 Street
New York, N.Y. 10010

Cover art by Alan Gutierrez

ISBN: 0-812-53552-9
CAN. ED.: 0-812-53553-7

Printed in the United States of America

Acknowledgments

"Introduction" by Poul Anderson copyright © 1985 by Poul Anderson.

"Out of the Darkness" copyright © 1961 by Davis Publications, Inc. First published in February 1961, *Ellery Queen Mystery Magazine*, volume 37, number 2. Reprinted by permission of the author.

"The Man in the Mailbag" copyright © 1959 by Galaxy Publishing Corporation. First published in April 1959, *Galaxy*.

"The Hard Way" copyright © 1963 by Conde Nast Publications. First published in January 1963, *Analog*.

"Perfectly Adjusted" copyright © 1955 by Columbia Publications. First published in July 1955, *Science Fiction Stories*.

"Steel Brother" copyright © 1952 by Street and Smith Publications, Inc. First published in February 1952, *Astounding*.

"The Childe Cycle Status Report" copyright © 1979 by Gordon R. Dickson. First published in *SFWA Bulletin*, Fall 1979.

"A Conversation With Gordon R. Dickson" by Sandra Miesel copyright © 1978 by Algol Magazine. Part was first published in Spring 1978, *Algol*.

Contents

Introduction

by Poul Anderson

Over the years, Gordon R. Dickson and I have written quite a few pieces about each other, for convention programs and the like. Requests to do this are very natural, it being well-known that we are old friends and occasional collaborators. The actual writing has always been a pleasant little task—for me, at least, and I hope for Gordy too. Still, eventually and inevitably one comes to feel that one has nothing more to say, and next time somebody else with a fresh viewpoint should get the job.

Thus I admit having hesitated for a moment when invited to introduce this book. However, as soon as it became clear what the project was, I accepted with delight and, what's more, a sense of having been honored. Of course, it's a challenge and even a danger. My words are going to be right in the same volume as his. They'll suffer by comparison. Yet, conceivably, they may throw an extra bit of light on their subject. If nothing else, an undertaking like this deserves an honest effort on the part of everybody concerned.

It is a noble gesture by the New England Science Fiction Association, publishing a book of Dickson writings on the occasion of the author's being guest of honor at the 1984

World Science Fiction Convention in Los Angeles. The gesture is twice meaningful because that guest of honorship is so grotesquely overdue. We owe the Los Angeles people heartfelt thanks for their recognition of Gordon R. Dickson's stature in science fiction. Not that that has been in question for many years. But—without reflecting in any way on his predecessors, all of whom have been worthy—throughout that time I felt it was a discredit to the system of world conventions, that we were consistently failing to pay our highest respects to one of the finest makers that our field has ever known.

Now, at last!

This collection will give you some idea of my reason for advancing the claim. As if you didn't already know. . . . But there is the sad fact that a certain percentage of convention goers these days read little or nothing. They watch the tube and the movies, turn the pages of comic books, and that's about it. Others are literate, but so new to science fiction, often because of youth, that they are unaware of most of its classics and of who the real giants are among those still working today. In either case, through these stories they can meet a great writer. As for the majority, those for whom the name "Gordon R. Dickson" already is charged with magic, why, here's a splendid review of the past, overview of the present, and prospectus for the future.

Publishing resources are finite. The only way really to show what the author can do would be through a uniform edition of his collected works. This small volume can merely hint at his diversity and, by including items from a time span of some thirty years, his continuous development, his lifelong striving toward ever higher peaks.

I do not propose to discuss the contents. Those speak for themselves. Rather let me say something about the context, the entire body of Gordon R. Dickson's art, and about the man himself.

The latter is not really necessary to the former. Nobody alive has met, say, Shakespeare, and indeed our knowledge of him as a person is slight. That doesn't interfere with our appreciation of his writings. Yet it would be fascinating to learn what happened to him throughout his years on earth, and just where he got those crazy ideas. (I don't mean the plots; their sources are well documented. I mean the characters, the situations. Kipling's poem "The Craftsman" offers some wonderful speculations, but they are only speculations.) Gordy, happily, is still with us. But not all his admirers can meet him face to face. Those who can't may enjoy a few remarks about him as a human being, which he most thoroughly is.

There is no point in my giving a biographical sketch, because you will find his own autobiographical notes in the account of the Childe cycle which this book includes. Excellent notes they are, too, clear, concise, neither boastful nor bashful. From them you'll get some idea of his intellectual side. People do, though, have other aspects than that, so let me reminisce a bit.

Toward the end of 1947, the Minneapolis Fantasy Society began meeting again. This had been a fan club consisting mainly of boys, among whose activities were the writing of so-called "silly stories" and sitting worshipfully at the feet of Clifford D. Simak. I hasten to add that that kindly and modest gentleman has never sought adulation; he simply couldn't avoid becoming a father figure. America entered the war; presently most members of the MFS—including Gordy—went into military service; and when at last they came back home and agreed to reconstitute the organization, they were no longer boys but young men. A few had settled elsewhere or died, and various newcomers appeared.

I was one, then in my senior year at the University of Minnesota and rather lonely. When a letter of mine was published in a magazine, I got an invitation to join the

group. That first evening was unforgettable: meeting Mr.
Simak himself, going on with kindred spirits to drink beer
and talk, then after the bars closed to drink coffee and talk
until the sun rose on my course back to my lodgings. . . .
In the time that followed, friendships were formed that
will endure as long as a single party remains to remember.
Such was mine with Gordy.

From the beginning, his goal in life had been to write.
That was not mine, except perhaps as a sideline; I hoped to
become a physicist. However, when I graduated in 1948 it
was into a recession. Jobs were hard to find and there was
no money left for postgraduate studies. Having sold a few
stories while still in college, and being a bachelor who had
had no chance to develop expensive tastes, I thought I'd
support myself by writing while looking around for steady
employment. Somehow that while got longer and longer.
Surely Gordy's example helped me realize at length that
writing was what I, too, was actually cut out for.

I had rented a light-housekeeping room. For a time,
Gordy had a room in the same place. Although our work
habits were dissimilar, more evenings than not one of us
would knock on the door of the other—"Am I interrupt-
ing? Uh, if you're through for the day, why don't we go
get a beer?"—and likely as not we'd find somebody else
in the bar, and it would be talk and chess and discordant
song till closing time.

For both of us, this was a hand-to-mouth existence.
Soon Gordy found it more practical to move back to his
mother's home. Needless to say, he paid his share of
expenses there, and in later years has devotedly seen to the
well-being of that charming and courageous lady. Otherwise nothing changed much, on the surface. The MFS
gradually ceased to be an organized club and became just a
circle of friends, but they were close and got together
often. Once I returned from some expedition and heard
that Gordy had come around to visit, and waited for me as

long as possible before leaving. He'd used my typewriter to whack out a *Morte d'Arthur* parody which is still among my cherished keepsakes: wildly comical, unprintably bawdy.

Humor was, and is, a vital part of his character. It has always been gentle, and not uncommonly directed at himself. For instance, he was among the several co-authors of a *Macbeth* burlesque done for a Hallowe'en party, and played the role of doddering old King Dickson—and afterward the king's ineffectual ghost—to such perfection that the performance was repeated next year by popular demand.

His own misadventures may have inspired some of this. I hope he won't mind my remarking that in those days he was not exactly the best-organized person I have ever met. (Nor was I.) And a good thing, too. His basic ambition, to write, was a steady flame within him, but on occasion he would fumble a bit or bite off more than he could chew. This was probably necessary. If you try all things, you are bound to fail at some, but you learn thereby. The person who never strays from a carefully planned path through life has a narrow soul.

Memories come crowding. We were young, not yet broken to harness, kicking up our heels. We two and Ted Cogswell, taking over the bar car on a train to Chicago . . . a street in the small hours after the taverns had closed, I striding along carrying Gordy in my arms—heaven knows why, as he was neither disabled nor a beautiful woman— bawling out "*Die Beiden Grenadiere*" at the top of my lungs while Ollie Saari ran ahead of us flapping his arms to see if he could fly . . . the German Dinner Club, whose members gorged on sausage and sauerkraut and bierkaese and pumpernickel, and when the host's wife came back to the apartment the smell nearly knocked her over . . . pounding out nonsensical stories turn by turn at the typewriter, not for sale but because it was fun . . . softball in summer, rough touch football in autumn, Nanks vs. Geeps . . . cross-country trips to conventions, fishing on the multitudinous lakes, wild celebration when a check came in sufficient for a little more than beans and beer. . . . It wasn't pure joy, of course. We experienced the frustrations of being poor, we had our disappointments in love, we got screwed up, down, and sideways by assorted publishers and copy editors, for back then science fiction writers were at the bottom of the totem pole. On the whole, life has vastly improved since, for both Gordy and myself. Nevertheless I am very glad to have had those years.

That was when his own career was getting started, about which more will follow. Here I should mention our collaborations. They originated with a farcical time travel story and went on to the earlier parts of the "Hoka" series. Now, collaborations resemble marriages in that no two are alike. In Gordy's and my case, we'd kick an idea around conversationally until we thought we'd know what we were doing. Then he, having the more imaginative sense of humor, would turn out a first draft. I, having perhaps the more methodical mind, would rewrite, tying up loose ends and adding whatever bits of business occurred to me. Usually that was enough. We have afterward continued in this fashion, although Gordy doesn't really need anyone to make his logic four-square for him.

These subsequent joint efforts have been few and far between, partly because I moved to California in 1953 while Gordy, whose heart is in the Upper Midwest, stayed in Minneapolis. Far too seldom since have we come together. This has not eroded the bond between us. Whenever I have visited his town, his hospitality has been boundless; I hope my wife and I have shown him a good time on our turf; always we are instantly at home with each other. May there be many more such meetings.

As his income and prestige began to grow, Gordy began to take more thought about the practical aspects than either of us had done before. In due course he had his business

organized to a degree which only a handful of his colleagues can even imagine, let alone accomplish. Today he
lives in a house comfortable and gracious. The work space
within it is better equipped than most offices of any kind.
An assistant frees him from such chores as consume the
time, energy, and spirit of most of us. He is a shrewd
negotiator with publishers and producers. Without being
hypochondriacal, by care and diligence he copes with the
ills that flesh is heir to. All this is to the end of enabling
him to realize his creative dreams.

Not that he is a recluse or a fanatic. On the contrary, he
is one of the world's great bon vivants. Hardly ever have I
wined and dined better than under Gordy's leadership, and
certainly never in better company. He sings and plays the
guitar well, has composed a number of ballads that are
popular in "filk" circles, and—ladies tell me—swings a
goodly shoe on the dance floor. His friends are legion,
because he travels widely, especially to science fiction
conventions. There he is always amiable, always accessi-
ble even to the lowliest neo-fan, always himself.

I cannot but wonder if this may be the reason that his
honors at the principal annual gathering come so belatedly.
We take too much for granted the things that are simply
and continuously there, like sunshine, fresh air, and stars.

This may even be true of Gordy's writing. It has by no
means gone unnoticed or unappreciated—except, to some
degree, among critics, and who in his right mind pays any
attention to them? Readers respond to the traditional virtues that his work embodies, as they have responded since
'Omer smote 'is bloomin' lyre. These virtues include solid
plots, believable backgrounds, three- and four-dimensional
characters; but this sounds pretty dull, and anything by
Dickson is anything but. Let's say instead that he is among
the best *storytellers* we have ever had. So, for example, the
sheer vigor and colorfulness of the Childe Cycle has evoked

quite a cult, with songs and uniformed Dorsai Irregulars and everything else.

Yet Gordon R. Dickson is far more than a spinner of yarns with which we can pass an occasional agreeable hour. He understands that if we want sermons we can best go to church, if we want a course in philosophy we can best go to college. What he has to teach is much more subtle and goes much more deep. Therefore, as his medium he uses tales that grip the emotions and engage the mind. It is the only possible one.

Repeat: these are damn good narratives. You can read and enormously enjoy them for their action, invention, people, way with words. But if you read them over again, or just sit and think about them for a while, you'll realize they have shown you something that at the time you were not aware you were seeing.

Oh, yes, Gordy's done his share of stories that are funny or suspenseful or ingenious and little else. What's wrong with that? Neither writers nor readers can forever sail close-hauled in half a gale; sometimes we want, need, to clip along lee rail under on a broad reach, or ghost wing and wing before the lightest and balmiest of breezes. How fondly I recall such comedies as "Zeepsday," such adventures as "The Hard Way," even such grimnesses as "The Monkey Wrench"—to name only three fairly short items.

But from the first, Gordon R. Dickson was ranging farther. As an illustration, consider "Computers Don't Argue," which opens hilariously with a book club subscriber trying to straighten out a minor problem and closes with a stark warning that is still more appropriate today than it was when he wrote it. "Black Charlie" has as much to say about what art really is and means as do, in their quite different ways, Merejcovski's *The Romance of Leonardo da Vinci* and van Loon's *R.v.R. St. Dragon and the George*, although a gorgeous romp, has its elements of heroism and tragedy. *Naked to the Stars* is a searing and thundering denunciation of militarism. The author is, however, no pacifist, but sympathizes with the decent soldier, recognizes what need we sometimes have of him, and looks unflinchingly at the often agonizing dilemmas he confronts. "Call Him Lord" is about loves and duties in conflict, a motif which pervades the Childe stories.

Their gigantic cycle has become what the creator regards as his true lifework. If I refrain from commenting on it, that is largely because his essay in the present volume does so far better than I could hope to. Besides, it is still growing—like Yggdrasil, with roots in unknown depths and crown in the heavens, boughs bearing worlds and leaves enshadowing mystery. Nobody else has ever dared anything like this.

Some people suppose that an outstanding writer is a menace to other writers, that he or she will crowd them out. This is dead wrong. Literature, like every art, is not a zero-sum game. The enemy is the bad writer, who harms the reputation of his entire field. The good one enhances it, thereby attracting readership for everybody else, too. Perhaps more importantly, the excellent writer inspires colleagues to do better than they thought they were able. For these things we are all of us, readers and writers alike, in the debt of Gordon R. Dickson. At long last we are paying him the homage that is his due by right of achievement.

Whatever genre he writes, common concerns flash through all of Gordon Dickson's work. Here in a mystery story he dramatizes a proposition—later elaborated in Necromancer— *that intention determines the significance of an action. This is an ethical principle dating back to the medieval philosopher Peter Abelard. The hero's response to challenge also illustrates the scholastic notion that vice and virtue are essentially habits. When put to the test, his well-trained conscience shows "an affirming flame."*

Out of the Darkness

The bright sun of noon slanted through the lower-floor window of the lighthouse and lay square across the letter he was writing. But the pen wavered in his fingers and the inked lines blurred through the quick, soft tears of age. He blinked his eyes clear and read again: "—*so thank you again, Maddy, but I cannot come. It would not work out. You have always been a wonderful niece to me and I would like to see the boys again; but after twenty-nine years my heart is hear*"

He paused to cross out the last word and write it correctly. In little things he was failing too. He licked dry lips and his throat was stiff with pain. He went on: "*here. Possibly they can find something for me to do on shore around the harbor up at Lynd. I do not see why they could not let me stay at least a few years more but it is the*"

*government that sets the retirement age and they do not
make exceptions, even if you have a perfect record."*

He stopped, drew a heavy breath, then set the pen to
paper again.

*I will try to come East for a short visit after they have
put a new man on here. But do not count on it too much. If
something should happen or you should hear of my early
demise—for I am not as young as I used to be, Maddy,
and it is true that anything can happen. God bless you and
the boys. It is hard for me to imagine that they are both
grown up now and have homes of their own. I think of you
all often.*

> *Your loving uncle,*
> *Charles Merriot Blyne*

He folded the letter, put it in an envelope, addressed and
stamped it. Leaving it there to lie in the sunlight, he got
slowly up from the walnut writing table and turned to the
tall, old cupboard on the wall behind him. Around him,
the old-fashioned furniture of the lighthouse parlor, waxed
and polished to a finer sheen by the timeless years, breathed
permanence. He thought, fumbling with the knob on the
cupboard, that it would stay on when he was gone; and the
sudden delicate chime of the square clock on the mantel
above the fireplace, striking the third quarter of the hour,
pierced him with an almost unbearable cruelty.

He opened the cupboard and took out a thick glass
tumbler and a thick-bellied bottle of rye whiskey. His
hands shook as he set them on the table. The top of the
bottle had been unsealed; but the high level of the liquid,
seen through the dark glass, showed nothing taken. In
twenty-nine years no liquor had been poured in this building, on this small rocky island. He had kept his light in
perfect order, in strict accordance with the regulations—

and now they were turning him out, and only because of an arbitrary figure of years.

He closed his eyes against the inner hurt, opened them, and picked up the bottle. More steadily than he had held the pen, he poured half a glassful of the whiskey. He set the bottle down and reached for the glass. It was a little distance, but twenty-nine years of habit weighed down his hand. He could not touch it—not just yet. He let his hand drop and turned away from the table.

He wandered across the room and looked out to the south. The weather was fair and the barometer high. Far shoreward, he could see the faint line of the coast, stretching away, curving away to the south and Bellisle Point. Past that point and past his lighthouse the coastwise ships had gone safely all these years up to the big harbor at Lynd—millions of dollars worth of cargo and thousands of lives, all dependent on him. If his light had ever failed, there would have been a boat out from the mainland in two hours to see what had gone wrong. But it had never failed—not in twenty-nine years.

Tonight it would be fair, with a bright moon. And no ocean-going vessels were scheduled to pass until eleven that night; and the sleek yacht out there belonged to some fabled man of millions whose strange network of commerce ran underground even in the open light of day, and all over the world.

But by the time the yacht passed, the light would be burning again. Those on shore who watched would have noticed its failure to go on at dusk—his first dereliction of duty in almost a generation of years. They would come out to encounter his protest and set the light to work again. Yes, everything would be as it was—except for him. Except for him.

He roused suddenly from his thoughts. Caught in the long rays of the afternoon sunlight, a small cabin cruiser he had thought to be quartering past his rock had turned and was now making for his landing. It was an ordinary inboard cruiser built for fair weather and inshore fishing; and there were two men visible in the open cockpit. And there was no doubt about it, they were headed right for his landing.

Starting, he turned back and hurried across the room. He snatched up bottle and glass, held them clumsily in one arm and jerked open the cupboard door. It swung wide and he thrust them in. There was a clatter and a small multitude of odds and ends rolled out to scatter on the rug below—medicine bottles, pill boxes, a roll of adhesive tape and another of bandage. Sweating, he dropped to his knees and began to gather them in, scratching the small objects together, cramming them into his hands.

One empty pill box had flipped under the table and he had to crawl after it. He rose with burdened arms and shoved everything helter-skelter out of sight in the cupboard and closed the cupboard door just as feet sounded on the cement walk leading to the front door. Then the door opened without the courtesy of a knock and a tall, broad-shouldered young man in waterproof jacket and duck pants stood looking in, his broad mouth curved in a pleasant grin.

"You Blyne?" said the young man. He had a harsh, not unpleasing voice, and there was a sort of friendly contempt in the brown eyes under his wavy hair. He wore a sweat shirt under the jacket.

"Yes," said the old man.

"You alone here?"

"That's right," said Charles Blyne. "What is it?"

The man with the grin turned his head. "All right," he said to someone outside the house. The young man came the rest of the way in, followed by a short stocky man in early middle-age with a quiet face and thinning black hair. The stocky man wore a suit with a trench coat over it. He closed the door behind him.

"What is it?" demanded the old lighthouse keeper.

"Nothing for you to worry about," said the young one. "Nothing at all. Just sit down, Blyne. Take it easy." He began to circle the room. In a moment he came to the door leading to the second story and the light above. He pulled the door open, looked at the stairs going up, nodded, and shut the door again. He turned back to the old man, who was still standing.

"Sit down," he said.

The old man felt his knees suddenly weaken. He sat—in the same chair in which he had been writing his letter a few minutes before. He looked for the letter now, then remembered he had put it with the bottle and the glass in the cupboard. His hands clenched into two knubbled fists.

"What's your business?" he said. "What's your business here?"

The stocky older man was taking off his trench coat, shaking the dampness of spray from it, hanging it methodically on the clothes tree inside the door. The young one unzipped his jacket and came across the room to sit down at the table opposite Blyne.

"Now we're just going to stay for a while," he said. "Nothing for you to get excited about."

"You can't come on Coast Guard property like this," said the old man, a quaver in his voice.

"We'll be gone by midnight," said the young man.

"I'll have to ask you to leave," said Blyne determinedly.

The young man shook his head. He turned to the other. "You'd better take a look upstairs."

"Right." The stocky man opened the door to the tower, and they heard his steps going up.

"Now I'll tell you what," said the young man, looking across the table at Blyne. "That boat of yours has a hole in the bottom—that is, it has now—and ours is padlocked to the dock. So I think it's all right for you to go around the rock, if you want. And you can come and go in this bottom floor as much as you like. But no going above stairs. When it's time to light the light, one of us'll go upstairs with you and bring you down again.''

"Do you know this is a Federal offense—this is trespass?" cried Blyne. The young man patted him on the shoulder and stood up.

"Easy," he said. "Take it easy, old man."

The stocky man came down.

"All clear," he said. "The big boat's already in position. It'll be dark in half an hour."

Blyne got up and crossed the room to them.

"Listen to me—" he said shakily.

"Here," the young man turned him about and shoved him toward the door. His strong hand opened the door and his other palm pushed Blyne through. "Go walk around a little bit. You'll feel better."

Blyne found himself on his own front walk, his own door shut behind him. He whirled about, but the quick flame of anger in him sputtered helplessly, and died. Buttoning his jacket automatically, he went slowly down the walk toward the landing.

When he got there he saw that his own boat was now sunk—all except for a section of the bow which was held out of water by the mooring chain. The strangers' cabin cruiser rolled next to it in the slight waves, its mooring chain fast around one of the pilings of the dock and secured by a lock inboard. The lock was visible and far too heavy for him to break.

He stood there, feeling the evening chill bite through his jacket. The sunset was fading. The waves had gone gray. A broad band of rose held the western horizon, but this was slipping, off and down, around the world and out of sight.

All small boats had gone in. Two miles to the south, halfway to Bellisle Point, there was the low gray hull of a commercial fishing boat, red-washed by the late rays of light. It was close inshore, lying idle where there would be no fishing. As he watched, the sunset light slipped off and it disappeared in the gathering gloom that came quickly across the water.

He went back up the concrete walk, up the rock slope to the lighthouse. The yellow gleam of the windows and the chugging of the generator, muted behind the thick stone walls, greeted him as he approached the door. He opened it and stepped inside, into the well-known room now cozy with electric light. The young man and his companion were settled—the stocky man in the wing chair and the young man stretched out on the couch. The young man had his shoes off.

Blyne thought of the revolver in the dresser drawer of his bedroom upstairs, but he put the thought away with a weary sort of despair.

"What are you up to?" he asked them, standing squarely in the middle of the room. "What's this all about?"

"Now don't you worry about it," said the young man, unmoving on the couch. "Just pretend everything's normal."

"I've got to turn the light on," he said.

"Good. You do that," said the young man. He looked across at the stocky man. "Go up with him."

Without a word the stocky man followed Blyne upstairs. Passing the first floor landing, Blyne looked down the hall to his closed bedroom door and again thought of the revolver. But the stocky man's footsteps were close behind him and Blyne kept on climbing the clean, well-varnished steps.

At the top he went rather hesitantly to the big lamp and fussed for several moments with the panels and mirrors, as if searching them for some defect. Meanwhile, he was thinking desperately for a means of using the light itself as a signal—but nothing came to him.

Finally, in defeat, he crossed the room, threw the switch that would activate the submarine power cable running underwater to the mainland, and set the light to going, sending out its steady six flashes every quarter minute.

Heavily descending the stairs with the silent man behind him, Blyne came out on the ground level and saw that the young man had produced a deck of cards. He was sitting at the table, shuffling and reshuffling them.

"Gin?" he said to the stocky man.

The stocky man grunted and pulled up a chair. "Five bucks a game," he said. It was the first time Blyne had heard him speak and at the unexpected sound of his voice the old man jumped in spite of himself, although the voice itself was ordinary enough.

The young man shifted his chair slightly so as to hold both the upstairs and the outside door within his field of vision, and began to deal. Blyne sat down on one end of the couch. He looked at his hands, lying loose-skinned and big-veined in his lap. Then suddenly he stood up.

"I'm going outside," he said.

"Okay." The young man nodded, not looking up from the game.

Blyne buttoned his jacket and went out. As he closed the front door behind him, the night darkness flowed in around him. He felt cold and his head was clearing. He had not stopped to think until now. When the men had first come he had felt guilty—because of the bottle—then bewildered, then stunned. He had been too wrapped up in his own problem. And now—

He looked toward the mainland and saw the far lights of the shore buildings. The waves were washing with their steady noise against the rock. The tide would be rising. Above, the moon had risen, but she was a sickle moon, and the sky would be slightly overcast after all. The sea was dark. He looked off toward Bellisle Point and strained his eyes to make out the lights of the commercial fishing boat that had been lying in line with it. As he watched there was a faint fugitive gleam from high on its single mast. Something was going on aloft there.

The night wind blew chilly about Blyne. He thought, no man comes and takes over a lighthouse unless he has a need for a lighthouse. And the need for a lighthouse is to light ships away from danger—or to fail to light them away from it. The kelp-cold smell of the sea came up in his nostrils. He remembered the yacht that would be coming along before midnight, on its easy step down the coast.

He remembered now all that he had read about the man on the yacht—the strange multimillionaire who had made his first fortune before he was twenty-one. He had come up out of the Levant to flash with a rich and strangely secret gleam from time to time on the front pages of newspapers. A man of legend whose career, perversely, had attracted Blyne as any completely incomprehensible thing attracts—and fascinates. It had been something to read about a man like that, a man so different from a solitary, Puritan-minded lighthouse keeper. His name, Blyne remembered, standing in the darkness and the wind, was Nagi—Lester Nagi.

Would such a man have enemies? Blyne wondered. Enemies who played gin rummy, waiting in a lighthouse? Enemies who anchored a fishing boat with a false light that could bring a million dollar yacht onto rocks that would sink her? All it would take was fifteen minutes of darkness from his own light and a false light blinking six flashes every quarter hour. Then the sudden striking on the rocks and—perhaps the man somehow deserved to die.

How sacred was the life of a stranger?—and the light-house keeper was amazed at his thought.

The wind and the night gave him no answer. He went back inside. The two men were immersed in the slap and shift of the cards. Casually he slipped out of his jacket as he walked across the room in the direction of the door to the upstairs and the two telephones to the mainland—one in his bedroom and one beside the lamp at the tower's top. He laid his hand on the knob.

"That's far enough," said the young man.

Blyne turned about with his hand still on the knob. The young man was leaning across the table toward him, still smiling, a ridiculously small gun in his large hand.

"You can't operate the light without me," said Blyne. He jerked open the door, hurling himself up the stairs. Behind him there was an explosion and something slammed against his left shoulder, knocking him off balance. He fell and slid down the steps back onto the carpet.

He felt suddenly dizzy and a little sick, as if he had hit his head on something. He was aware of the two men lifting him up and placing him on the couch.

"Leave me be," he said thickly. The young man's face, smiling, bobbed like a balloon in front of him, then steadied; and the room came back to normal.

"You see," said the young man gently. "Now if you'd done right you wouldn't have been hurt."

Blyne put a hand up to his shoulder. It felt numb.

"Just a scratch," said the young man. "I shoot good." But the other man was already ripping Blyne's sleeve and binding a wad of cloth against the shoulder. Very quickly he was finished.

"Good for a couple hours," he said, speaking for the second time. "By then we'll be out of here."

"What do you want me for?" said Blyne. "What do you want me to do?"

"Just cut the light when we say so—for a few minutes. It won't be long now." The young man stood up, smiling down at him. "That's not so much, is it?"

Blyne stared at the wall. He felt his world turn and steady. The shock of being shot had cleared everything up. The immediate future was a tunnel down which he was groping, guided only by the single rope of conscience. Clumsily he pushed to his feet and staggered a little, over to the cupboard. He opened it and closed his good hand on the bottle and the glass. Turning, he set them on the table and unscrewed the bottle cap.

"I need a drink—" he said.

Later that night the Coast Guard patrol boat that happened to be up along this part of the coast on special business finally found time to investigate the diaphone of the lighthouse. The diaphone had been sending out the moaning grunt of its fog warning for an hour—though the night was clear. The patrol boat would have got around to it sooner except for its special business and the wild goose chase that had led it past a fishing boat with a tall mast and a surprising turn of speed.

When it approached the lighthouse rock, all the lights were on. They were white in the tower and brilliant on the landing where an old man stood in a bloody shirt. The lighthouse foghorn moaned above them. A young ensign was the first to reach the old man and he saw that Blyne's eyes were glazed with shock. He put out his hand, but Blyne waved it away.

"No," the old man said dully. "No. I want to live."

A tall man with a lieutenant's bars came up behind the ensign.

"We better get you to the doctor," he said.

"No—" Blyne shook his head. He lurched away from them, up the slope toward the lighthouse. "Here—"

They followed, along the cement path and in through the door. What they saw in the room brought them up short. Two men lay sprawled over the table, an empty bottle of whiskey between them.

"I never knew their names," Blyne murmured. "Never knew—"

"It's them!" said the ensign.

He stepped forward, but the lieutenant caught his

arm. "Don't touch them." He turned to Blyne. "What happened?"

"Them?" murmured Blyne. "You know— Who are they?"

"The two we're after," said the lieutenant. "We've been chasing them all night. What happened here?"

"You know?" said Blyne. "They were going to wreck the ship?"

"What ship?" cried the ensign. "These two are spies trying to get out of the country. Nagi was going to pick them up and—"

"Clauson!" The lieutenant's voice chopped like an axe across the conclusion of the ensign's sentence.

"They wanted me to turn off the light." Blyne swayed. "For a signal? Then what about the boat, the fishing boat? What was that for?"

"What happened?" The voice of the lieutenant cracked like a whip through the fog surrounding Blyne's thoughts. "How'd they get drunk?"

"Drunk?" Blyne looked at the two men and choked suddenly on laughter that sounded something like a sob. "They're dead."

"Dead?" The two Coast Guard officers stared.

"I never knew their names. And I killed them."

"You?" The lieutenant turned on him.

"The whiskey." The old man sat down suddenly and heavily in the wing chair. "It was for me. It was full of sleeping pills."

The lieutenant and the ensign stared at each other.

"For you?" said the lieutenant.

Blyne nodded.

"They were retiring me. I—" His voice stumbled. "I wouldn't know what to do. So I picked a time when someone would be due by who would make a fuss about the light, if it wasn't on. This man, Nagi— And then I was going to kill myself." He looked at the two younger men, appealingly. "And then—when these two came, I couldn't do—what I shouldn't. But I was going to drink the whiskey anyway, to kill myself, so they wouldn't know how to handle the light, how to turn it off, without me."

The lieutenant took a step forward and stared at the old man's eyes. There was a still glaze on them.

"Then what happened?" said the lieutenant. "You offered it to them, instead?"

"No, no!" Blyne's voice broke. "I was going to drink it myself—because of all the people on that boat." He stared at the two coast guardsmen with a tragic face. His voice rose. "But they took it away from me! They wouldn't listen to me. They took it away from me and wouldn't let me have any, and drank it all themselves. They drank it—every drop!"

Perhaps Gordon Dickson's memories of his own golden-furred teddy bear inspired the Hokas, those cuddly aliens whose imitative antics he and Poul Anderson chronicled in Earthman's Burden *and* Hoka! *But the Hokas' giant cousins, the Dilbians, tap other childhood recollections: canny backwoods Canadians and the bear that didn't eat young Gordy when the two met in a berry patch. Dickson's usual humor strategy places rational beings in irrational situations. But "The Man in the Mailbag" thrusts a bemused human into the paws of creatures so madly logical they would drive even Mr. Spock to a padded cell.*

The Man in the Mailbag

The Right Honorable Joshua Guy, Ambassador Plenipotentiary to Dilbia, was smoking tobacco in a pipe. The fumes from it made John Tardy cough and strangle—or, at least, so it seemed.

"Sir?" wheezed John Tardy.

"Sorry," said Joshua, knocking the pipe out in an ashtray where the coals continued to smolder only slightly less villainously than before. "Thought you heard me the first time. I said that naturally as soon as we knew you were being assigned to the job, we let out word that you were deeply attached to the girl."

"To—" John gulped air. Both men were talking Dilbian, to exercise the command of the language John had had hypnoed into him on his way here from the Belt Stars, and

14

the Dilbian nickname for the missing Earthian female sociologist came from his lips automatically—"this Greasy Face?"

"Miss Ty Lamorc," nodded Joshua, smoothly slipping into Basic and then out again. "Greasy Face, if you prefer. By the by, you mustn't go taking all these Dilbian names at face value. The two old gentlemen you're going to meet—Daddy Shaking Knees and Two Answers—aren't what they might sound like. Daddy Shaking Knees got his name from holding up one end of a timber one day in an emergency—after about forty-five minutes, someone noticed his knees beginning to tremble. And Two Answers is a tribute to the Dilbian who can come up with more than one answer to a problem."

About to ask Joshua about his own Dilbian nickname of Little Bite, John Tardy shifted to safer ground. "What about this Schlaff fellow who—"

"Heiner Schlaff," interrupted Joshua Guy, frowning, "made a mistake. You'd think anyone would know better than to lose his head when a Dilbian picks him up. After the first time one picked up Heinie, he wasn't able to step out onto the street without some Dilbian lifting him up to hear him yell for help. The Squeaking Squirt, they called him—very bad for Earth-Dilbian relations." He looked severely at John. "I don't expect anything like that from you." The ambassador's eye seemed to weigh John's chunky body and red hair.

"No, no," said John hastily.

"Decathlon winner in the Olympics four years back, weren't you?"

"Yes," said John. "But what I really want is to get on an exploration team to one of the new planets. I'm a fully qualified biochemist and—"

"I read your file. Well," Joshua Guy said, "do a good job here and who knows?" He glanced out the window beside him at the sprawling log buildings of the local

Dilbian town of Humrog, framed against the native conifers and the mountain peaks beyond. "But it's your physical condition that'll count. You understand *why* you have
to go it alone, don't you?"

"They told me back on Earth. But if you can add
anything—"

"Headquarters never understands the fine points of these
situations," said Joshua, almost cheerfully. "To put it
tersely—we want to make friends with these Dilbians.
They're the race nearest to ours in intelligence that we've
run across so far. They'd make fine partners. Unfortunately we don't seem to be able to impress them very
much."

"Size?" asked John Tardy.

"Well, yes—size is probably the biggest stumbling block.
The fact that we're about lap-dog proportions in relation to
them. But it shows up even more sharply in a cultural
dissimilarity. They don't give a hang for our mechanical
gimmicks and they're all for personal honor and a healthy
outdoors life." He looked at John. "You'll say, of course,
why not a show of force?"

"I should think—" began John.

"But we don't want to fight them—we want to make
friends with them. Let me give you an Earth-type analogy.
For centuries, humans have been able to more or less tame
most of the smaller wild animals. The large ones, however, being unused to knuckling under to anyone—"

Beep! signaled the annunciator on Joshua's desk.

"Ah, they're here now." Joshua Guy rose. "We'll go
into the reception room. Now remember that Boy-Is-She-
Built is old Shaking Knees' daughter. It was the fact that
the Streamside Terror wanted her that caused all this ruckus
and ended up with the Terror's kidnapping Ty Lamorc."

He led the way through the door into the next room.
John Tardy followed, his head, in spite of the hypno
training, still spinning a little with the odd Dilbian names—in

particular Boy-Is-She-Built, the Basic translation of which was only a pale shadow of its Dilbian original. While not by any means a shy person, John rather hesitated to look a father in the eye and refer to the female child of his old age as—further reflections were cut short as he entered the room.

"Ah, there, Little Bite!" boomed the larger of the two black-furred monsters awaiting them. The one who spoke stood well over two and a half meters in height—at least eight feet tall. "This the new one? Two Answers and I came right over to meet him. Kind of bright-colored on top, isn't he?"

John Tardy blinked. But Joshua Guy answered equably enough.

"Some of us have that color hair back home," he said. "This is John Tardy—John, meet Shaking Knees. And the quiet one is Two Answers."

"*Quiet!*" roared the other Dilbian, bursting into gargantuan roars of laughter. "Me *quiet!* That's good!" He bellowed his merriment.

John stared. In spite of the hypno training, he could not help comparing these two to a couple of very large bears who had stood up on their hind legs and gone on a diet. They were leaner than bears—though leanness is relative when you weigh upward of a thousand pounds—and longer-legged. Their noses were more pug, their lower jaws more humanlike than ursinoid in the way of chin. But their complete coat of thick black hair and their bearishness of language and actions made the comparison almost inevitable—though in fact their true biological resemblance was closer to the humans themselves.

"Haven't laughed like that since old Souse Nose fell in the beer vat!" snorted Two Answers, gradually getting himself under control. "All right, Bright Top, what've you got to say for yourself? Think you can take the Streamside Terror with one hand tied behind your back?"

"I'm here," said John Tardy, "to bring back—er—Greasy Face, and—"

"Streamside won't just hand her over. Will he, Knees?" Two Answers jogged his companion with a massively humorous elbow.

"Not that boy!" Shaking Knees shook his head. "Little Bite, I ought never have let you talk me out of a son-in-law like that. Tough? Rough? Tricky? My little girl'd do all right with a buck like that."

"I merely," demurred Joshua, "suggested you make them wait a bit. Boy-Is-She-Built is still rather young—"

"And, boy, is she built!" said Shaking Knees in a tone of fond, fatherly pride. "Still, it's hard to see how she could do much better." He peered suddenly at Joshua. "You wouldn't have something hidden between your paws on this?"

Joshua Guy spread his hands in a wounded manner. "Would I risk one of my own people? Maybe two? All to start something that would make the Terror mad enough to steal Greasy to pay me back?"

"Guess not," admitted Shaking Knees. "But you Shorties are shrewd little characters." His words rang with honest admiration.

"Thanks. The same to you," said Joshua. "Now about the Terror—"

"He headed west through the Cold Mountains," replied Two Answers. "He was spotted yesterday a half-day's hike north, pointed toward Sour Ford and the Hollows. He probably nighted at Brittle Rock Inn there."

"Good," said Joshua. "We'll have to find a guide for my friend here."

"Guide? Ho!" chortled Shaking Knees. "Wait'll you see what *we* got for you." He shouldered past Two Answers, opened the door and bellowed, "Bluffer! Come on in!"

There was a moment's pause, and then a Dilbian even leaner and taller than Shaking Knees shoved his way into the room, which, with this new Dilbian addition, became decidedly crowded.

"There you are," said Shaking Knees, waving a prideful paw. "What more could you want? Walk all day, climb all night, and start out fresh next morning after breakfast. Little Bite, meet the Hill Bluffer!"

"That's me!" boomed the newcomer, rattling the walls. "Anything on two feet walk away from me? Not over solid ground or living rock! When I look at a hill, it knows it's beat, and it lays out flat for my trampling feet!"

"Very good," said Joshua dryly. "But I don't know about my friend here keeping up if you can travel like that."

"Keep up? Hah!" guffawed Shaking Knees. "No, no, Little Bite—don't you recognize the Bluffer here? He's the postman. We're going to mail this half-pint friend of yours to the Terror. Only way. Cost you five kilos of nails."

"Nobody stops the mail," put in the Hill Bluffer.

"Hmm," said Joshua. He glanced at John Tardy. "Not a bad suggestion. The only thing is how you plan to carry him—"

"Who? Him?" boomed the Bluffer, focusing on John. "Why, I'll handle him like he was a week-old pup. I'll wrap him in some real soft straw and tuck him in the bottom of my mailbag and—"

"Hold it," interrupted Joshua. "That's just what I was afraid of. If you're going to carry him, you'll have to do it humanely."

"I won't wear it!" the Hill Bluffer was still roaring, two hours later. The cause of his upset, a system of straps and pads arranged into a rough saddlebag that would ride between his shoulders and bear John, lay on the crushed rock of Humrog's main street. A few Dilbian bystanders had gathered to watch and their bass-voiced comments were not of the sort to bring the Hill Bluffer to a more reasonable frame of mind.

"Listen, you tad!" Shaking Knees was beginning to get a little hot under the neck-fur himself. "This is your mother's uncle's first cousin speaking. You want me to speak to the great-grandfathers of your clan—"

"Arright—arright—arright!" snarled the Hill Bluffer. "Buckle me up in the obscenity thing!"

"That's better!" growled Shaking Knees, simmering down as John Tardy and Joshua Guy went to work to put the saddle on. "Not that I blame you, but—"

"Don't feel so bad at that," said the Hill Bluffer sulkily, wriggling his shoulders under the straps in experimental fashion.

"You'll find it," grunted Joshua, tugging on a strap, "easier to carry than your regular bag."

"That's not the point," groused the Hill Bluffer. "A postman's got dignity. He just don't wear—" He exploded suddenly at a snickering onlooker. *"What's so funny, you? Want to make something out of it? Just say the—"*

"I'll take care of him!" roared Shaking Knees, rolling forward. "What's wrong with you, Split Nose?"

The Dilbian addressed as Split Nose swallowed his grin rather hastily as the Humrog village chief took a hand in the conversation.

"Just passing by," he growled defensively, backing out of the crowd.

"Well, just pass on, friend, pass on!" boomed Shaking Knees. He was rewarded by a hearty laugh from the crowd, and Split Nose rolled off down the street with every indication his hairy ears were burning.

John had taken advantage of this little by-play to mount into the saddlebag. The Hill Bluffer grunted in surprise and looked back at him.

"You're light enough," he said. "How is it? All right back there?"

"Feels fine," said John, unsuspecting.

"Then so long, everybody!" boomed the Hill Bluffer,

and, without further warning, barreled off down the main street in the direction of the North Trail, the Cold Mountains and the elusive but dangerous Streamside Terror.

Had it not been for the hypno training, John Tardy would not have been able to recognize this fast and unexpected start for the Dilbian trick it was. He realized instantly, however, that the Hill Bluffer, having lost his enthusiasm for the job at first sight of the harness which was to carry John, was attempting a little strategy to get out of it. Outright refusal to carry John was out of the question, but if John should object to the unceremoniousness of his departure, the Bluffer would be perfectly justified—by Dilbian standards—if he threw up his hands and refused to deliver a piece of mail that insisted on imposing conditions on him. John shut his mouth and hung on.

All the same, it was awkward. John had intended to work out a plan of action with Joshua Guy before he left. Well, there was always the wrist-phone. He would call Joshua at the first convenient opportunity.

Meanwhile, it was developing that the Hill Bluffer had not exaggerated his ability to cover ground. One moment they were on the main street of Humrog, and the next upon a mountain trail, green pinelike branches whipping by as John Tardy plunged and swayed to the Hill Bluffer's motion like a man on the back of an elephant. It was no time for abstract thought. John clung to the straps before him, meditating rather bitterly on that natural talent of his for athletics which had got him into this, when by all rights he should be on an exploration team on one of the frontier planets right now. He was perfectly qualified, but just because of that decathlon win . . .

He continued to nurse his grievances for something better than an hour, when he was suddenly interrupted by the Hill Bluffer's grunting and slowing down. Peering

forward over the postman's shoulder, John discovered another Dilbian who had just stepped out of the woods before
them. The newcomer was on the shaggy side. He carried
an enormous triangular-headed axe and had some native
herbivore roughly the size and shape of a musk-ox slung
casually over one shoulder.

"Hello, woodsman," said the Hill Bluffer, halting.

"Hello, postman." The other displayed a gap-toothed
array of fangs in a grin. "Got some mail for me?"

"You!" the Hill Bluffer snorted.

"Not so funny. I could get mail," growled the other.
He peered around at John. "So that's the Half Pint Posted."

"Oh?" said the Hill Bluffer. "Who told you?"

"The Cobbly Queen, that's who!" retorted the other,
curling the right side of his upper lip in the native equivalent of a wink. John Tardy, recalling the Cobblies were the
Dilbian equivalent of fairies, brownies, or what-have-you,
peered at the woodsman to see if he was serious. John
decided he wasn't. Which still left the problem of how he
had recognized John.

Remembering the best Dilbian manners were made of
sheer brass, John Tardy horned in on the conversation.

"Who're you?" he demanded of the woodsman.

"So it talks, does it?" The woodsman grinned. "They
call me Tree Weeper, Half Pint. Because I chop them
down, you see."

"Who told you about me?"

"Oh, that'd be telling," grinned Tree Weeper. "Say,
you know why they call him the Streamside Terror, Half
Pint? It's on account of he likes to fight alongside a
stream, pull the other feller in and drown him."

"I know," said John shortly.

"Do you now?" said the other. "Well, it ought to be
something to watch. Good going to you, Half Pint, and
you too, postman. Me for home."

He turned away into the brush alongside the trail and it

swallowed him up. The Hill Bluffer took up his route again without a word.

"Friend of yours?" inquired John, when it became apparent the Hill Bluffer was not going to comment on the meeting.

"Friend?" the Hill Bluffer snorted angrily. "*I'm* a public official!"

"I just thought—" said John. "He seemed to know things."

"That hill hopper! Somebody ahead of us told him!" growled the Bluffer. But he fell unaccountably silent after that and said no more for the next three hours, until—the two of them having left Humrog a couple of hours past noon—they pulled up in the waning sunlight before the roadside inn at Brittle Rock, where they would spend the night.

The first thing John Tardy did, after working some life back into his legs, was to stroll off to the limits of the narrow, rocky ledge on which the inn stood—Brittle Rock was hardly more than a wide spot in the narrow mountain gorge up which their road ran—and put in a call to Joshua Guy with the phone on his wrist. As soon as Joshua got on the beam, John relievedly explained the reason behind his call. It did not go over, apparently, very well.

"Instructions?" floated the faintly astonished voice of the ambassador out of the receiver. "What instructions?"

"The ones you were going to give me. Before I took off so suddenly—"

"But there's absolutely nothing I can tell you," interrupted Joshua. "You've had your hypno training. It's up to you. Find the Terror and get the girl back. You'll have to figure out your own means, my dear fellow."

"But—" John stopped, staring helpless at the phone.

"Well, good luck, then. Call me tomorrow. Call me anytime."

"Thanks," said John.

"Not at all. Luck. Good-by."

"Good-by."

John Tardy clicked off the phone and walked somberly back to the inn. Inside its big front door, he found a wide common room filled with tables and benches. The Hill Bluffer, to the amusement of a host of other travelers, was arguing with a female Dilbian wearing an apron.

"How the unmentionable should *I* know what to feed him?" the Hill Bluffer was bellowing. "Give him some meat, some beer—anything!"

"But you haven't had the children dragging in pets like I have. Feed one the wrong thing and it dies. And then they cry their little hearts—"

"Talking about me?" John Tardy broke in.

"Oh!" gasped the female, glancing down and retreating half a step. "It talks!"

"Didn't I say he did?" demanded the Bluffer. "Half Pint, what kind of stuff do you eat?"

John fingered the four-inch tubes of food concentrate at his waist. Dilbian food would not poison him, though he could expect little nourishment from it, and a fair chance of an allergic reaction from certain fruits and vegetables. Bulk was all he needed to supplement the concentrates.

"Just give me a little beer," he said.

The room buzzed approval. This little critter, they seemed to feel, could not be too alien if he liked to drink. The female brought him a wastebasket-sized wooden mug that had no handles and smelled like the most decayed of back-lot breweries. John took a cautious sip and held the bitter, sour, flat-tasting liquid in his mouth for an indecisive moment.

He swallowed manfully. The assembled company gave vent to rough-voiced approval, then abruptly turned their attention elsewhere. Looking around, he saw that the Hill Bluffer had gone off somewhere. John climbed up on a nearby bench and got to work on his food concentrates.

After finishing these, he continued to sit where he was for the better part of an hour, but the Hill Bluffer did not return. Struck by a sudden thought, John Tardy climbed down and went back toward the kitchen of the inn. Pushing his way through a hide curtain, he found himself in it—a long room with a stone fire-trough down the center, carcasses hanging from overhead beams, and a dozen or so Dilbians of both sexes equally immersed in argument and the preparation of food and drink. Among them was the female who had brought John the beer.

He stepped into her path as she headed for the front room with a double handful of full mugs.

"Eeeeek!" she exclaimed, or the Dilbian equivalent, stopping so hastily she spilled some of the beer. "There's a good little Shorty," she said in a quavering, coaxing tone. "Good Shorty. Go back now."

"Was the Terror really here last night?" John asked.

"He stopped to pick up some meat and beer, but I didn't see him," she said. "I've no time for hill-and-alley brawlers. Now shoo!"

John Tardy shooed.

As he was heading back to his bench, however, he felt himself scooped up from behind. Looking back over his shoulder, he saw he was being carried by a large male Dilbian with a pouch hanging from one shoulder. This individual carried him to a table where three other Dilbians sat and dropped him on it. John Tardy instinctively got to his feet.

"There he be," said the one who had picked him up. "A genuine Shorty."

"Give him some beer," suggested one with a scar on his face, who was seated at the table.

They did. John prudently drank some.

"Don't hold much," commented one of the others at the table, examining the mug John had set down after what had been actually a very healthy draft for a human. "I wonder if he—"

"Couldn't. Not at that size," replied the one with the pouch. "He's chasing that female Shorty, though. You reckon—?"

Scarface regretted that they did not have the Shorty female there at the moment. Her presence, in his opinion, would have provided the opportunity for interesting and educative experimentation.

"Go to hell!" said John in Basic. He then made the most forceful translation he could manage in Dilbian.

"Tough character!" said the pouched one, and they all laughed. "Better not get tough with me, though."

He made a few humorous swipes at John's red head that would have split it on contact. They laughed again.

"I wonder," said Scarface, "can he do tricks?"

"Sure," John answered promptly. He hefted his still-full mug of beer. "Watch. I take a firm grip, rock back, and—" He spun suddenly on one heel, sloshing a wave of beer into their staring faces. Then he was off the table and dodging among Dilbian and table legs toward the front entrance. The rest of the guests, roaring with laughter, made no attempt to halt him. He ducked into the outer darkness.

Fumbling in the gloom, he made his way around the side of the inn and dropped down on a broken keg he found there. He was just making up his mind to stay there until the Hill Bluffer came and found him, when the back kitchen door opened and closed very softly, off to his left.

He slipped off the keg into deeper shadow. He had caught just a glimpse out of the corner of his eye, but he had received the impression of a Dilbian female in the doorway. There was no sound now.

He began to creep backward. Dilbia's one moon was not showing over these latitudes at this season of the year, and the starlight gave only a faint illumination. He stumbled suddenly over the edge of an unseen slope and froze, remembering the cliff edge overhanging the gorge below.

A faint reek of the Dilbian odor came to his nostrils—and a sound of sniffing. Dilbians were no better than humans when it came to a sense of smell, but each had a perceptible odor to the nostrils of the other—an odor partly dependent on diet, partly on a differing physiological makeup. The odor John Tardy smelled was part-pine, part-musk.

The sniffing ceased. John held his breath, waiting for it to start again. The pressure built up in his chest, and finally he was forced to exhale. He turned his head slowly from side to side.

Silence.

Only the inner creak of his tense neck muscles turning. There! Was that something? John began to creep back along the edge beside him.

There was a sudden rush, a rearing up of some huge dark shape in the darkness before him. He dodged, felt himself slipping on the edge, and something smashed like a falling wall against the side of his head, and he went whirling down and away into star-shot darkness.

He opened his eyes to bright sunlight.

The sun, just above the mountain peaks, was shining right in his eyes. He blinked and started to roll over, out of its glare, into—

—And grabbed in a sudden cold sweat for the stubby trunk of a dwarf tree growing right out of the cliffside.

For a second then, he hung there, sweating and looking down. He lay on a narrow ledge and the gorge was deep below. How deep, he did not stop to figure. It was deep enough.

He twisted around and looked up the distance of a couple of meters to the ledge on which the inn was built. It was not far. He could climb it. After a little while, with his heart in his throat, John Tardy did.

When he came back around the front of the inn, in the morning sunlight, it was to find the Bluffer orating at a sort of open-air meeting, with the four who had harried John standing hangdog between two axemen and before an elderly Dilbian judgelike on a bench.

"—the mail!" the Hill Bluffer was roaring. "The mail is sacred! Anyone daring to lay fist upon the mail in transit—"

John, tottering forward, put an end to the trial in progress.

Later on, after washing his slight scalp-wound and having taken on some more food concentrates and flat beer for breakfast, John Tardy climbed back up on the Bluffer's back and they were under way once more. Their route today led from Brittle Rock through the mountains to Sour Ford and the Hollows. The Hollows, John had learned, was clan-country for the Terror, and their hope was to catch him before he reached it. The trail now led across swinging rope suspension bridges and along narrow cuts in the rock—all of which the Hill Bluffer took not only with the ease of one well accustomed to them, but with the abstraction of one lost in deep thought.

"Hey!" said John, at last.

"Huh? What?" grunted the Hill Bluffer, coming to suddenly.

"Tell me something," said John, reaching out for anything to keep his carrier awake. "How'd the ambassador get the name Little Bite?"

"You don't know that?" exclaimed the Hill Bluffer. "I thought you Shorties all knew. Well, it was old Hammertoes down at Humrog."

The Bluffer chuckled. "Got drunk and all worked up about Shorties. 'Gimme the good old days,' he said, and went down to just make an example of Little Bite—Shorty One, we called him then. He pushes the door open far as it'll go, but Little Bite's got it fixed to only open part way. So there's Hammertoes, with only one arm through the door, feeling around and hollering, 'All right, Shorty! You can't get away! I'll get you—' when Little Bite picks up something sharp and cuts him a couple times across the knuckles. Old Hammertoes yells bloody murder and yanks his hand back. Slam goes the door.''

The Hill Bluffer chortled to himself. "Then old Hammertoes comes back uptown, sucking his knuckles. 'What happened?' says everybody. 'Nothing,' says Hammertoes. 'Something must've happened—look at your hand,' everybody says. 'I tell you nothing happened!' yells Hammertoes. 'He wouldn't let me in where I could grab hold of him, so I come away. And as for my hand, that's got nothing to do with it. He didn't hurt my hand hardly at all. He just give it a little bite!' ''

The Hill Bluffer's laughter rolled like thunder between the mountain walls. "Old Hammertoes never did live that down. Every time since, whenever he goes to give somebody a hard time, they all tell him, 'Look out, Hammertoes, or I'm liable to give you a little bite!' ''

John Tardy found himself laughing. Possibly it was the time and place of the telling, possibly the story, but he could see the situation in his mind's eye and it was funny.

"You know," said the Bluffer over one furry shoulder when John stopped laughing, "you're not bad for a Shorty." He fell silent, appeared to wrestle with himself for a moment, then came to a stop and sat down in a convenient wide spot on the trail.

"Get off," he said. "Come around where I can talk to you."

John complied. He found himself facing the seated Dilbian, their heads about on a level. Behind the large, black-furred skull, a few white clouds floated in the high blue sky.

"You know," the Bluffer said, "the Streamside Terror's mug's been spilled."

"Spilled?" echoed John—then remembered this as a

Dilbian phrase expressing loss of honor. "By me? He's never even seen me."

"By Little Bite," the Bluffer said. "But Little Bite's a Guest in Humrog and the North Country. The Terror couldn't call him to account personally for speaking against Shaking Knees giving the Terror Boy-Is-She-Built. He had to do something, though, so he took Greasy Face."

"Oh," said John.

"So you got to fight the Terror if you want Greasy back."

"*Fight?*" John blurted.

"Man's got his pride," said the Bluffer. "That's why I can't figure you out. I mean you aren't bad for a Shorty. You got guts—like with those drunks last night. But you fighting the Terror—I mean *hell!*" said the Bluffer, in deeply moved tones.

Silently, John Tardy found himself in full agreement with the postman.

"So what're you going to do when you meet Streamside?"

"Well," said John, rather inadequately, "I don't exactly know—"

"Well," growled the Bluffer in his turn, "not my problem. Get on." John went around behind his furry back. "Oh, by the way, know who it was tried to pitch you over the cliff?"

"Who?" asked John.

"The Cobbly Queen—Boy-Is-She-Built!" translated the Bluffer as John looked blank. "She heard about you and got ahead of us somehow . . ." The Bluffer's voice trailed off into a mutter. "If they're thinking of monkeying with the mail . . ."

John paid no attention. He had his own fish to fry, and very fishy indeed they smelled just at the moment. Swaying on top of the enormous back as they took off again, he found himself scowling over the situation. Headquarters had said nothing about his being expected to fight some monstrous free-style scrapper of an alien race—a sort of gargantuan Billy the Kid with a number of kills to his credit. Joshua Guy had not mentioned it. Just what was going on here, anyway?

Abruptly casting aside the security regulation that recommended a "discreet" use of the instrument, John lifted the wrist that bore his wrist-phone to his lips.

"Josh—" he began, and suddenly checked. A fine trickle of sweat ran coldly down his spine.

The phone was gone.

He had the rest of the morning to ponder this new development in the situation, and a good portion of the afternoon. He might have continued indefinitely if it had not been for a sudden interruption in their journey.

They had crossed a number of spidery suspension bridges during the course of the day, and now they had come to another one, somewhat longer than any met so far. If this had been the only difference, John might have been left to his thoughts. But this bridge was different.

Somebody had fixed it so they couldn't get across.

It happened that their end of the bridge had its anchors sunk in a rock face a little back and some seven or eight meters above their heads. All that had been done, simply enough, was to tighten the two main support cables at the far end. The sag of the span had straightened out, lifting the near end up above them, out of reach.

The Hill Bluffer bellowed obscenely across the gap. There was no response from the windlass on the far side, or the small hut beyond.

"What's happened?" John Tardy asked.

"I don't know," said the Bluffer, suddenly thoughtful. "It isn't supposed to be rucked up except at night, to keep people from sneaking over and not paying toll."

He reached as high as he could, but his fingertips fell far short.

"Lift me up," suggested John.

They tried it, but even upheld by the ankles, at the full stretch of the Bluffer's arms, John was rewarded only by a throat-squeezing view of the Knobby River below.

"It'll take five days to go around by Slide Pass," growled the Bluffer, putting John down.

John went over to examine the rock face. What he discovered about it did not make him happy, though perhaps it should have. It was climbable. Heart tucked in throat, he began to go up it.

"Hey! Where're you going?" bellowed the Hill Bluffer.

John did not answer. He needed his breath; anyway, his destination was obvious. The climb up the rock was not bad for someone who had had some mountain experience, but a reaction set in when he wrapped his arms around the rough six-inch cable. He inched his way upward and got on top, both arms and both legs wrapped around the cable, and began a worm-creep toward the bridge end, floating on nothingness at a rather remarkable distance—seen from this angle—ahead of him.

It occurred to him, after he had slowly covered about a third of the cable-distance in this fashion, that a real hero in a place like this should stand up and tightrope-walk to the bridge proper. This, in addition to impressing the Bluffer, would shorten the suspense considerably. John Tardy concluded he must be a conservative and went on crawling.

Eventually he reached the bridge, crawled out on it and lay panting for a while, then got up and crossed the gorge. At the far end, he knocked loose the lock on the windlass with a heavy rock, and the bridge banged down into position, raising a cloud of dust.

Through this same cloud of dust, the Hill Bluffer was shortly to be seen advancing with a look of grim purpose. He stalked past John and entered the hut—from which subsequently erupted thunderous crashes, thuds and roars.

John Tardy looked about for a place of safety. He had never seen two Dilbians fight, but it was only too apparent now what was going on inside.

He was still looking around, however, when the sound ceased abruptly and the Hill Bluffer emerged, dabbing at a torn ear.

"Old slaver-tongue," he growled. "*She* got at him."

"Who?" asked John.

"Boy-Is-She-Built. Well, mount up, Half Pint. Oh, by the way, that was pretty good."

"Good? What was?"

"Climbing across the bridge that way. Took guts. Well, let's go."

John climbed back up into his saddlebag and thought heavily.

"You didn't kill him?" he asked, as they started out once more.

"Who? Old Winch Rope? Just knocked a little sense into him. Hell, there's got to be somebody to work the bridge. Hang on now. It's all downhill from here and it'll be twilight before we hit the ford."

It was indeed twilight before they reached their stopping place at Sour Ford. John Tardy, who had been dozing, awoke with a jerk and sat up in his saddle, blinking.

In the fading light, they stood in a large, grassy clearing semicircled by forest. Directly before them was a long low log building, and behind it a smooth-flowing river with its farther shore shrouded in tree shadow and the approaching dusk.

"Get down," said the Bluffer.

Stiffly, John Tardy descended, stamped about to restore his circulation, and followed the Bluffer's huge bulk through the hide-curtain of the doorway to the building's oil-lamp lit interior.

John discovered a large room like that at the Brittle Rock Inn—but one that was cleaner, airier, and filled with travelers a good deal less noisy and drunken. Gazing around for the explanation behind this difference, John caught sight of a truly enormous Dilbian, grizzled with age and heavy with fat, seated like a patriarch in a huge chair behind a table at the room's far end.

John and the Bluffer found a table and set about eating. But as soon as they were through, the postman led John up to the patriarch.

"One Man," said the Bluffer in a respectful voice, "this here's the Half Pint Posted."

John Tardy blinked. Up close, One Man had turned out to be even more awe-inspiring than he had seemed from a distance. He overflowed the carved chair he sat in, and the graying fur on top of his head all but brushed against a polished staff of hardwood laid crosswise on pegs driven into the wall two meters above the floor. His massive forearms and great pawlike hands were laid out on the table before him like swollen clubs of bone and muscle. But his face was almost Biblically serene.

"Sit down," he rumbled in a voice so deep it sounded like a great drum sounding far off somewhere in a woods. "I've wanted to see a Shorty. You're my Guest, Half Pint, for as long as you wish. Anyone tell you about me?"

"I'm sorry—" began John.

"Never mind." The enormous head nodded mildly. "They call me One Man, Half Pint, because I once held blood feud all by myself—being an orphan—with a whole clan. And won." He looked calmly at John. "What you might call an impossible undertaking."

"Some of them caught him on a trail once," put in the Hill Bluffer. "He killed all three."

"That was possible," murmured One Man. His eyes were still on John. "Tell me, Half Pint, what are you Shorties doing here, anyhow?"

"Well—" John blinked. "I'm looking for Greasy Face—"

"I mean the entire lot of you," One Man said. "There must be some plan behind it. Nobody asked you all here, you know."

"Well—" said John again, rather lamely, and proceeded to try an explanation. It did not seem to go over very well, a technological civilization being hard to picture with the Dilbian vocabulary.

One Man nodded when John Tardy was through. "I see. If that's the case, what makes you think we ought to like you Shorties?"

"Ought to?" said John, jolted into a reactive answer, for he did not have red hair for nothing. "You don't ought to! It's up to you."

One Man nodded. "Pass me my stick," he said.

One of the Dilbians standing around took down the staff from its pegs and passed it to him. He laid it on the table before him—a young post ten centimeters in thickness—grasping it with fists held over two meters apart.

"No one's ever been able to do this but me," he said.

Without lifting his fists from contact with the table, he rotated them to the outside. The staff sprang upward in the center like a bow, and snapped.

"Souvenir for you," said One Man, handing the pieces to John. "Good night."

He closed his eyes and sat as if dozing. The Bluffer tapped John on a shoulder and led him away, off to their sleeping quarters.

Once in the inn dormitory, however, John found himself totally unable to sleep. He had passed from utter bone-weariness into a sort of feverish wide-awakedness, through which the little episode with One Man buzzed and circled like a persistently annoying fly.

What had been the point of all that talk and wood-breaking?

Suddenly and quietly, John sat up. Beside him, on his heap of soft branches, the Bluffer slept without stirring, as did the rest of the dormitory inhabitants. A single lamp burned high above, hanging from the rooftree. By its light, John got out and examined the broken pieces of wood. There was a little node or knot visible just at the point of breakage. A small thing, but—

John frowned. He seemed surrounded by mysteries. The more he thought of it, the more certain he was that One Man had been attempting to convey some message to him. What was it? For that matter, what was going on between humans and Dilbians, and what had his mission to rescue Greasy Face to do with the business of persuading the recalcitrant Dilbians into a partnership? If that was indeed the aim, as Joshua Guy had said.

John swung out of the pile of boughs and to his feet. One Man, he decided, owed him a few more—and plainer—answers.

He went softly down the length of the dormitory and through the door into the common room of the inn.

There were few Dilbians about—they went early to bed. And One Man was also nowhere to be seen. He had not come into the dormitory, John knew. So either he had separate quarters, or else he had stepped outside for some reason . . .

John Tardy crossed the room and slipped out through the inn entrance. He paused to accustom his eyes to the darkness and moved off from the building to get away from the window light. Slowly the night took shape around him, the wide face of the river running silver-dark in the faint light of the stars, and the clearing pooled in gloom.

He circled cautiously around the inn to its back. Unlike Brittle Rock, the backyard here was clear of rubbish, sloping gradually to the river. It was given over to smaller huts and outbuildings. Among these the darkness was more profound and he felt his way cautiously.

Groping about in this fashion, quietly, but with some small, unavoidable noise, he saw a thin blade of yellow light. It cut through the parting of two leather curtains in the window of a hut close by him. He stepped eagerly toward it, about to peer through the crack, when, from deep wall shadow, a hand reached out and took his arm.

"Do you *want* to get yourself killed?" hissed a voice.

And, of course, it was human. And, of course, it spoke in Basic.

Whoever had hold of him drew him deeper into the shadow and away from the building where they stood. They came to another hut whose door stood ajar on an interior blackness, and John was led into this darkness. The hand let go of his arm. The door closed softly. There was a scratch, a sputter, and an animal-oil lamp burst into light within the place.

John squinted against the sudden illumination. When he could see again, he found himself looking into the face of one of the best-looking young women he had ever seen.

She was a good fifteen centimeters shorter than he, but at first glance looked taller by reason of her slim outline in the tailored coveralls she wore. To John Tardy, after two days of Dilbians, she looked tiny—fragile. Her chestnut hair swept back in two wide wings on each side of her head. Her eyes were green above sharply marked cheekbones that gave her face a sculptured look. Her nose was thin, her lips firm rather than full, and her small chin was determined.

John blinked. "Who—?"

"I'm Ty Lamorc," she whispered fiercely. "Keep your voice down!"

"Ty Lamorc? *You?*"

"Yes, yes!" she said impatiently. "Now—"

"Are y-you sure?" stammered John. "I mean—"

"Who were you expecting to run into way out here in—oh, I see!" She glared at him. "It's that Greasy Face name the Dilbians gave me. You were expecting some horror."

"Certainly not," said John stoutly.

"Well, for your information, they just happened to see me putting on makeup one day. That's where the name came from."

"Well, naturally. I didn't think it was because—"

"I'll bet! Anyway, never mind that now. The point is, what are *you* doing out here? Do you *want* to get knocked on the head?"

"Who'd knock—" John Tardy stiffened. "The Terror's here!"

"No, no!" She sounded annoyed. "Boy-Is-She-Built is."

"Oh." John frowned. "You know, I still don't get it—her angle on all this, I mean."

"She loves him, of course," said Ty Lamorc. "Actually, they make an ideal couple, by Dilbian standards. Now let's get you back to the inn before she catches you. She won't follow you in there. You're a Guest."

"Now wait—" John took a deep breath. "This is silly. I came out here to find you. I've found you. Let's head back right now. Not to Humrog—"

"You don't," interrupted Ty with feeling, "understand a blasted thing about these people, Half Pint—I mean, Tardy."

"John."

"John, you don't understand the situation. The Streamside Terror left me here with Boy-Is-She-Built because I was slowing him down. That Hill Bluffer of yours is too fast for him, and he wanted to be sure to be in his own clan-country before you caught up with him, in case there would be—" her voice faltered a little—"repercussions to what happens when you meet. It's all a matter of honor, and that's the point. *You're a piece of mail, John.* Don't you understand? The Hill Bluffer's honor is involved, too."

"Oh," said John. He was silent for a while. "You mean he'd insist on delivering me?"

"What do you think?"

"I see." John was silent again. "Well, to blazes with it," he said at last. "Maybe we can make it across a bridge and cut the ropes and get away from it all. We can't leave you here."

Ty Lamorc did not reply at once. When she did, it was with a pat on his arm.

"You're nice," she said softly. "I'll remember that. Now get back to the inn." And then she had blown out the lamp and he could hear her go.

Next morning, One Man was still nowhere to be seen. Nor, in the half hour that elapsed before they got going, did John Tardy catch any glimpse of Ty, or a female Dilbian who might be Boy-Is-She-Built. He mounted into the Hill Bluffer's mailbag with his mind still engrossed by the happenings of the night before, and it continued to be engrossed as they began their third day of journey.

They were descending now into a country of lower altitudes, though they were still in hill country. The ground was more gently hollowed and crested, and several new varieties of trees appeared.

But John had no time to consider this. He rode through the cool hours of the morning and into noon's heat still trying to find a common solution to the riddles that occupied his mind—about One Man, about the abduction of Ty Lamorc, and about his own peculiar lack of briefing.

"Tell me," said John finally to the Hill Bluffer, "is it a fact no other Dilbian could break that stick of One Man's that same way?"

"Nobody ever can," replied the Bluffer, as they rounded a small hill and plunged through a thin belt of trees. "Nobody ever will."

"Well, you know," said John, "back where I come

from, we have a trick with something called a phone directory—"

He stopped. For the Hill Bluffer himself had stopped, with a jolt that almost pitched John from the mailbag. John sat up, looked around the Dilbian's head—and stared.

They had passed through the woods. They had emerged into a small valley in which a cluster of buildings stood in the brown color of their peeled and weathered logs, haphazardly about a stream that ran the valley's length. Beyond these houses there was a sort of natural amphitheater made by a curved indentation of the far rock wall of the valley. Past this the path went when it emerged from between the buildings and plunged into the trees again.

However, none of this claimed John's attention after the first second. He blinked, instead, at a living wall of five large Dilbians with axes.

"Who do you think you're stopping?" bellowed the Hill Bluffer.

"Clan Hollow's in full meeting," responded the central axeman. "The Great-Grandfathers want to see you both. You come with us."

The axemen formed around the Bluffer and John. They led off down and through the village and beyond to the amphitheater that was swarming with Dilbians of all ages. Several hundred of them were there, and more accumulating, below a ledge of rock where six ancient Dilbians sat.

"This is the mail!" stormed the Hill Bluffer as soon as they were close. "Listen, you Clan Hollows—"

"Be quiet, postman!" snapped the old Dilbian at the extreme right of the line as it faced John and the Bluffer. "Your honor will be guarded. Call the meeting."

"Great-Grandfathers of Clan Hollows, sitting in judgment upon a point of honor!" chanted a young Dilbian standing just below the ledge. He repeated the cry six times.

There was a stir in the crowd. Looking around, John

saw Ty Lamorc. With her was a plump young female that was most likely Boy-Is-She-Built. Boy-Is-She-Built was currently engaged in herding Ty to the foot of the ledge. She accomplished this and immediately began talking.

"I'm Boy-Is-She-Built," she announced.

"We know you," said the Great-Grandfather on the right end.

"I'm speaking here for the Streamside Terror, who's waiting over at Glenn Hollow for the Shorty known as the Half Pint Posted. That Shorty over there. His mug has been spilled—the Terror's, I mean. This Shorty belongs to him—the male over there, I mean. Not that this female Shorty here with me doesn't belong to him, too. He took her fair and square, and it serves those Shorties right. After all, nobody has more honor than the Terror—"

"That's enough," said the judge. "We will decide—"

"I should think you wouldn't even have to call a meeting over it. After all, it's perfectly plain—"

"I said *that's enough!* Be quiet, female!" roared the end judge.

"Well?" interjected one of the other judges testily. "We've heard the arguments. The Shorties are both here. What's left to say?"

"Can I speak?" boomed a new voice, and the crowd parted to let One Man come up before the ledge of rock. The Great-Grandfathers thawed visibly as only great men can in the company of their peers.

"One Man is always welcome to speak," piped an ancient who had not spoken before, and whose voice, with age, had risen almost to the pitch of a human baritone.

"Thank you," said One Man. He raised his head and his voice rose with it, carrying easily out over the assembled Dilbians. "Just think this over. That's what I've got to say. Think deep about it—because it may be Clan Hollows' decision here is going to be binding on just about everybody—us and Shorties alike."

He waved to the judges and went back into the crowd.

"Thanks, One Man," said the right-end judge. "Now, having heard from everybody important who had something to say, here's our opinion. This is a matter concerning the honor of the Streamside Terror—"

"How about me?" roared the Hill Bluffer. "The mail must—"

"Hold your jaw about the mail!" snapped the right-end judge. "As I was saying, Terror's mug was spilled by the Guest in Humrog. Quite properly, the Terror then spilled the mug of the Guest by stealing off one of the Guest's household. This by itself is a dispute between individuals not touching Clan Hollows. But now here comes along a Shorty who wants to fight Terror for the stolen Shorty. And the question is, can Clan Hollows honorably allow the Terror to do so?"

He paused for a moment, as if to let the point sink in on the crowd.

"For us to do this in honor," he continued, "the combat mentioned must be a matter of honor. And this point arises—is honor possible between a man and a Shorty? We Great-Grandfathers have sat up a full night finding an answer, and to do so we have had to ask ourselves, 'What *is* a Shorty?' That is, is it the same thing as us, a being capable of having honor and suffering its loss?"

He paused again. The crowd muttered its interest.

"A knotty question," said the spokesman, with a touch of complacency in his voice. "But your Great-Grandfathers have settled it."

The crowd murmured this time in admiration.

"What makes honor?" demanded the spokesman rhetorically. "Honor is a matter of rights—rights violated and rights protected. Have the Shorties among us had any rights? Guest-rights, only. Failing Guest-rights, can one imagine a Shorty defending and maintaining its rights in our world?"

A chortle broke out in the crowd and spread through its listening ranks at the picture conjured up.

"Silence!" snapped another of the judges. "This is *not* a house-raising."

The crowd went silent.

"Your display of bad manners," said the right-end judge severely, "has pointed up the same conclusion we came to—by orderly process of discussion. It is ridiculous to suppose a Shorty existing as an honor-bound equal in our world. Accordingly, the rules of honor are not binding. Both Shorties here will be returned unharmed to the Guest in Humrog. The Terror has lost no honor. The matter is closed."

He stood up. So did the other five Great-Grandfathers.

"This meeting," he said, "is ended."

"Not yet it isn't!" bellowed the Hill Bluffer.

He plunged forward to the edge of the rock bench, hauling John Tardy along by the slack in John's jacket.

"What do you all know about Shorties?" he demanded. "I've seen this one in action. When a bunch of drunks at Brittle Rock tried to make him do tricks like a performing animal, he fooled them all and got away. How's that for defending his honor? On our way here, the Knobby Gorge Bridge was cranked up out of our reach. He risked his neck climbing up to get it down again, so's not to be slowed in getting his paws on the Terror. How's that for a willingness to defend his rights? I say this Shorty here's as good as some of us any day. Maybe he isn't any bigger'n a two-year-old baby," roared the Hill Bluffer, "but I'm here today to tell you he's all guts!"

He spun on John. "How about it, Shorty? You want Greasy Face handed back to you like scraps from a plate—"

John's long cogitations at last paid off. These and something just witnessed in the Clan Meeting had thrown the switch he had been hunting for.

"Show me that skulking Terror!" he shouted.

The words had barely passed his lips when he felt himself snatched up. The free air whistled past his face. The Hill Bluffer had grabbed him in two huge hands and was now running toward the far woods with him, like a football player with a ball. A roar of voices followed them; looking back, John saw the whole of Clan Hollows in pursuit.

John blinked. He was being jolted along at something like fifty kilometers an hour, and the crowd was coming along behind at the same rate. Or were they? For a long second, John hesitated, then allowed himself to recognize the inescapable fact. All praise to the postman—the Bluffer was outrunning them!

John felt the thrill of competition in his own soul. He and the Hill Bluffer might be worlds apart biologically, but, by heaven, when it came to real competition . . .

Abruptly, the shadow of the further forest closed about them. The Hill Bluffer ran on dropped needles from the conifers, easing to a lope. John Tardy climbed over his shoulder into the mailbag and hung on.

The forest muffled the roar of pursuit. They descended one side of a small hollow and, coming up the other, the Bluffer dropped to his usual ground-eating walk. On the next downslope, he ran again. And so he continued, alternating his pace as the ground shifted.

"How far to the Terror?" asked John.

"Glen Hollow," puffed the Hill Bluffer. He gave the answer in Dilbian units that worked out to just under eight kilometers.

About ten minutes later, they broke through a small fringe of trees to emerge over the lip of a small cuplike valley containing a meadow split by a stream which, in the meadow's center, spread into a pool. The pool was a good fifty meters across and showed the sort of color that indicates a fair depth. By the poolside, a male Dilbian was just looking up at the sound of their approach.

John leaned forward and said quietly to the Hill Bluffer, "Put me down by the deepest part of the water." Reaching to his waist, he loosened the buckle of the belt threaded through the loops on his pants.

The Hill Bluffer grunted and continued his descent. At the water's margin, some dozen meters from the waiting Dilbian, he stopped.

"Hello, postman," said the Dilbian.

"Hello, Terror," answered the Bluffer. "Mail."

The Terror looked curiously past the Bluffer's head at John.

"So that's the Half Pint Posted, is it?" he said. "They let you come?"

"No, we just came," said the Bluffer.

While the Terror stared at John Tardy, John had been examining the Terror. The other Dilbian did not, at first glance, seem to live up to his reputation. He was big, but nowhere near the height of the Hill Bluffer, nor the awe-inspiring massiveness of One Man. John noted, however, with an eye which had judged physical capabilities among his own race, the unusually heavy boning of the other's body, the short, full neck, and, more revealing than any of these, the particularly *poised* balance exhibited by the Terror's thick body.

John Tardy threw one quick glance at the water alongside and slid down from the Bluffer's back. The Bluffer moved off and, with no attempt at the amenities, the Streamside Terror charged.

John turned and dived deep into the pool.

He expected the Terror to follow him immediately, reasoning the other was too much the professional fighter to take chances, even with a Shorty. And, indeed, the water-shock of the big body plunging in after John made him imagine the Terror's great clawed hands all but scratching at his heels. John stroked desperately for depth and distance. He did have a strategy of battle, but it all depended on time and elbow room. He changed direction underwater, angled up to the surface, and, flinging the water from his eyes with a jerk of his head, looked around him.

The Terror, looking the other way, had just broken water four meters off.

John dived again and proceeded to get rid of boots, pants and jacket. He came up again practically under the nose of the Terror and was forced to dive once more. But this time, as he went down, he trailed from one fist the belt he had taken from his trousers, waving in the water like a dark stem of weed.

Coming up the third time at a fairly safe distance, John discovered the Terror had spotted him and was coming after him. John grinned to himself and dove, as if to hide again. But under the water he changed direction and swam directly at his opponent. He saw the heavy legs and arms churning toward him overhead. They moved massively but relatively slowly through the water, and in this he saw the final proof he needed. He had guessed that, effective as the Terror might be against other Dilbians, in the water his very size made him slow and clumsy in comparison to a human—in possibly all but straightaway swimming.

Now John let his opponent pass him overhead. Then, as it went by, he grabbed the foot. And pulled.

The Terror instinctively checked and dived. John, flung surfaceward, let go and dived—this time behind and above the Dilbian. He saw the great back, the churning arms, and then, as the Terror turned once more toward the surface, John closed in, passing the belt around the thick neck and twisting its leather length tight.

At this the Terror, choking, should have headed toward the surface, giving John a chance to breathe. The Dilbian did, John got his breath—and there the battle departed from John's plan entirely.

John had simply failed to give his imagination full rein.

He had, in spite of himself, been thinking of the Dilbian in human terms—as a very big man, a man with vast but not inconceivable strength. It is not inconceivable to strangle a giant man with a belt. But how conceivable is it to strangle a grizzly?

John was all but out of reach, stretched at arm's-length by his grip on the belt, trailing like a lamprey attached to a lake trout. But now and then the Terror's huge hand, beating back at him through the water, brushed against him. Only brushed—but each impact slammed John about like a chip in the water. His head rang. The water roared about him. His shoulder numbed to a blow and his ribs gave to another.

His senses began to fog; and he tightened his grip on the belt—for it was, in the end, kill or be killed. If he did not do for the Terror, there was no doubt the Terror would . . . do for . . . him . . .

Choking and gasping, he found his hands no longer on the belt, but clawing at the grassy edge of the pond. Hands were helping him. He pulled himself up on the slippery margin. His knees found solid ground. He coughed water and was suddenly, ungracefully sick. Then he blacked out.

He came around after an indeterminate time to find his head in someone's lap. He blinked upward and a blur of color slowly turned into the face of Ty Lamorc, very white and taut—and crying.

"What?" he croaked.

"Oh, shut up!" she said. She was wiping his damp face with a rag of cloth that was nearly as wet as he was.

"No—" he managed. "I mean—what're *you* doing here?" He tried to sit up.

"Lie down!"

"I'm all right—I think." He struggled into sitting position. The whole area of Glen Hollow, he saw, was aswarm with Dilbians. A short way off, a knot of them were gathered on the pool-bank around something.

"What—?" he began.

"The Terror, Half Pint," said a familiar voice, and he looked up at the looming figure of the Hill Bluffer, mountainous from this angle. "He's still out. It's your fight, all right." He went off, and they could hear him informing the other group down the bank that the Shorty was up and talking.

John Tardy looked at Ty.

"What happened?" he asked.

"They had to pull him out. You made it to shore by yourself." She found a handkerchief somewhere, wiped her eyes and blew her nose vigorously. "You were wonderful."

"*Wonderful?*" said John, still too groggy for subtlety. "I was out of my head to even think of it!" He felt his ribs gingerly. "I better get back to Humrog and have an X-ray of this side."

"Oh, are your ribs broken?"

"Maybe just bruised. Wow!" said John, coming on an especially tender spot.

"Oh!" wept Ty. "You might have been killed! And it's all my fault!"

"*Your* fault?" said John. He spotted the massive figure of One Man breaking away from the group around the fallen Terror and hissed quickly at her. "Hurry. Help me up." She assisted him clumsily to his feet. "Tell me, did they find anything around the Terror's neck when they pulled him out?"

She stared at him and wiped her eyes. "Why, no. What should they find around his neck?"

"Nothing," whispered John. "Well!" he said as One Man rolled up to a halt before them. "What do *you* think of the situation?"

"I think, Half Pint," said One Man, "that it's all very interesting. Very interesting indeed. I think you Shorties may be getting a few takers now on this business of going off into the sky and learning things.''

"You do, eh? How about you, for one?''

"No-o,'' said One Man slowly. "No, I don't think me. I'm a little too old to jump at new things that quick. Some of the young ones'll be ready, though. The Terror, for one, possibly. He's quite a bright lad, you know. Of course, now that you've done the preliminary spadework, I may put in a good word for you people here and there.''

"Mighty nice of you—*now,*'' said John, a little bitterly.

"Nothing wins like a winner, Half Pint,'' rumbled One Man. "You Shorties should have known that. Matter of fact, I'm surprised it took you so long to show some common sense. You just don't come in and sit down at a man's table and expect him to take your word for it that you're one of the family. As I said to you once before, who asked you Shorties to come here, anyway, in the first place? And what made you think we had to like you? What if, when you were a lad, some new kid moved into your village? He was half your size, but he had a whole lot of shiny new playthings you didn't have, and he came up and tapped you on the shoulder and said, 'C'mon, from now on we'll play *my* sort of game!' How'd you think *you'd* have felt?''

He eyed John shrewdly out of his hairy face.

"I see,'' said John, after a moment. "Then why'd you help me?''

"Me? Help you? I was as neutral as they come. What're you talking about?''

"We've got something back home called a phone directory—a book like those manuals Little Bite has down at Humrog. It's about this thick—'' he measured with thumb and forefinger. "And for one of us Shorties, you'd say it was a physical impossibility to pick it up and tear it in two. But some of us can do it.'' He eyed One Man. "Of course, there's a trick to it.''

"Well, now," said One Man judiciously, "I can believe it. Directories, thick sticks, or first-class hill-and-alley scrappers—there's a trick to handle almost any of them. Not that I'd ever favor a Shorty over any of us in the long run—don't get that idea." He looked around them. The Streamside Terror was being helped out of the Glen and most of the crowd was already gone. "We'll have to get together for a chat one of these days, Half Pint. Well, see you in the near future, Shorties."

John Tardy wiped a damp nose with the back of his hand and stared after One Man. Then he turned to Ty Lamorc.

"Now," he said, "what'd you mean—it was all your fault?"

"It was," she said miserably. "It was all my idea. Earth knew we weren't getting through to the Dilbians, so they sent me out. And I—" she gulped—"I recommended they send out a man who conformed as nearly as possible to the Dilbian psychological profile and we'd get him mixed up in a Dilbian emotional situation—to convince them we weren't the utter little aliens we seemed to be. They've got a very unusual culture here. They really have. I never thought Boy-Is-She-Built would catch up with you and nearly kill you and take your wrist-phone away. You were supposed to be able to stay in contact with Joshua Guy so he could always rescue you from the other end."

"I see. And why," queried John, very slowly and patiently, "did you decide not to let *me* in on what was going on?"

"Because," she wailed, "I thought it would be better for you to react like the Dilbians in a natural, extroverted, uncerebral way!"

"I see," said John again. They were still standing beside the pool. He picked her up—she was quite light and slender—and threw her in. There was a shriek and a satisfying splash. John turned and walked off.

After half a dozen steps, he slowed down, turned and went back. She was clinging to the bank.

"Here," he said gruffly, extending his hand.

"Thag you," she said humbly, with her nose full of water, as he hauled her out.

Gordon Dickson's predilection for aliens with "black, shining noses" is so marked, it has drawn critical comment. However, this feature is by no means limited to a gentle, otter-like Black Charlie (Alien Art) or a perky, squirrel-like Peep (Arcturus Landing): cuteness is as cuteness does. There is nothing cute in the behavior of feline marsupial Kator Secondcousin of "The Hard Way." Nevertheless, he demonstrates Dickson's notable gift for extrapolating alien behavior from that of real animals. (The book-length version of this story, The Alien Way, incorporates actual scientific references in its text.) The author's success is founded on factual knowledge as well as genuine empathy with the creatures he uses as models—the very factors that shape the plot of "The Hard Way."

The Hard Way

Kator Secondcousin, cruising in the neighborhood of a Cepheid variable down on his charts as 47391L, but otherwise known to the race he was shortly to discover as *A Ursae Min.*—or Polaris, the pole star—suddenly found himself smiled upon by a Random Factor. Immediately— for although he was merely a Secondcousin, it was of the family of Brutogas—he grasped the opportunity thus offered and locked the controls while he set about planning his Kingdom. Meanwhile, he took no chances. He fastened a tractor beam on the artifact embodying the Random Factor. It was a beautiful artifact, even in its fragmentary condition, fully five times as large as the two-man scout in which he and Aton Maternaluncle—of the family Ochadi—had been making a routine sampling sweep of debris in the galactic drift. Kator locked it exactly in the center of his viewing screen and leaned back in his pilot's chair. A polished bulkhead to the left of the screen threw back his own image, and he twisted the catlike whiskers of his round face thoughtfully and with satisfaction, as he reviewed the situation with all sensible speed.

The situation could hardly have been more ideal. Aton Maternaluncle was not even a connection by marriage with the family Brutogas. True, he, like the Brutogasi, was of the Hook persuasion politically, rather than Rod. But on the other hand the odds against the appearance of such a Random Factor as this to two men on scientific survey were astronomical. It canceled out Ordinary Duties and Conventions almost automatically. Aton Maternaluncle— had he been merely a disinterested observer rather than the other half of the scout crew—would certainly consider Kator a fool not to take advantage of the situation by integrating the Random Factor positively with Kator's own life pattern. *Besides*, thought Kator, watching his own reflection in the bulkhead and stroking his whiskers, *I am young and life is before me*.

He got up from the chair, loosened a tube on the internal ship's recorder, and extended the three-inch claws on his stubby fingers. He went back to the sleeping quarters behind the pilot room. Back home the door to it would never have been unlocked—but out here in deep space, who would take precautions against such a farfetched situation as this the Random Factor had introduced?

Skillfully, Kator drove his claws into the spinal cord at the base of Aton's round skull, killing the sleeping man instantly. He then disposed of the body out the air lock, replaced the tube in working position in the recorder, and wrote up the fact that Aton had attacked him in a fit of sudden insanity, damaging the recorder as he did so. Finding Kator ready to defend himself, the insane Aton had then leaped into the air lock, and committed suicide by discharging himself into space.

After all, reflected Kator, as he finished writing up the account in the logbook, *While Others Still Think, We Act* had always been the motto of the Brutogasi. He stroked his whiskers in satisfaction.

A period of time roughly corresponding to a half hour later—in the time system of that undiscovered race to whom the artifact had originally belonged—Kator had got a close-line magnetically hooked to the blasted hull of the artifact and was hand-over-hand hauling his spacesuited body along the line toward it. He reached it with little difficulty and set about exploring his find by the headlight of his suit.

It had evidently been a ship operated by people very much like Kator's own human kind. The doors were the right size, the sitting devices were sittable-in. Unfortunately it had evidently been destroyed by a pressure-warp explosion in a drive system very much like that aboard the scout. Everything not bolted down in it had been expelled into space. No, not everything. A sort of hand carrying-case was wedged between the legs of one of the sitting devices. Kator unwedged it and took it back to the scout with him.

After making the routine safety tests on it, Kator got it open. And a magnificent find it turned out to be. Several items of what appeared to be something like cloth, and could well be garments, and what were clearly ornaments or perhaps badges of rank, and a sort of coloring-stick of soft red wax. But these were nothing to the real find.

Enclosed in a clear wrapping material formed in bag-shape, were a pair of what could only be foot-protectors

with soil still adhering to them. And among the loose soil
in the bottom of the bag, was the tiny dried form of an
organic creature.

A dirt-worm, practically indistinguishable from the dirt-
worms at home.

Kator lifted it tenderly from the dirt with a pair of
specimen tweezers and sealed it into a small cube of clear
plastic. This, he thought, slipping it into his belt pouch,
was his. There was plenty in the wreckage of the ship and
in the carrying-case for the examiners to work on back
home in discovering the location of the race that had built
them all. This corpse—the first of his future subjects—was
his. A harbinger of the future, if he played his knuckle-
dice right. An earnest of what the Random Factor had
brought.

Kator logged his position and the direction of drift the
artifact had been taking when he had first sighted it. He
headed himself and the artifact toward Homeworld, and
turned in for a well-earned rest.

As he drifted off to sleep, he began remembering some
of the sweeps he and Aton had made together before this,
and tears ran down inside his nose. They had never been
related, it was true, even by the marriage of distant connection. But Kator had grown to have a deep friendship for
the older Ruml, and Kator was not the sort that made
friends easily.

Only, when a Kingdom beckons, what can a man do?

Back on the Ruml Homeworld—capital planet of the
seven star-systems where the Ruml were in power—an
organization consisting of some of the best minds of the
race fell upon the artifact that Kator had brought back, like
robber wasps upon the honey-horde of a wild bees hive,
where the hollow tree trunk hiding it has been split open
by lightning. Unlike the lesser races and perhaps the unknown ones who had created the artifact, there was no

large popular excitement over the find, no particular adulation of its discoverer. The artifact could well fail to pan out for a multitude of reasons. Perhaps it was not even of this portion of the galaxy. Perhaps it had been wandering the lightless immensity of space for a million years or more; and the race that had created it was either dead or gone to some strange elsewhere. As for the man who had found it—he was no more than a second cousin of an acceptable, but not great house. And only a few seasons adult, at that.

Only one individual never doubted the promise of reward embodied in the artifact. And that was Kator.

He accepted the reward in wealth that he was given on his return. He took his name off the scout list, and mortgaged every source of income available to him—even down to his emergency right of demand on the family coffers of the Brutogasi. And that was a pledge he would eventually be forced to redeem, or be cut off from the protection of family relationship—which was equivalent to being deprived of the protection of the law among some other races.

He spent his mornings, all morning, in a *salle d'armes*, and his afternoons and evenings either buttonholing or entertaining members of influential families. It was impossible that such activity could remain uninterpreted. The day the examination of the artifact was completed, Kator was summoned to an interview with The Brutogas—head of the family, that individual to whom Kator was second cousin.

Kator put on his best kilt and weapons-harness and made his way at the appointed hour down lofty echoing corridors of white marble to that sunlit office which he had entered, being only a second cousin, only on one previous occasion in his life—his naming day. Behind the desk in the office on a low pedestal squatted The Brutogas, a shrewd, heavy-bodied, middle-aged Ruml. Kator bowed, stopping before the desk.

"We understand," said The Brutogas, "you have ambitions to lead the expedition shortly to be sent to the Homeworld of the Muffled People."

"Sir?" said Kator, blandly.

"Quite right," said The Brutogas, "don't admit anything. I suppose though you'd like to know what's been extracted in the way of information about them from that artifact you brought home."

"Yes, sir," said Kator, standing straight, "I would."

"Well," said the head of the family, flicking open the lock on a report that lay on the desk before him, "the deduction is that they're about our size, biped, of a comparable level of civilization but probably overloaded with taboos from an earlier and more primitive stage. Classified as violent, intractable, and probably extremely dangerous. You still want to lead that expedition?"

"Sir," said Kator, "if called upon to serve—"

"All right," said The Brutogas, "I respect your desire not to admit your goal. Not that you can seriously believe after all your politicking through the last two seasons that anybody can be left in doubt about what you're after." He breathed out through his nose thoughtfully, stroked his graying cat-whiskers that were nearly twice the length of Kator's, and added, "Of course it would do our family reputation no harm to have a member of our house in charge of such an expedition."

"Thank you, sir."

"Don't mention it. However, the political climate at the moment is not such that I would ordinarily commit the family to attempting to capture the Keysman post in this expedition—or even the post of Captain. Something perhaps you don't know, for all your conversations lately, is that the selection board will be a seven-man board and it is a practical certainty that the Rods will have four men on it to three of our Hooks.''

Kator felt an unhappy sinking sensation in the region of his liver, but he kept his whiskers stiff.

''That makes the selection of someone like me seem pretty difficult, doesn't it, sir?''

''I'd say so, wouldn't you?''

''Yes, sir.''

''But you're determined to go ahead with it anyhow?''

''I see no reason to change my present views about the situation, sir.''

''I guessed as much.'' The Brutogas leaned back in his chair. ''Every generation or so, one like you crops up in a family. Ninety-nine per cent of them end up familyless men. And only one in a million is remembered in history.''

''Yes, sir.''

''Well, you might bear in mind then that the family has no concern in this ambition of yours and no intention of officially backing your candidacy for Keysman of the expedition. If by some miracle you should succeed, however, I expect you will give due credit to the wise counsel and guidance of your family elders on an unofficial basis.''

''Yes, sir.''

''On the other hand, if your attempt should somehow end up with you in a scandalous or unfavorable position, you'd better expect that that mortgage you sold one of the—Chelesi, wasn't it?—on your family rights will probably be immediately called in for payment.''

The sinking sensation returned in the region of Kator's liver.

''Yes, sir.''

''Well, that's all. Carry on, Secondcousin. The family blesses you.''

''I bless the family,'' said Kator, automatically, and went out feeling as if his whiskers had been singed.

* * *

Five days later, the board to choose officers for the Expedition to the Homeworld of the Muffled People, was convened. The board sent out twelve invitations for Keysman, and the eleventh invitation was sent to Kator.

It could have been worse. He could have been the twelfth invited.

When he was finally summoned in to face the six-man board—from the room in which he had watched the ten previous candidates go for their interviews—he found the men on it exactly as long-whiskered and cold-eyed as he had feared. Only one member looked at him with anything resembling approval—and this was because that member happened to be a Brutogas, himself, Ardof Halfbrother. The other five judges were, in order from Ardof at the extreme right behind the table Kator faced, a Cheles, a Worna (both Hooks, politically, and therefore possible votes at least for Kator), and then four Rods—a Gulbano, a Ferth, a Achobka, and The Nelkosan, head of the Nelkosani. The last could hardly be worst. Not only did he outrank everyone else on the board, not only was he a Rod, but it was to the family he headed that Aton Maternaluncle, Kator's dead scoutpartner, had belonged. A board of inquiry had cleared Kator in the matter of Aton's death. But the Nelkosani could hardly have accepted that with good grace, even if they had wanted to, without losing face.

Kator took a deep breath as he halted before the table and saluted briefly with his claws over the central body region of his heart. Now it was make or break.

"The candidate," said The Nelkosan, without preamble, "may just as well start out by trying to tell us whatever reasons he may have to justify awarding such a post as Keysman to one so young."

"Honorable Board Members," said Kator, clearly and distinctly, "my record is before you. May I point out, however, that training as a scout, involving work as it does both on a scientific and ship-handling level, as well as associating with one's scoutpartner . . .''

He talked on. He had, like all the candidates, carefully prepared and rehearsed the speech beforehand. The board listened with the mild boredom of a body which has heard such speeches ten times over already—with the single exception of The Nelkosan, who sat twisting his whiskers maliciously.

When Kator finally concluded the board members turned and looked at each other.

"Well?" said The Nelkosan. "Shall we vote on the candidate?"

Heads nodded down the line. Hands reached for ballot chips—black for acceptance, white for rejection—the four Rods automatically picking up black, the three Hooks reaching for white. Kator licked his whiskers furtively with a dry tongue and opened his mouth before the chips were gathered—

"I appeal!" he said.

Hands checked in midair. The board suddenly woke up as one man. Seven pairs of gray eyes centered suddenly upon Kator. Any candidate might appeal—but to do so was to call the board wrong upon one of its actions, and that meant somebody's honor was due to be called in question. For a candidate without family backing to question the honor of elders such as sat on a board of selection was to put his whole future in jeopardy. The board sat back on its collective haunches and considered Kator.

"On what basis, if the candidate pleases?" inquired The Nelkosan, in far too pleasant a tone of voice.

"Sir, on the basis that I have another reason to urge for my selection than that of past experience," said Kator.

"Interesting," purred The Nelkosan, glancing down the table at the other board members. "Don't you think so, sirs?"

"Sir, I do find it interesting," said Ardof Halfbrother,

The Brutogas, in such an even tone that it was impossible to tell whether he was echoing The Nelkosan's hidden sneer, or taking issue with it.

"In that case, candidate," The Nelkosan turned back to Kator, "by all means go ahead. What other reason do you have to urge? I must say"—he glanced down the table again—"I hope it justifies your appeal."

"Sir, I think it will." Kator thrust a hand into his belt pouch, withdrew something small, and stepping forward, put it down on the table before them all. He took his hand away, revealing a cube of clear plastic in which a small figure floated.

"A dirt worm?" said The Nelkosan, raising his whiskers.

"No, sir," said Kator. "The body of a being from the planet of the Muffled People."

"*What?*" Suddenly the room was in an uproar and there was not a board member there who was not upon his feet. For a moment pandemonium reigned and then all the voices died away at once as all eyes turned back to Kator, who was standing once more at attention before them.

"Where did you get this?"

It was The Nelkosan speaking and his voice was like ice.

"Sirs," said Kator, without twitching a whisker, "from the artifact I brought back to Homeworld two seasons ago."

"And you never turned it in to the proper authorities or reported the fact you possessed it?"

"No, sir."

There was a moment's dead silence in the room.

"*You know what this means?*" The words came spaced and distinct from The Nelkosan.

"I realize," said Kator, "what it would mean ordinarily—"

"Ordinarily!"

"Yes, sir. Ordinarily. My case, however," said Kator, as self-possessedly as he could, "is not ordinary. I did not take this organism from the artifact for the mere desire of possessing it.''

The Nelkosan sat back and touched his whiskers gently, almost thoughtfully. His eyelids drooped until his eyes were almost hidden.

"You did not?" he murmured softly.

"No, sir," said Kator.

"Why did you take it, if we may ask?"

"Sir," said Kator, "I took it after a great deal of thought for the specific purpose of exhibiting it to this board of selection for Keysman of the Expedition to the planet of the Muffled People."

His words went out and seemed to fall dead in the face of the silence of the watching members of the board. A lengthening pause seemed to ring in his ears as he waited.

"For," said the voice of The Nelkosan, breaking the silence at last, "what reason did you choose to first steal this dead organism, and then plan to show it to us?"

"Sir," said Kator, "I will tell you."

"Please do," murmured The Nelkosan, almost closing his eyes.

Kator took a deep breath.

"Elders of this board," he said, "you, whose responsibility it is to select the Keysman—the man of final authority, on ship and off—of this expedition, know better than anyone else how important an expedition like this is to all our race. In ourselves, we feel confident of our own ability to handle any situation we may encounter in space. But confidence alone isn't enough. The Keysman in charge of this expedition must not merely be confident of his ability to scout these aliens we have named the Muffled People because of their habit of wrapping themselves in cloths. The Keysman you pick must in addition be able to perform his task, not merely well or excellently—but *perfectly,* as laid down in the precepts of The Morahnpa, he who originally founded a kingdom for our race on the third planet of Star 12A, among the lesser races there.''

"Our candidate," interrupted The Nelkosan from beneath his half-closed eyes, "dreams of founding himself a kingdom?''

"Sir!" said Kator, standing stiffly. "I think only of our race.''

"You had better convince us of that, candidate?''

"I shall, sir. With my culminating argument and explanation of why I took the dead alien organism. I took it, sirs, to show to you. To convince you beyond doubt of one thing. Confidence is not enough in a Keysman. Skill is not enough. *Perfection*—fulfillment of his task without a flaw, as defined by The Morahnpa—is what is required here. And for perfection a commitment is required beyond the ordinary duty of a Keysman to his task.''

Kator paused. He could tell from none of them whether he had caught their interest or not.

"I offer you evidence of my own commitment in the shape of this organism. So highly do I regard the need for success on this expedition, that I have gambled with my family, my freedom, and my life to convince you that I will go to any length to carry it through to the point of perfection. Only someone willing to commit himself to the extent I have demonstrated by taking this organism should be your choice for Keysman on this Expedition!''

He stopped talking. Silence hung in the room. Slowly, The Nelkosan uncurled himself and reaching down the table, gathered in the cube with the worm inside and brought it back to his own place and held it.

"You've made your gesture, candidate," he said, with slitted eyes. "But who can tell whether you meant anything more than a gesture, now that you've given the organism back to us?" He lifted the cube slightly and turned it so that the light caught it. "Tell us, what does it mean to you now, candidate?''

The matter, Kator thought with a cold liverish sense of fatalism, was doomed to go all the way. There was no other alternative now. He looked at The Nelkosan.

"I'll kill you to keep it!" he said.

After that, the well-oiled machinery of custom took over. The head of a family, or a member of a selection board, or anyone in authority of course did not have to answer challenges personally. That would be unfair. He could instead name a deputy to answer the challenge for him. The heads of families in particular usually had some rather highly trained fighters to depute for challenges. That this could also bring about an unfair situation was something that occurred only to someone in Kator's position.

The selection board adjourned to the nearest *salle d'armes*. The deputy for The Nelkosan—Horaag Adoptedson—turned out to be a man ten seasons older than Kator, half again as large and possessing both scars and an air of confidence.

"I charge you with insult and threat," he said formally to Kator as soon as they were met in the center of the floor.

"You must either withdraw that or fight me with the weapons of my choice," said Kator with equal formality.

"I will fight. What weapons?"

Kator licked his whiskers.

"Double-sword," he said. Horaag Adoptedson started to nod— "And shields," added Kator.

Horaag Adoptedson stopped nodding and blinked. The board stared at each other and the match umpire was questioned. The match umpire, a man named Bolf Paternalnephew, checked the books.

"Shields," he announced, "are archaic and generally out of use, but still permissible."

"In that case," said Kator, "I have my own weapons and I'd like to send for them."

The weapons were sent for. While he waited for them,

Kator saw his opponent experimenting with the round, target-shaped shield of blank steel that had been found for him. The shield was designed to be held in the left hand while the right hand held the sword. Horaag Adoptedson was trying fencing lunges with his long, twin-bladed sword and trying to decide what to do with the shield which he was required to carry. At arm's length behind him the shield threw him off balance. Held before him, it restricted his movements.

Kator's weapons came. The shield was like the one found for his opponent, but the sword was as archaic as the shield. It was practically hiltless, and its parallel twin blades were several times as wide as the blades of Horaag's sword, and half the length. Kator slid his arm through a wide strap inside the shield and grasped the handle beyond it. He grasped his archaically short sword almost with an underhand grip and took up a stance like a boxer.

The board murmured. Voices commented to the similarity between Kator's fighting position and that of figures on old carvings depicting ancestral warriors who had used such weapons. Horaag quickly fell into a duplicate of Kator's position—but with some clumsiness evident.

"Go!" said the match umpire. Kator and Horaag moved together and Kator got his shield up just in time to deflect a thrust from Horaag's long sword. Kator ducked down behind his shield and moved in, using his short sword with an underhand stabbing motion. Horaag gave ground. For a few moments swords clanged busily together and on the shields.

Horaag circled suddenly. Kator, turning, tripped and almost went down. Horaag was instantly on top of him. Kator thrust the larger man off with his shield. Horaag, catching on, struck high with his shield, using it as a weapon. Kator slipped underneath, took the full force of the shield blow from the stronger man and was driven to one knee. Horaag struck down with his sword. Kator

struck upward from his kneeling position and missed.
Horaag shortened his sword for a death-thrust downward
and Kator, moving his shorter double blade in a more
restricted circle, came up inside the shield and sword-guard
of the bigger man and thrust Horaag through the shoulder.
Horaag threw his arms around his smaller opponent to
break his back and Kator, letting go of his sword handle in
these close quarters, reached up and clawed the throat out
of his opponent.

They fell together.

When a bloody and breathless Kator was pulled from
under the body of Horaag and supported to the table which
had been set up for the board, he saw the keys to every
room and instrument of the ship which would carry the
Expedition to the planet of the Muffled People, lying in
full sight, waiting for him.

The ship of the Expedition carried fifty-eight men, including Captain and Keysman. Shortly after they lifted
from the Ruml Homeworld, just as soon as they were the
distance of one shift away from their planetary system,
Kator addressed all crew members over the intercommuni-
cations system of the ship.

"Expedition members," he said, "you all know that as
Keysman, I have taken my pledge to carry this Expedition
through to a successful conclusion, and to remain impartial
in my concern for its Members, under all conditions. Let
me now reinforce that pledge by taking it again before you
all. I promise you the order of impartiality which might be
expected by strange but equal members of an unknown
family; and I commit myself to returning to Homeworld
with the order of scouting report on this alien race of
Muffled People that only a perfect operation can provide.
I direct all your attentions to that word, *perfect*, and a
precept laid down by an ancestor of ours, The Morahnpa—*if
all things are accomplished to perfection, how can failure*

attend that operation in which they are accomplished? I have dedicated myself to the success of this Expedition in discovering how the Muffled People may be understood and conquered. Therefore I have dedicated myself to perfection. I will expect a like dedication from each one of you."

He turned away from the communications board and saw the ship's Captain, standing with arms folded and feet spread a little apart. The Captain's eyes were on him.

"Was that really necessary, Keysman?" said the Captain. He was a middle-aged man, his chest-strap heavy with badges of service. Kator thought that probably now was as good a time as any to establish their relationship.

"Have you any other questions, Captain?" he asked.

"No, sir."

"Then continue with your normal duties."

"Yes, sir."

The Captain inclined his head and turned back to his control board on the other side of the room. His whiskers were noncommittal.

Kator left the control room and went down the narrow corridor to his own quarters. Locking the door behind him—in that allowance of luxury that only the Keysman was permitted—he went across to the small table to which was pinned the ring holding his Keys, his family badge, and the authorization papers of the Expedition.

He rearranged these to make room in the center. Then he took from his belt pouch and put in the place so provided the clear plastic cube containing the alien worm. It glittered in that position under the overhead lights of the room; and the other objects surrounded it, thought Kator, like obsequious servants.

There was only one quarrel on the way requiring the adjudication of the Keysman, and Kator found reason to execute both men involved. The hint was well taken by the rest of the Expedition and there were no more disputes. They backtracked along the direction calculated on their Homeworld to have been the path of the artifact, and found themselves after a couple of nine-day weeks midway between a double star with a faint neighbor, Star Unit 439LC&W—and a single yellow star which was almost the twin of the brighter partner of the double star, Star 44OL.

The Ruml investigations of the artifact had indicated the Muffled People's Homeworld to be under a single star. The ship was therefore turned to the yellow sun.

Traces of artificially produced radio emissions were detected well out from the system of the yellow sun. The ship approached cautiously—but although the Ruml discovered scientific data-collecting devices in orbit as far out as the outer fringes of the planetary system surrounding the yellow sun, they found no warning stations or sentry ships.

Penetrating cautiously further into the system, they discovered stations on the moons of two larger, outer planets, some native ship activity in an asteroid belt, and light settlements of native population on the second and fourth planets. The third planet, on the other hand, was swarming with aliens.

The ship approached under cover of that planet's moon, ducked around to the face turned toward the planet, at nightfall, and quickly sealed itself in, a ship's length under the rock of the moon's airless surface. Tunnels were driven in the rock and extra workrooms hollowed out.

Up until this time the ship's captain had been in some measure in command of the Expedition. But now that they were down, all authority reverted to the Keysman. Kator spent a ship's-day studying the plan of investigation recommended by the Ruml Homeworld authorities, and made what changes he considered necessary in them. Then he came out of his quarters and set the whole force of the expedition to building and sending out collectors.

These were of two types. The primary type were simply lumps of nickel-iron with a monomolecular surface layer sensitized to collect up to three days worth of images, and provided with a tiny internal drive unit that would explode on order from the ship or any attempt to block or interfere with the free movement of the device. Several thousand of these were sent down on to the planet and recovered with a rate of necessary self-destruction less than one tenth of one per cent. Not one of the devices was even perceived, let alone handled, by a native. At the end of five weeks, the Expedition had a complete and detailed map of the world below, its cities and its ocean bottoms. And Kator set up a large chart in the gathering room of the ship, listing Five Phases, numbered in order. Opposite Phase One, he wrote Complete to Perfection.

The next stage was the sending down of the secondary type of collectors—almost identical lumps of nickel iron, but with cargo-carrying space inside them. After nine weeks of this and careful study of the small species of alien life returned to the Expedition Headquarters on the moon, he decided that one small flying blood-sucking insect, one crawling, six-legged pseudo-insect—one of the arthropoda, an arachnid or *spider*, in Muffled People's classification—and a small, sharp-nosed, long-tailed scavenging animal of the Muffled People's cities, should be used as live investigators. He marked Phase Two as Complete to Perfection.

Specimens of the live investigators were collected, controlling mechanisms surgically implanted in them, and they were taken back to the planet's surface. By the use of scanning devices attached to the creatures, Expedition members remote-controlling them from the moon were able to investigate the society of the Muffled People at close hand.

The live investigators were directed by their controller into the libraries, factories, hospitals. The first two phases of the investigation had been cold matters of collecting, collating and filing data. With this third phase, and the on-shift members of the Expedition living vicarious insect and animal lives on the planet below, a spirit of adventure began to permeate the fifty-six men remaining on the moon.

The task before them was almost too great to be imagined. It was necessary that they hunt blindly through the civilization below until chance put them on the trail of the information they were after concerning the character and military strength of the Muffled People. The first six months of this phase produced no evidence at all of military strength on the part of the Muffled People—and in his cabin alone Kator paced the floor, twitching his whiskers. The character of the Muffled People as a race was emerging more clearly every day and it was completely at odds with such a lack of defensive elements. And so was the Muffled People's past history as the Expedition had extracted it from the libraries of the planet below.

He called the Captain in.

"We're overlooking something," he said.

"I'll agree with that, Keysman," said the Captain. "But knowing that doesn't solve our problem. In the limited time we've had with the limited number of men available, we're bound to face blank spots."

"Perfection," Kator said, "admits of no blank spots."

The Captain looked at him with slitted eyes.

"What does the Keysman suggest?" he said. ". . . Sir."

"For one thing," Kator's eyes were also slitted, "a little more of an attitude of respect."

"Yes, sir."

"And for another thing," said Kator, "I make the suggestion that what we're looking for must be underground. Somewhere the Muffled People must have a source of military strength comparable to our own—their civilization and their past history is too close to our own for there not to be such a source. If it had been on the surface of the

planet or in one of the oceans, we would've discovered it
by now. So it must be underground."

"I'll have the men check for underground areas."

"You'll do better than that, Captain. You'll take every
man and put them in a hookup with the long-tailed scavenging animals, and run their collectors underground. In
all large blank areas."

"Sir."

The Captain went out. The change in assignment was
made and two shifts later—by sheer luck or coincidence—
the change paid off. One of the long-tailed animal collectors was trapped aboard a large truck transporting food.
The truck went out from one of the large cities in the
middle of the western continent of the planet below and at
about a hundred and fifty of the Muffled People's miles
from the city turned into a country route that led to an
out-of-operation industrial manufacturing complex. It trun-
dled past a sleepy farm or two, across a bridge over a
creek and down a service road into the complex. There it
drove into a factory building and unloaded its food onto a
still and silent conveyor belt.

Then it left.

The collector, left with the food, suddenly felt the conveyor belt start to move. It carried the food deep into the
factory building, through a maze of machinery, and delivered it onto a platform, which dropped without warning
into the darkness of a deep shaft.

And it was at this point that the Ruml in contact with the
collector, called Kator. Kator did not hesitate.

"Destroy it!" he ordered.

The Ruml touched a button and the collector stiffened
suddenly and collapsed. Almost immediately a pinpoint of
brilliance appeared in the center of its body and in a
second it was nothing but fine gray ash, which blew back
up the shaft on the draft around the edges of the descending platform.

While the rest of the men of the Expedition there present in the gathering room watched, Kator walked over to the chart he had put up on the wall. Opposite Phase Three, with a clear hand he wrote *Complete to Perfection*.

Kator allowed the Expedition a shift in which to celebrate. He did not join the celebration himself or swallow one of the short-lived bacterial cultures that temporarily manufactured ethyl alcohol in the Ruml stomachs from carbohydrates the Expedition Members had eaten. Intoxication was an indulgence he could not at the moment permit himself. He called the Captain into conference in the Keysman's private quarters.

"The next stage," Kator said, "is, of course, to send a man down to examine this underground area."

"Of course, sir," said the Captain. The Captain had swallowed one of the cultures, but because of the necessity of the conference had eaten nothing for the last six hours. He thought of the rest of the Expedition gorging themselves in the gathering room and his own hunger came sharply on him to reinforce the anticipation of intoxication.

"So far," said Kator, "the Expedition has operated without mistakes. Perfection of operation must continue. The man who goes down on to the planet of the Muffled People must be someone whom I can be absolutely sure will carry the work through to success. There's only one individual in this Expedition of whom I'm that sure."

"Sir?" said the Captain, forgetting his hunger suddenly and experiencing an abrupt chilliness in the region of his liver. "You aren't thinking of me, are you, Keysman? My job with the ship, here—"

"I am not thinking of you."

"Oh," said the Captain, breathing freely. "In that case . . . while I would be glad to serve . . ."

"I'm thinking of myself."

"*Keysman!*"

It was almost an explosion from the Captain's lips. His whiskers flattened back against his face.

Kator waited. The Captain's whiskers slowly returned to normal position.

"I beg your pardon, sir," he said. "Of course, you can select whom you wish. It's rather unheard of, but . . . Do you wish me to act as Keysman while you're down there?"

Kator smiled at him.

"No," he said.

The Captain's whiskers twitched slightly, involuntarily, but his face remained impassive.

"Who, then, sir?"

"No one."

This time the Captain did not even explode with the word of Kator's title. He merely stared, almost blindly at Kator.

"No one," repeated Kator, slowly. "You understand me, Captain? I'll be taking the keys of the ship with me."

"But—" the Captain's voice broke and stopped. He took a deep breath. "I must protest officially, Keysman," he said. "It would be extremely difficult to get home safely if the keys were lost and the authority of a Keysman was lacking on the trip back."

"It will be impossible," said Kator, evenly. "Because I intend to lock ship before leaving."

The Captain said nothing.

"Perfection, Captain," remarked Kator in the silence, "can imply no less than utter effort and unanimity— otherwise it isn't perfection. Since to fail of perfection is to fail of our objective here, and to fail of our objective is to render the Expedition worthless—I consider I am only doing my duty in making all Members of the Expedition involved in a successful effort down on the planet's surface."

"Yes, sir," said the Captain woodenly.

"You'd better inform the Expedition of this decision of mine."

"Yes, sir."

"Go ahead then," said Kator. The Captain turned toward the door. "And Captain—" The Captain halted with the door half open, and looked back. Kator was standing in the middle of the room, smiling at him. "Tell them I said for them to enjoy themselves—this shift."

"Yes, sir."

The Captain went out, closing the door behind him and cutting off his sight of Kator's smile. Kator turned and walked over to the table holding his keys, his family badge, his papers and the cube containing the worm. He picked up the cube and for a moment held it almost tenderly.

None of them, he thought, would believe him if he told them that it was not himself he was thinking of, but of something greater. Gently, he replaced the cube among the other precious items on the table. Then he turned and walked across the room to squat at his desk. While the sounds of the celebration in the gathering room came faintly through the locked door of his quarters, he settled down to a long shift of work, planning and figuring the role of every Member of the Expedition in his own single assault upon the secret place of the Muffled People.

The shift after the celebration, Kator set most of the Expedition Members to work constructing mechanical burrowing devices which could dig down to, measure and report on the outside of the underground area he wished to enter. Meanwhile, he himself, with the help of the Captain and two specialists in such things, attacked the problem of making Kator himself into a passable resemblance of one of the Muffled People.

The first and most obvious change was the close-clipping of Kator's catlike whiskers. There was no pain or discomfort involved in this operation, but so deeply involved were the whiskers in the sociological and psychological patterns of the adult male Ruml that having them trimmed down to the point of invisibility was a profound emotional shock. The fact that they would grow again in a matter of months—if not weeks—did not help. Kator suffered more than an adult male of the Muffled People would have suffered if the normal baritone of his voice had suddenly been altered to a musical soprano.

The fact that the whiskers had been clipped at his own order somehow made it worse instead of better.

The depilation that removed the rest of the fur on Kator's head, bad as it was, was by contrast a minor operation. After the shock of losing the whiskers, Kator had been tempted briefly to simply dye the close gray fur covering the skull between his ears like a beanie. But to do so would have been too weak a solution to the fur problem. Even dyed, his natural head-covering bore no relationship to human hair.

Still, dewhiskered and bald, Kator's reflection in a mirror presented him with an unlovely sight. Luckily, he did, now, look like one of the Muffled People after a fashion from the neck up. The effect was that of a pink-skinned oriental with puffy eyelids over unnaturally wide and narrow eyes. But it was undeniably native-like.

The rest of his disguise would have to be taken care of by the mufflings he would be wearing, after the native fashion. These complicated body-coverings, therefore, turned out to be a blessing in disguise, with pun intended. Without them it would have been almost impossible to conceal Kator's body-differences from the natives.

As it was, foot-coverings with built-up undersurfaces helped to disguise the relative shortness of Kator's legs, as the loose hanging skirt of the sleeved outside upper-garment hid the unnatural—by Muffled People physical standards—narrowness of his hips. Not a great deal could be done about the fact that the Ruml spine was so connected to the Ruml pelvis that Kator appeared to walk with his upper body at an angle leaning forward. But heavy padding widened the narrow Ruml shoulders and wide sleeves hid the fact that the Ruml arms, like the Ruml legs, were normally designed to be kept bent at knee and elbow-joint.

When it was done, Kator was a passable imitation of a Muffled Person—but these changes were only the beginning. It was now necessary for him to learn to move about in these hampering garments with some appearance of native naturalness.

The mufflings were hideously uncomfortable—like the clinging but lifeless skin of some loathsome creature. But Kator was as unyielding with himself as he was with the other Expedition Members. Shift after shift, as the rest of the Expedition made their burrowing scanners, sent them down and collected them back on the moon to digest the information they had discovered, Kator tramped up and down his own quarters, muffled and whiskerless—while the Captain and the two specialists compared his actions with tapes of the natives in comparable action, and criticized.

Intelligent life is inconceivably adaptable. There came a shift finally when the three watchers could offer no more criticisms; and Kator himself no longer felt the touch of the mufflings about his body for the unnatural thing it was.

Kator announced himself satisfied with himself; and went to the gathering room for a final briefing on the information the burrowing mechanisms had gathered about the Muffled People's secret place. He stood—a weird-looking Ruml figure in his wrappings while he was informed that the mechanisms had charted the underground area and found it to be immense—half a native mile in depth, twenty miles in extent and ten in breadth. Its ceiling was an eighth of a mile below the surface and the whole underground area was walled in by an extremely thick casing of native concrete stiffened by steel rods.

The mechanisms had been unable to scan through the

casing and, since Kator had given strict orders that no attempt was to be made to burrow or break through the casing for fear of alarming the natives, nothing was discovered about the interior.

What lay inside, therefore, was still a mystery. If Kator was to invade the secret place, therefore, he would have to do so blind—not knowing what in the way of defenders or defenses he might discover. The only open way in was down the elevator shaft where the food shipments disappeared.

Kator stood in thought, while the other Members of the Expedition waited around him.

"Very well," he said at last. "I consider it most likely that this place has been set up to protect against invasion by others of the natives, themselves—rather than by someone like myself. At any rate, we will proceed on that assumption."

And he called them together to give them final orders for the actions they would have to take in his absence.

The face of the planet below them was still in night when Kator breached the moon surface just over the site of the Expedition Headquarters and took off planetward in a small, single-man ship. Behind him, the hole in the dust-covered rock filled itself in as if with a smooth magic.

His small ship lifted from the moon and dropped toward the darkness of the planet below.

He came to the planet's surface, just as the sun was beginning to break over the eastern horizon and the fresh chill of the post-dawn drop of temperature was in the air. He camouflaged his ship, giving it the appearance of some native alder bushes, and stepped from it for the first time onto the alien soil.

The strange, tasteless atmosphere of the planet filled his nostrils. He looked toward the rising sun and saw a line of trees and a ramshackle building blackly outlined against the redness of its half-disk. He turned a quarter-circle and began to walk toward the factory.

Not far from his ship, he hit the dirt road running past the scattered farms to the complex. He continued along it with the sun rising strongly on his left, and after a while he came to the wooden bridge over the creek. On this, as he crossed it, his footcoverings fell with a hollow sound. In the stillness of the dawn these seemed to echo through the whole sleeping world. He hurried to get off the planks back onto dirt road again; and it was with an internal lightening of tension that he stepped finally off the far end of the bridge.

"Up early, aren't you?" said a voice.

Kator checked like a swordsman, just denying in time the impulse that would have whirled him around like a discovered thief. He turned casually. On the grassy bank of the creek just a few feet below this end of the bridge, an adult male native sat.

A container of burning vegetation was in his mouth, and smoke trickled from his lips. He was muffled in blue leg-coverings and his upper body was encased in a worn, sleeved muffling of native leather. He held a long stick in his hands, projecting out over the waters of the creek, and as Kator faced him, his lips twisted upward in the native fashion.

Kator made an effort to copy the gesture. It did not come easily, for a smile did not mean humor among his people as much as triumph, and laughter was almost unknown except in individuals almost at the physical or mental breaking point. But it seemed to satisfy the native.

"Out for a hike?" said the native.

Kator's mind flickered over the meaning of the words. He had drilled himself, to the point of unconscious use, in the native language of this area. But this was the first time he had spoken native to a real native. Strangely, what caught at his throat just then was nothing less than embarrassment. Embarrassment at standing whiskerless before this native—who could know nothing of whiskers, and what they meant to a Ruml.

"Thought I'd tramp around a bit," Kator answered, the alien words sounding awkward in his mouth. "You fishing?"

The native waggled the pole slightly, and a small colored object floating on the water trembled with the vibration sent from the rod down the line attached to it.

"Bass," said the native.

Kator wet his nonexistent whiskers with a flicker of his tongue, and thought fast.

"Bass?" he said. "In a creek?"

"Never know what you'll catch," said the native. "Might as well fish for bass as anything else. You from around here?"

"Not close," said Kator. He felt on firmer ground now. While he knew something about the fishing habits and jargon of the local natives—the matter of who he was and where from had been rehearsed.

"City?" said the native.

"That's right," said Kator. He thought of the planet-wide city of the Ruml Homeworld.

"Headed where?"

"Oh," said Kator, "just thought I'd cut around the complex up there, see if I can't hit a main road beyond and catch a bus back to town."

"You can do that, all right," said the native. "I'd show you the way, but I've got fish to catch. You can't miss it, anyway. Ahead or back from here both brings you out on the same road."

"That so?" said Kator. He started to move off. "Well, thanks."

"Don't mention it, friend."

"Good luck with your bass."

"Bass or something—never tell what you'll catch."

Kator waved. The native waved and turned back to his contemplation of the creek. Kator went on.

Only a little way down the dirt road, around a bend and through some trees, he came on the wide wire gate where the road disappeared into the complex. The gate was closed and locked. Kator glanced about him, saw no one and took a small silver cone from his pocket. He touched the point of the cone to the lock. There was a small, upward puff of smoke and the gate sagged open. Kator pushed through, closed the gate behind him and headed for the building which the truck holding the Ruml collector had entered.

The door to the building also was locked. Kator used the cone-shaped object on the lock of a small door set into the big door and slipped inside. He found himself in a small open space, dim-lit by high windows in the building. Beyond the open space was the end of the conveyor belt on which the food boxes had been discharged, and a maze of machinery.

Kator listened, standing in the shadow of the door. He heard nothing. He put away the cone and drew his hand-gun. Lightly, he leaped up on to the still conveyor belt and began to follow it back into the clutter of machinery.

It was a strange, mechanical jungle through which he found himself traveling. The conveyor belt was not a short one. After he had been on it for some minutes, his listening ears caught sound from up ahead. He stopped and listened.

The sound was that of native voices talking.

He went on, cautiously. Gradually he approached the voices, which did not seem to be on the belt but off it to the right some little distance. Finally, he drew level with them. Kneeling down and peering through the shapes of the machinery, he made out a clear area in the building about thirty feet off the belt. Behind the cleared area was a glassed-in cage in which five humans, wearing blue uniforms and weapon harnesses supporting handguns, could be seen—sitting at desks and standing about talking.

Kator lowered his head and crept past like a shadow on the belt. The voices faded a little behind him and in a little distance, he came to the shaft and the elevator platform on to which the conveyor belt discharged its cargo.

Kator examined the platform with an eye already briefed on its probable construction. It was evidently remotely controlled from below, but there should be some kind of controls for operating it from above—if only emergency controls.

Kator searched around the edge of the shaft, and discovered controls set under a plate at the end of the conveyor belt. Using a small magnetic power tool, he removed the plate covering the connections to the switches and spent a moment or two studying the wiring. It was not hard to figure it out from this end—but he had hoped to find some kind of locking device, such as would be standard on a Ruml apparatus of this sort, which would allow him to prevent the elevator being used after he himself had gone down.

But there was no such lock.

He replaced the plate, got on to the platform and looked at the controls. From this point on it was a matter of calculated risk. There was no way of telling what in the way of guards or protective devices waited for him at the bottom of the shaft. He had had his choice of trying to find out with collectors previously and running the risk of alerting the natives—or of taking his chances now. And he had chosen to take his chances now.

He pressed the button. The platform dropped beneath him, and the darkness of the shaft closed over his head.

The platform fell with a rapidity that frightened him. He had a flashing mental picture of it being designed for only nonhuman materials—and then thought of the damageable fruits and vegetables among its food cargo came to mind and reassured him. Sure enough—after what seemed like a much longer drop than the burrowing scanners had reported the shaft to have—the platform slowed quickly but evenly to a gentle halt and emerged into light from an opening in one side of the shaft.

Kator was off the platform the second it emerged, and racing for the nearest cover—behind the door of the small room into which he had been discharged. And no sooner than necessary. A lacework of blue beams lanced across the space where he had been standing a tiny part of a second before.

The beams winked out. The smell of ozone filled the room. For a moment Kator stood frozen and poised, gun in hand. But no living creature showed itself. The beams had evidently been fired automatically from apertures in the wall. And, thought Kator with a cold feeling about his liver, the spot he had chosen to duck into was about the only spot in the room they had not covered.

He came out from behind the door, slipped through the entrance to which it belonged—and checked suddenly, catching his breath.

He stood in an underground area of unbelievable dimensions, suddenly a pygmy. No, less than a pygmy, an ant among giants, dimlit from half a mile overhead.

He was at one end of what was no less than an underground spacefield. Towering away from him, too huge to count, were the brobdingnagian shapes of great spaceships. He had found it—the secret gathering place of the strength of the Muffled People.

From up ahead came the sound of metal on other metal and concrete, sound of feet and voices. Like a hunting animal, Kator slipped from the shadow of one great shape to the next until he came to a spot from which he could see what was going on.

He peered out from behind the roundness of a great, barrel-thick supporting jack and saw that he was at the edge of the field of ships. Beyond stretched immense emptiness, and in a separate corner of this, not fifty feet from where Kator stood, a crew of five natives in green one-piece mufflings were dismounting the governor of a phase-shift drive from one of the ships, which had been taken out of the ship and lowered to the floor here, apparently for servicing. A single native in blue with a weapons harness and handgun stood by them.

As Kator stopped, another native in blue with weapons harness came through the ranked ships from another direction. Kator shrank back behind the supporting jack. The second guard came up to the first.

"Nothing," he said. "May have been a short up in the powerhouse. Anyway, nothing came down the shaft."

"A rat, maybe?" said the first guard.

"No. I looked. The room was empty. It would've got caught by the beams. They're checking upstairs, though."

Kator slipped back among the ships.

The natives were alerted now, even if they did not seriously suspect an intruder like himself. Nonetheless, a great exultation was welling up inside him. He had prepared to break into one of the ships to discover the nature of its internal machinery. Now—thanks to the dismantled unit he had seen being worked on, that was no longer necessary. His high hopes, his long gamble, were about to pay off. His kingdom was before him.

Only two things were still to be done. The first was to make a visual record of the place to take Home; and the other was to get himself safely out of here and back to his small ship.

He took a hand recorder from his weapons belt and adjusted it. This device had been in operation recording his immediate vicinity ever since he had set foot outside his small ship. But adjustments were necessary to allow it to

record the vast shapes and spaces about him. Kator made
the necessary adjustments and for about half an hour flitted
about like an entertainment-maker, taking records not only
of the huge ships, and their number, but of everything else
about this secret underground field. It was a pity, he
thought, that he could not get up to also record the structure of the ceiling lost overhead in the brightness of the
half-mile-distant light sources. But it went without saying
that the Muffled People would have some means of letting
the ships out through the apparently solid ground and
buildings overhead.

Finished at last, Kator worked his way back to the room
containing the elevator shaft. Almost, in the vast maze of
ships and jacks, he had forgotten where it was, but the
sense of direction which had been part of his scoutship
training paid off. He found it and came at last back to its
entrance.

He halted there, peering at the platform sitting innoc-
uously waiting at the shaft bottom. To cross the room to it
would undoubtedly fire the automatic mechanism of the
blue beams again—which, aside from the danger that posed,
would this time fully alert the blue-clad natives with the
weapons harnesses.

For a long second Kator stood, thinking with a rapidity
he had hardly matched before in his life. Then a farfetched scheme occurred to him. He knew that the area
behind the door was safe. From there, two long leaps
would carry him to the platform. If he, with his different
Ruml muscles, could avoid that single touching of the
floor, he might be able to reach the platform without
triggering off the defensive mechanism. There was a way
but it was a stake-everything sort of proposition. If he
missed, there would be no hope of avoiding the beams.

The door opened inward, and it was about six feet in
height, three and a half feet in width. From its most

inward point of swing it was about twenty-two feet from the platform. Reaching in, Kator swung it at right angles to the entrance, so that it projected into the room. Then he backed up and took off his foot coverings, tucking them into pouches of his mufflings.

He got down on hands and feet and arched his back. His claws extended themselves from fingers and toes, clicking on the concrete floor. For a moment he felt a wave of despair that the clumsy mufflings hampering him would make the feat impossible. But he resolutely shoved that thought from his mind. He backed up further until he was a good thirty feet from the door.

He thought of his kingdom and launched himself forward.

He was a young adult Ruml in top shape. By the time he had covered the thirty feet he was moving at close to twenty miles an hour. He launched himself from a dozen feet out for the entrance and flew to the inmost top edge of the door.

He seemed barely to touch the door in passing. But four sets of claws clamped on the door, making the all-important change in direction and adding additional impetus to his flying body. Then the platform and the shaft seemed to fly to meet him and he slammed down on the flat surface with an impact that struck the breath from his body.

The beams did not fly. Half-dazed, but mindful of the noise he had made in landing, Kator fumbled around the edge of the shaft for the button he had marked from the doorway, punched it, and felt the platform thrust him upward.

On the ride up he recovered his breath. He made no attempt to replace the clumsy foot-coverings and drew his handgun, keeping it ready in his hand. The second the platform stopped at the top of the shaft he was off it and running noiselessly back along the conveyor belt at a speed which no native would have been able to maintain in the crouched position in which Kator was holding himself.

There were sounds of natives moving all about the factory building in which he was—but for all that he was half-persuaded that he still might make his escape unobserved, when a shout erupted only about a dozen feet away within the maze of machinery off to his left.

"Stop there! You!"

Without hesitation, Kator fired in the direction of the voice and dived off the conveyor belt into a tangle of gears at his right. Behind him came a groan and the sound of a falling body and a blue beam lanced from another direction through the spot where he had stood a second before.

A dozen feet back in the mechanical maze, Kator clung to a piece of ductwork and listened. His first impression had been that there were a large number of the natives searching the building. Now he heard only three voices, converging on the spot where the first voice had hailed him.

"What happened?"

"I thought I saw something—" the voice that had hailed Kator groaned. "I tried to get a clear shot and I slipped down in between the drums, here."

"You jammed in there?"

"I think my leg's broke."

"You say you saw something?"

"I thought I saw something. I don't know. I guess that alarm had me seeing things—there's nothing on the belt now. Help me out of here, will you!"

"Give me a hand, Corry."

"Easy—take it *easy!*"

"All right . . . All right. We'll get you in to the doctor."

Kator clung, listening, as the two who had come up later lifted their hurt companion out of wherever he had fallen, and carried him out of the building. Then there was nothing but silence; and in that silence, Kator drew a deep breath. It was hardly believable; but for this, too, the

Morahnpa had had a saying—*Perfection attracts the Random Factor—favorably as well as unfavorably*.

Quietly, Kator began to climb back toward the conveyor belt. Now that he could move with less urgency, he saw a clearer route to it. He clambered along and spotted a straight climb along a sideways-sloping, three-foot-wide strip of metal filling the gap between what seemed to be the high side of a turbine and a narrow strip of darkness a foot wide alongside more ductwork. The strip led straight as a road to the open area where the conveyor belt began, and there was the door where Kator had originally entered.

Perfection attracts the Random Factor. . . . Kator slipped out on the strip of metal and began to scuttle along it. His claws scratched and slipped. It was slicker than he had thought. He felt himself sliding. Grimly, in silence, he tried to hold himself back from the edge of darkness. Still blunting his claws ineffectually on the polished surface, he slid over the edge and fell—

To crashing darkness and oblivion.

When he woke, he could not at first remember where he was. It seemed that he had been unconscious for some time but far above him the light still streamed through the high windows of the building at the same angle, almost, as when he had emerged from the platform on his way out. He was lying in a narrow gap between two vertical surfaces of metal. Voices suddenly struck strongly on his ear—the voices of two natives standing in the open space up ahead between Kator and the door.

"Not possible," one of the voices was saying. "We've looked everywhere."

"But you left the place to carry Rogers to the infirmary?"

"Yes, sir. But I took him in myself. Corry stood guard outside the door there. Then, when I came back we searched the whole place. There's no one here."

"Sort of a funny day," said the second voice. "First,

that short or whatever it was, downstairs, and then Rogers thinking he saw someone and breaking his leg." The voice moved off toward the door. "Well, forget it, then. I'll write it up in my report and we'll lock the building behind us until an inspector can look it over."

There was the sound of the small door in the big truck door opening.

"What's anybody going to steal, anyway?" said the first voice, following the other through the door. "Put a half million tons of spaceship under one arm and carry it out?"

"Regulations . . ." the second voice faded away into the outdoors as the door closed.

Kator stirred in his darkness.

For a moment he was afraid he had broken a limb himself. But his leg appeared to be bruised, rather than broken. He wriggled his way forward between the two surfaces until some other object blocked his way. He climbed up and over this—more ductwork yet, it seemed—and emerged a second later into the open area.

The local sun was well up in the center of the sky as he slipped out of the building. No one was in sight. At a half-speed, limping run, Kator dodged along in the shade of an adjoining building; and a couple of minutes later he was safely through the gate of the complex and into the safe shelter of the trees paralleling the dirt road—headed back toward his ship.

The native fisherman was no longer beside the creek. No one at all seemed to be in sight in the warm day. Kator made it back to his ship; and, only when he was safely inside its camouflaged entrance, did he allow himself the luxury of a feeling of safety. For—at that—he was not yet completely safe. He simply had a ship in which to make a run for it, if he was discovered now. He throttled the feeling of safety down. It would be nightfall before he could risk taking off. And that meant that it must be nightfall before he took the final step in securing his kingdom.

He got rid of the loathsome mufflings he had been forced to wear and tended to his wrenched leg. It was painful, but it would be all right in a week at most. And he could use it now for any normal purpose. The recorder he had been carrying was smashed—that must have happened when he had the fall in the building. However, the record of everything he had done up to that moment would be still available within the recording element. No more was needed back Home. Now, if only night would fall!

Kator limped restlessly back and forth in the restricted space of the small ship as the shadows lengthened. At last, the yellow sun touched the horizon and darkness began to flood in long shadows across the land. Kator sat down at the communications board of his small ship and keyed in voice communication alone with the Expedition Headquarters on the moon.

The speaker crackled at him.

"Keysman?"

He said nothing.

"Keysman? This is the Captain. Can you hear us?"

Kator held his silence, a slight smile on his Ruml lips.

"*Keysman!*"

Kator leaned forward to the voice-collector before him. He whispered into it.

"No use—" he husked brokenly, "natives . . . surrounding me here. Captain—"

Kator paused. There was a moment's silence, and then the Captain's voice broke in.

"Keysman! Hold on. We'll get ships down to you and—"

"No time—" husked Kator. "Destroying self and ship. Get Home . . ."

He reached out to his controls and sent the little ship leaping skyward into the dark. As it rose, he fired a cylindrical object back into the ground where it had lain. And, three seconds later, the white, actinic glare of a phase-shift explosion lighted the landscape.

But by that time, Kator was drilling safely upward through the night darkness.

He took upwards of four hours, local time, to return to the Expedition Headquarters. There was no response as he approached the surface above the hidden ship and its connected network of rooms excavated out of the undersurface. He opened the passage that would let his little ship down in, by remote control, and left the small ship for the big one.

There was no one in the corridors or in the outer rooms of the big ship. When Kator got to the gathering room, they were all there, lying silent. As he had expected, they had not followed his orders to return to the Ruml Homeworld. Indeed, with the ship locked and the keys lost with their Keysman, they could not have raised ship except by an extreme butchery of their controls, or navigated her once they had raised her. They had assumed, as Kator had planned, that their Keysman—no doubt wounded and dying on the planet below—had been half-delirious and forgetful of the fact he had locked the ship and taken her keys.

With a choice between a slow death and a fast, they had taken the reasonable choice; and suicided politely, with the lesser ranks first and the Captain last.

Kator smiled, and went to examine the ship's recorder. The Captain had recited a full account of the conversation with Kator, and the Expedition's choice of action. Kator turned back to the waiting bodies. The Expedition's ship had cargo space. He carried the dead bodies into it and set the space at below freezing temperature so that the bodies could be returned to their families—that in itself would be a point in his favor when he returned. Then he unlocked the ship, and checked the controls.

There was no great difference between any of the space-going vessels of the Ruml; and one man could handle the large Expedition ship as well as the smallest scout. Kator set a course for the Ruml Homeworld and broke the ship free of the moon's surface into space.

As soon as he was free of the solar system, he programmed his phase shift mechanism, and left the ship to take itself across immensity. He went back to his own quarters.

There, things were as they had been before he had gone down to the planet of the Muffled People. He opened a service compartment to take out food, and he lifted out also one of the alcohol-producing cultures. But when he had taken this last back with the food to the table that held his papers, badges, and the cube containing the worm, he felt disinclined to swallow the culture.

The situation was too solemn, too great, for drunkenness.

He laid the culture down and took up the cube containing the worm. He held it to the light above the table. In that light the worm seemed almost alive. It seemed to turn and bow to him. He laid the cube back down on the table and walked across to put his smashed recording device in a resolving machine that would project its story onto a life-size cube of the room's atmosphere. Then, as the lights about him dimmed, and the morning he had seen as he emerged from his small ship the morning of that same day, he hunkered down on a seat with a sigh of satisfaction.

It is not every man who is privileged to review a few short hours in which he has gained a Kingdom.

The Expedition ship came back to the Ruml Homeworld, and its single surviving occupant was greeted with the sort of excitement that had not occurred in the lifetime of anyone then living. After several days of due formalities, the moment of real business arrived, and Kator Secondcousin Brutogas was summoned to report to the heads of the fifty great families of the Homeworld. Now those families would number fifty-one, for The Brutogas would after this day—at which he was only an invited observer—be listed among their number. Fifty-one long-whiskered male Rumls, therefore, took their seats in a half-circle facing a small stage, and out onto that stage came Kator Secondcousin to salute them all with claws over the region of his heart.

"Keysman," said the eldest family head present, "give us your report."

Kator saluted again. His limp was almost gone now but his whiskers were barely grown a few inches. Also, he seemed to have lost weight and aged on the Expedition.

"My written report is before you, sirs," he said. "As you know we set up a headquarters on the moon of the planet of the Muffled People. As you know, my Captain and men, thinking me dead, suicided. As you know, I have returned."

He stopped talking and saluted again. The family heads waited in some surprise. Finally, the eldest broke the silence.

"Is that *all* you have to say, Keysman?"

"No, sirs," said Kator. "But I'd like to show you the recording I made of the secret place of the Muffled People before I say anything further."

"By all means," said the eldest family head. "Go ahead."

Kator saluted again, and put the smashed recorder into a resolving machine at one edge of the stage. He stood beside it while the heads of the great families watched the incidents from Kator's landing to the moment of his fall in the factory building that had smashed the recorder.

"After I fell," said Kator, as he switched the resolving machine off beside him, "I came to hear two natives discussing the fact they had been unable to find anyone prowling about. They left, and I got away, back to my small ship. From then on, it was simple. I waited until darkness ensured that it was safe for me to take off unnoticed. Then I armed the device I had rigged to simulate a small phase-shift explosion, and called Expedition Headquarters. As I'd planned, my voice-message and my imitation explosion with its indication that the ship's keys were lost for good, left the rest of the Expedition no choice but polite suicide. I gave them ample time to do so before I re-entered the Expedition ship and headed her Home."

Kator stopped talking. There was a remarkable silence from the fifty-one faces staring at him for a long moment—and then a rising mutter of question and incredulity. The strong voice of the eldest family head cut across this.

"Are you telling us you *planned* the suicides of your Captain and men?"

Kator's face twisted in a sudden, apparently uncontrollable fashion. Almost as if he had been ready to laugh.

"Yes, sir," he said. "I planned it."

There was another dead silence.

"In the name of . . . *why?*" burst out the eldest. At one side of the half-circle of faces, the face of The Brutogas looked stricken with paralysis.

Kator's face twisted again.

"Our ancestor, The Morahnpa," he said, "once ensured the conquest of a world and a race by his own individual actions. Because of this, and to encourage others who might do likewise, the principle was laid down that whoever might match The Morahnpa's action, might have, as The Morahnpa did, complete sovereignty over the *natives* of such a conquered world, after the conquest was accomplished. That is—other men might be entitled to take their advantages of the world and race itself. But its true conqueror, during his lifetime, would be the final authority on the planet."

"What's history got to do with this?" It was noticeable that the use of Kator's title of Keysman had begun to be forgotten by the eldest of the family heads. "The Morahnpa not only earned his right to a world, he was in such a position that the world could not be taken without his assistance.''

"Or the Muffled People's world without mine," said Kator. "I had intended to return with a situation that was quite clear-cut. I left our base on the moon unhidden when I returned. It would be bound to be discovered within a limited time. During that limited time, I would offer my knowledge of where the place of strength of the Muffled People was—in turn for the planet of the Muffled People being granted to me as my kingdom—as his world was to The Morahnpa.''

"In that case," said the eldest, "you made a mistake in showing us your recording.''

"No," said Kator. "I've renounced my ambition.''

"Renounced?" The fifty-one faces watched Kator without moving as the eldest spoke. "Why?"

Kator's face twitched again.

"Let me show you the rest of the recording.''

"The rest—'' began the eldest. But Kator was already turning to the resolving machine. He turned it on.

For a second there was nothing to be seen—only the bright flicker of a destroyed recording. Then, this cleared magically and the fifty-one found themselves looking at a native of the Muffled People—the same who had spoken to Kator earlier on the recording.

He took the container of burning vegetation out of his mouth, knocked the vegetation out of it on a rock beside him, overhanging the creek, and put the pipe away. Then he addressed them in perfect Ruml.

"Greetings," he said. "To all, and particularly to those heads of leading families who are viewing this. As you possibly already know, I am a member of that race you Ruml refer to as Muffled People, but which are correctly called humans''—he pronounced the native word carefully for them—"*Heh-eu-manz*. With a little practice you'll find it not hard at all to say.''

There was the beginning of a babble from the semicircle of seats.

"*Quiet!*" barked the eldest head of family.

". . . We humans," the native was saying, smiling at them, "have quite a warlike history, but we really don't like wars. We prefer to be independent, but on good terms with our neighbors. Accordingly, let me show you some of the means we've developed to obtain our preference."

The scene changed suddenly. The assembled Ruml saw before them one of the small, long-tailed, scavenging animals Kator had used as collectors. This was smaller than Kator's and white-furred. It was nosing its way up and down the corridors of a topless box—here being baffled by a dead end corridor, there finding an entrance through to an adjoining corridor.

"This," said the voice of the native, "is a device called a 'maze' used to test the intelligence of the experimental animal you see. This device is one of the investigative tools used in our study of a division of knowledge known as 'psychology'—which corresponds to a certain extent with the division of knowledge you Ruml refer to as Family-study."

The scene changed back to the native on the creekbank.

"Psychology teaches us humans many useful things about how other organisms must react—this is because it is founded upon basic and universal desires, such as the urge of the individual or the race to survive."

He lifted the pole he held.

"This," he said, "though it was used by humans long before we began to study psychology consciously, operates upon psychological principle—"

The view slid out along the rod, down the line attached to its tip, and through the surface of the water. It continued underwater down the line to a dirt worm like the one in Kator's cube. Then it moved off to the side a few inches and picked up the image of a native underwater creature possessing no limbs, but a fan-shaped tail and minor fans farther up the body. The creature swam to the worm and swallowed it. Immediately it began to struggle and a close-up revealed a barbed metal hook in the worm. The creature, however, for all its struggling was drawn up out of the water by the native, who hit it on the head and put it in a woven box.

"You see," said the native, cheerfully, "that this device makes use of the subject's—a 'fish' we call it—desire to survive, on a very primitive level. To survive the fish must eat. We offer it something to eat, but in taking it, the fish delivers itself into our hands, by fastening itself to the hook attached to our line.

"All intelligent, space-going races we have encountered so far seem to exhibit the universal desire to survive. To survive, most seem to believe that they must dominate any other race they encounter, or risk domination themselves. Our study of psychology shows that this is a false assumption. To maintain its domination over another intelligent race, a race must eventually bankrupt its resources, both physical and non-physical. However—it is entirely practical for one race to maintain its domination long enough to teach another race that domination is impractical.

"The worm on my hook," he said, "is known as 'bait.' The worm you found in the wreckage of the human spaceship was symbolic of the fact that the wreckage itself was bait. We have many such pieces of bait drifting outwards from our area of space here. And as I told Kator Secondcousin Brutogas, you never can tell what you'll catch. The object in catching, of course, is to be able to study what takes the bait. Now, when Kator Secondcousin took the spaceship wreckage in tow, there was a monitor only half a light-year away that notified us of that fact. Kator's path home was charted and we immediately went to work, here.

"When your expeditionary ship came, it was allowed to land on our moon and an extensive study was made not only of it, but of the psychology of the Rumls you sent aboard it. After as much could be learned by that method as possible, we allowed one of your collectors to find our underground launching site and for one of your people to come down and actually enter it.

"We ran a number of maze-level tests on Kator Secondcousin while he was making his entrance to and escaping from the underground launching site. You'll be glad to hear that your Ruml intelligence tests quite highly, although you aren't what we'd call maze-sophisticated. We had little difficulty influencing Kator to leave the conveyor belt and follow a route that would lead him onto a surface too slippery to cross. As he fell we rendered him unconscious—"

There was a collective sound, half-grunt, half-gasp, from the listening Ruml audience.

"And, during the hour that followed, we were able to make complete physical tests and studies of an adult male Ruml. Then Kator was put back where he had fallen and allowed to return to consciousness. Then he was let escape."

The human got up, picked up his rod, picked up his woven basket with the underwater creature inside, and nodded to them.

"We now," he said, "know all about you. And you, with the exception of Kator, know nothing about us. Because of what we have learned about your psychology, we are confident that Kator's knowledge will not be allowed to do you any good." He lifted a finger. "I have one more scene to show you."

He vanished, and they looked instead into the immensity of open space. The constellations were vaguely familiar and those who had had experience recognized the spatial area as not far removed from their own planetary system. Through this star-dimness stretched inconceivable great shape followed by great shape, like dark giant demons waiting.

"Kator," said the voice of the native, "should have asked himself why there was so much empty space in the underground launching area. Come see us on Earth whenever you're ready to talk."

The scene winked out. In the new glare of the lights, the fifty-one proud heads of families stared at Kator Second-cousin, who stared back. Then, as if at some unconscious signal, they rose as one man and swarmed upon him.

"You fools!" cackled Kator with a Ruml's mad laughter, as he saw them coming at him. "Didn't he say you wouldn't have any use of what I know?" He went down under their claws. "Force won't work against these people—that's what he was trying to tell you! Why do you have to take the bait just the way I did—"

But it was no use. He felt himself dying.

"All right!" he choked at them, as a red haze began to blot out the world about him. "Learn the hard way for yourselves. Killing me won't do any good . . ."

And of course he was quite right. It didn't.

Ancient Greek dramatists finished off their trilogies with "satyr plays," raunchy farces on the same theme to release the audience from sublimity, laughing. Hindsight recognizes "Perfectly Adjusted"—later expanded as Delusion World—*as the satyr play of the Childe Cycle's SF installment. (The Dragon and the George matches the historical one.) Romping here behind comic masks are Dorsai, Exotics, Friendlies, and the sundered halves of our racial psyche in what Dickson calls "one of those stories that just wrote itself."*

Perfectly Adjusted

The fictional hero who whips up a necessary invention on the spur of the immediate moment, is frequently cursed by his true-life counterpart, sadly embound and restricted by reality and his own human limitations. Probably none, however, has cursed so wildly well as did a certain knowledge trader by the name of Feliz Gebrod, on that unfortunate occasion when, halfway from the strait-laced world of Congerman, a Mark III plastic converter he had thrown together from memory, ran wild and vaporized most of his hat.

You see here the disadvantages of being a modern man. Had Feliz lived in the bad old days when all clothing was made of animal or vegetable fiber, he could have ripped up some other item of apparel and sewed or tied or glued it into some sort of head covering. Cast plastic, unfortunately, being in essence nothing more than a single giant molecule stretched out to whatever length is necessary, does not tear—even if you are half Micturian on your mother's side and can bend steel busbars when sufficiently annoyed. The only way to cut and shape it is with a Mark III plastic converter, which can mold, join, or separate with the greatest ease—when it is properly constructed, with a correct governor.

When it is improperly constructed, with an incorrectly-built governor, it is liable to vaporize large amounts of whatever it is aimed at. For example—a hat. Which, if you'll remember, is where we came in.

Feliz raved and swore and kicked the converter into a corner. Had there been a busbar at hand, he undoubtedly would have bent it. There were none, of course; small single-cabin spaceships do not run to busbars, any more than they run to spare hats. Its only cargo beyond the bare necessities of comfortable existence was the knowledge of skills and techniques that Feliz carried in his head with letter-perfect recall; these he would eventually sell on some planet that knew them not. But what use is an eidetic memory beneath your skull if there is no hat above it?

Absolutely none, if you are planning to land on the planet Congerman.

Congerman, unfortunately, was one of those worlds which have gone in extensively for nakedness taboos and an exaggerated moral code. On Congerman, the body is completely covered; the head, also—and the size of the hat is important. An individual with a large hat is respectable; one with a small hat, dubious (Feliz had been intending to enlarge his with the converter); and one who is hatless, impossible. Impossible, ethically, morally, spiritually, and legally. Without a hat, Feliz could *land* on Congerman; but none would do business with him thereafter, even if he wrapped himself up like a mummy. A true Congermanite would die rather than appear in public without a hat; and illogically, but quite humanly, they expected anybody else they associated with to follow the same tactics.

—And, as has been said, there was no spare hat aboard Feliz's ship. One outfit of spare clothing, he had—but no spare hat. The plans Feliz had once memorized of the Mark III converter had just proved to have an error in the section dealing with the governor. And that was that. The damage was done; there was, in fact, nothing to be done about it, but to grit one's teeth—which in Feliz's case caused his oversize jaw-muscles to stand out on each side of his face like cheek-pouched walnuts—and choose an alternate destination.

He turned to the Galactic Register, and, flipping it on, frowned from beneath shaggy brows at the screen as it reeled off the possible destinations within cruising distance. Hunched over the instrument, and still scowling with the remnants of his rage, Feliz was not a reassuring sight.

Operating on the principle that half a loaf is better than no bread at all, you would suppose that there would be virtues in possessing the superior Micturian mutation in even half your blood. Unfortunately, for Feliz, the virtues were lopsided ones. Full-blooded Micturians are very nicely-proportioned ten-foot giants, with a peculiar cellular structure that roughly doubles the tensile strength and rigidity of their flesh and bones. This cellular structure Feliz had inherited in only slightly watered-down condition; and also the strength, or most of the same, that went with it. Sadly, however, he was lacking in one respect that would have made life with the full-bloods tolerable. To put it bluntly, Feliz was, by Micturian standards, a dwarf—a mere six feet in height.

His head was normal size; so were his hands and feet— more or less. His shoulders, however, were abnormally broad for a human; and if you looked closely at the extremely loose cut of his tunic sleeves where they joined his body, and the great baggy trousers he wore, you might begin to suspect. There was a reason for the tailoring of these clothes—notably a bicep eight inches in diameter when relaxed, and a thigh twelve inches in diameter, under the same conditions. For all practical purposes his waist was so thick as to be indistinguishable from his chest; but the width of his shoulders and the loose tunic served to conceal this.

His face was quaintly humorous, its underlying features being composed of very large bones crammed together in a relatively small area. Literally, it might be said of Feliz that he was one of those men who are so ugly they just miss being handsome. The firm lips of his wide mouth concealed teeth a little too large to put people at ease when he smiled at them; his nose was short and wide, his eyebrows heavy, and his temples broad. A touch of gray streaked his unruly brown hair, and his eyes were a stormy blue.

Right at the moment, they were, indeed, perhaps a trifle more stormy than usual, for the Galactic Register, having hunted through its own files with mechanical patience, had produced one possible other destination—and one only. A world called, of all improbable names, Dunroamin. All others were outside the range of his ship without a stop to stock up on provisions—a very necessary part of the cargo. Feliz, because of his peculiar body-structure, had an enormous appetite.

He punched for a recheck. The Register clicked, whirred and emphatically refused to change its mind. Dunroamin, and Dunroamin only, it said in effect.

"Hell's boiling buckets!" said Feliz, and punched for more detailed information.

Dunroamin, the Register informed him, had been settled as recently as four hundred years before. It was a parklike

world with all the virtues of nature and none of her vices—
except for a few of the mild kind that titillate but do not
trouble seriously. It was thoroughly modern with regard to
the common language and behavior customs of the human
worlds. The people were monogamous, unmutated, and
healthy. The average male was etc. etc. etc. The average
female was etc. More statistics. They had so many cities,
so much of so many kinds of industry. And so forth.

A thoroughly desirable world, concluded the Register.
Unfortunately, they had officially closed their frontiers
some two hundred years before, pending the settlement of
some internal trouble; and the frontiers had never been
opened again. A landing would be in violation of local
law.

"Mother of Mephis!" yelled Feliz, thoroughly out of
temper, and stomped off to throw himself in the pilot's
chair and sit fuming for fifteen minutes. At the end of that
time he was cooled off enough to go back to the Register
and ask it why Dunroamin had closed its frontiers.

Reason unknown, said the Register.

"Well, to hell with them," said Feliz. "I'm going in
anyway!"

After all—all he wanted was a hat.

It was a desirable world—at least in appearance.

Feliz went into an orbit around the planet and looked it
over. Two hundred years without contact, eh? A knowledge trader like himself would have a lot to tell them; it
might be possible to do a little business while getting that
hat. Not that this was any substitute for Congerman, which
was still his main destination.

Meanwhile . . . He went dropping around Dunroamin,
picking out the cities, and looking it over, and plotting his
plans. It would probably be just as well to pick out some
out-of-the-way spot for a first landing. And then—

Feliz jumped suddenly as the alarm bell suddenly split

the silence of his small cabin. For a second he stared at the instrument as if doubting its existence, let alone the noise it was making. Then, returning somewhat to his senses, he dived for the communicator, wondering what other ship could possibly be sharing his rubberneck inspection of the planet below.

The screen clouded, wavered, and finally cleared (it had needed overhauling for six months now, that screen) to reveal something that could only be said to resemble a six or seven room house put together in a vacuum by someone who was either a child or a madman. For a long moment Feliz stared at it without comprehension, then memory of a former history course came to his mind.

"Sweet Susie," he breathed. "A space station!"

He punched assorted buttons. The space station dissolved to the image of a metal walled room and several individuals within it, one of whom leaned forward into the screen and howled at Feliz. He was not a prepossessing-looking character. His black uniform, shirt, breeches and bandolier had been natty once, but now were rumpled and food-stained. He needed a shave; and his black, lank hair needed a haircut.

"Out!" screamed this unwashed policeman. "Get out! We will destroy you. Man the guns! Fire at will! Blast him—"

And, around Feliz, the vacuum began to be filled with hurtling objects which, it struck the half-Micturian suddenly, were probably loaded with high explosive—an ancient and barbarous instrument of war. He snatched at his controls.

"He runs!" yelped the apparition in the speaker. "After him!"

This, of course, since the speaker was broadcasting from a station in free fall, was a manifest impossibility; but Feliz was in no position to appreciate the oddity of it. Acceleration kicked him back into the control seat as he fought for distance. The planet's night side reached sheltering arms toward him; and most of the shells were falling short behind when, just as he passed into the shelter of the penumbra, there was a heavy shock on the rear of his ship. The sound of an explosion transmitted through tortured metal, and he tumbled into the night side of Dunroamin, falling planetward.

Wobbling down on its nose jets, Feliz's ship tottered within a few feet of the ground, flipped, bounced, and stood upright. For a moment there was silence under the peaceful stars in the meadow, where the ship had landed; then slowly the hatch opened, and a battered Feliz crawled out to drop onto the turf with an ungracious grunt.

He looked at the sky. It was dark, of course, since he had come down on the night side of the world; but it shadowed a pleasant, warm summer night under conditions of near normal gravity; and a gentle wind was blowing. Feliz hitched up his baggy pants and went around to inspect the damage.

There was no moon in Dunroamin's sky, but the stars were bright. He discovered the explosion to have taken off about half of one of his stabilizer fins and jammed shut three of his main tubes. He could weld a new piece on the fin, but the tubes were beyond his repairing. No matter; now that he knew which ones they were, he could alter his firing pattern to balance the thrust. The fin, of course, was only necessary during takeoff and landings in atmosphere, anyway.

He went back through the hatch; regretfully tore out one of the ship's few partitions; folded it lengthwise to get it through the hatch; and debouched once more on the turf with this in one hand and a welding torch in the other. He set about repairing the fin.

He was still occupied at this about an hour and a half later when the night sky began to pale. Casting a glance upward, Feliz became aware that he had not fallen as far inside the dark area of the planet as he had thought, and that daylight would be soon upon him. Congratulating himself on the fact that he had gotten to work on the fin promptly, he put a few final touches on the repair job; then, torch in hand, headed back toward the hatch, the controls, and Congerman. Hat or no hat, a world where antiquated space stations opened fire without warning was no place for him.

As he reached for the hatch to open it, however, he suddenly became fully aware of a sound he had been hearing now for some time. It was a thin, recurrent little sound, which he had taken to be the ordinary ululation of some night creature, but which he recognized now—with a very definite sense of shock—to be the voice of some human crying. And, in fact, now that he listened closely, he became aware that the crier was a girl or at least a rather young woman—for, interspersed with the sobs were little comments—short and not uninteresting statements like "Oh dear—what will happen to me now?—I'm so hungry—why couldn't I stay adjusted?—" and more of the like.

Now there is nothing quite so disturbing to a man as the sight and sound of a woman crying. And even the sound is bad enough; there is something accusing and intensely irritating about it. The male feels in some way responsible, whether he is or not. He stands on one foot; he shuffles his feet. He feels like kicking something—preferably the woman who is doing the crying; but then we're none of us stone-age savages nowadays, are we? Of course not. So the resentment of the man settles on whatever is causing her to cry in the first place; and he feels like kicking *it*. If the woman has deliberately maneuvered the situation so that he believes himself to be responsible, he feels like kicking himself; which is, of course, insupportable and a tribute to the woman's ingenuity.

In this particular case Feliz could feel pretty certain that he was not the one responsible for the unknown woman's tears; but the general feeling of being accused, remained. He reached for the hatch cover, let go for a second time, cursed under his breath, slammed down his welding torch; and went to look for the tearful one.

He found her within fifty feet, sitting on a rock and weeping into her hands. He stood over her for several minutes without being able to attract the slightest attention from her, until her repeated statements that she was hungry drove him back to the ship. He rummaged in the food locker and came out with an oversized protein sandwich. He let himself out of the hatch, tramped back to her and thrust it into her hands.

"Here, blast it!" he said.

The girl looked up in surprise, stared at the sandwich in her hands and burst into a fresh wail.

"Now I'm getting tactile hallucinations!" she choked.

"Hallucinations!" exploded Feliz. "That's real, you idiot! Taste it!"

For the first time, she really looked up at him; and in the first pale half-light of approaching day, Feliz could see that she was, indeed, young; and, in fact, pretty. Blue eyes, somewhat reddened by the recent overactivity of her tear ducts, looked up at him from out of a pointed little face under a crown of fluffy hair—which, as far as Feliz could tell in that dim light, was a sort of pale blonde in color. She was dressed in sandals and a sort of striped cloak that half-covered a tunic and short skirt beneath.

"Oh, shut up!" she said. "If I hadn't paid any attentions to your h-hallucinations in the first place, I'd be in bed at home right now and I wouldn't have to be out here where nobody is—only I'm not here either—" and she trembled on the verge of going off again.

Feliz, with a great effort, restrained himself from arguing the question of his reality.

"What *are* you doing out here anyway?" he demanded.

"Where else can I go?" she sniffed dolefully. "I don't exist any more."

"You're out of your head," said Feliz, bluntly.

"No, I'm not," said the girl; "I'm out of my body, and that's worse." And she began to cry again.

"*Quit that!*" roared Feliz. And so effective was the volume of his voice that she did stop, staring up at him with a shocked expression.

"Look—" said Feliz, savagely. "Forget all this business about hallucinations and reality and tell me how you happen to be here."

"They disintegrated me because I kept seeing hallucinations," whimpered the girl. "Now nobody can see or hear me either—nobody real, that is."

Staring down at her, Feliz made up his mind. The girl was clearly insane, or the next thing to it. And on a backward planet like this with murderous space station operators there was no telling what they'd do with her. The best thing for him to do was to cart her along to Congerman, where they could treat her; the interstellar authorities could decide what was to be done with her after that.

"Here," he said, softening his voice, "you just come along with me—" And he reached for her. But before the thick ends of his fingers could touch her, she gave a sudden scream and tumbled backward off the stone in a frightened swirl of cloak and flashing limbs. Before he could move she had bounced to her feet and run off, still carrying the sandwich.

"Stop, dammit!" roared Feliz; and took off after her at a lumbering gallop.

II

The meadow was surrounded by trees; and the girl vanished almost immediately into these. Feliz Gebrod charged after her, tripped over a root in the false and tricky dawn illumination, fell sprawling, caught a flickering flash of cloak somewhere farther back in the depths of the wood, got up and galloped on again, expecting every minute to come up with her and not doing so—until shortness of wind forced him to halt.

He stopped, leaned against a tree and snorted for breath. His body was built for power rather than speed, though for a short distance he could move very fast indeed. Panting, lungs heaving, he told himself that he was a brass-bound idiot; that the girl, insane or not, obviously knew how to take care of herself; that, after all, this was her world—and it was all none of his business, anyway. The thing for him to do was forget her, return to the ship; and get out while the getting was still good.

But just where *was* the ship?

Jerked suddenly back to an appreciation of his surroundings, Feliz snapped upright, away from the tree trunk and looked about him. On all sides, leafy corridors stretched away into green dimness touched with brightness from the first rays of the sun. They all looked alike; they all looked like the way back to the ship. Feliz was lost.

This, thought Feliz, fuming furiously—some five minutes later, after casting around to pick up his bearings—was ridiculous. The ship must be just out of sight, in one direction or another; why, he hardly stepped away from it. To have lost his way in this baby forest! Feliz cursed savagely, then brought himself up short. Better to strike out at random than do nothing; damn that girl! He cast a despairing glance at the rising sun and slogged off in what he still hoped was the right direction.

After he had covered a little distance, however, it struck him that the trees he was passing looked definitely unfamiliar. After a pause to reconsider, he decided that the proper route led off to the right a little more, and altered his course accordingly.

Ten minutes later he changed it again.

Twenty minutes later he changed it for the fourth time.

An hour and a half later, completely bewildered, he was about to give up when he noticed that the trees seemed to be thinning out ahead. He plowed on, and, to his great relief, found that they did widen out and become sparser. They thinned and thinned, gave way to bushes of a rather sickening mauve color; and eventually Feliz emerged, to stand at the head of a gentle open slope. It ran away downhill to a small city below, hemmed about by wooded hills like the one he himself stood upon. To his right, a low, rustic stone wall marched down the tilt of the slope; and seated on the wall was a venerable gentleman in a scarlet kilt and tunic, with a long, white beard tucked into the belt at his waist.

"Greetings and good morning," said this oldster.

Feliz turned to look at him, half expecting that this one, too, would show indications of insanity. But the old man's eyes were bright and sensible. "Something about me surprises you?" he inquired, noting the suspicion in Feliz's stare.

"I just met a woman with a bad psychosis," said Feliz; "I was wondering about you."

The old man gave forth with a delightful chuckle. "Did you really?" he asked, the wrinkles dancing merrily around his old eyes as they crinkled with his laughter. "Well, you needn't worry about me. I'm perfectly adjusted." He sobered suddenly. "Pity more of us aren't. In fact"—he indicated the city below—"I'm the mayor down there."

"You are, huh?" said Feliz, becoming suddenly wary.

"Yes, indeed," he got up and slipped one long, thin

arm through Feliz's. "Hoska's the name; El Hoska. Come on down and meet my people. We see visitors so seldom."

"That's not surprising," grunted Feliz, thinking of the space station. "But," he added, restraining the mayor by the simple expedient of keeping his near three hundred pounds of bone and muscle planted solidly on motionless feet, "I've got to get back to my ship."

"That's too bad," said the mayor, releasing him. "However, if you must, you must. I will, though, be proud to tell people you passed by; would you care to give your name and profession?"

Feliz, caught in a cleft stick, hesitated. To identify himself might involve him with whatever authorities were concerned with the space station. On the other hand, refusal to identify yourself and/or giving a false identity to local authorities was an interstellar crime. He compromised with half an answer. "I'm a knowledge trader," he said.

"But this is magnificent!" cried El Hoska. "You positively *must* stay. You must come down and get acquainted. This is something entirely new. What *is* a knowledge trader?"

Feliz explained briefly.

"Just what we need worst!" cried the delighted mayor. "I am so delighted, I must express myself. Excuse me, but we don't believe in bottling up the emotions, here; I think I'll stand on my head."

He did so, skinny old legs waving in the air. It was an unlovely sight.

"Not bad for a man my age, eh?" he said, panting somewhat as he came upright again. "You should try it."

"Well, I've got to be going," gulped Feliz, firmly convinced by this latest act of lunacy that Dunroamin was no world for him. He started off, only to discover that—after a few strides toward the woods—his legs turned him firmly around and headed him back toward the city below.

"Hey!" yelled Feliz. "What are you doing to me?"

"The will of one is the will of all," said the mayor, coming up to walk gravely alongside him. "The desires of our community, their corporate will, is expressed through me. We are a simple people—" he continued modestly, as Feliz's captive feet continued to carry him on down the slope. "Though we live in the city, we are not of it. A clean mind—"

"I'll sue!" roared Feliz, furiously.

"—in a sound body are our only necessities, which is why you had the luck to bump into me on the hillside this morning. I had come up here to do my deep-breathing exercises. With a spiritual return to nature, has come a harmony between the flesh and the spirit which—"

He rambled on as they continued on down the hill, his bright old eyes agleam, his ancient voice expounding the philosophy of a natural life with the simple-hearted warmth of a gentle fanatic. While, captive by whatever psi faculty the old man controlled, Feliz strolled beside him, his feet obediently marching and his own tongue obediently dumb. And who could say that there was murder in his heart?

"Here," said the mayor, "you see our public square." He indicated a plastic-floored area with a wide sweep of his hand. Scowling, but helpless, Feliz was forced to look it over. It was almost deserted within its ring of low buildings, except for a few individuals dressed in bright colors like the old man, their clothes also cut like his and like the girl's he had seen earlier. Occasionally, a man in the black tunic-and-breeches costume of the men in the space station marched from one building across to another. But these paid no attention to the colorful strollers; or they to the black-clad individuals.

"Wait here," said the mayor, and Feliz felt the compulsion withdrawn from him. "Wander about and notice the fallen grandeur of these ancient buildings, now long ig-

nored and mostly fallen into disuse. Meanwhile I will
gather a few people that I am sure you will enjoy.'' And
he skipped away.

Feliz shook himself, feeling the compulsion which had
held him depart from his rebellious body. He scowled,
wondering at the power the fantastic old mayor wielded.
There were supposed to be a few isolated cultures on the
settled worlds who had matured in a psi sense to the point
where such shenanigans were possible. Feliz had never
bumped into any such before. He cut speculation suddenly
short in favor of action; the thing for him to do was get out
of this city while his feet still obeyed him. He turned on
his heel and almost ran head-on into two of the black-clad
men, who were carrying nightsticks in their hands.

"How did you sneak in here?" shouted one. "Spy,
you're under arrest."

"But I—" began Feliz.

"Oh, resisting arrest, eh?" roared the other. And the
two nightsticks descended as one on Feliz's head.

As he blacked out, Feliz's last thought was that Congerman was evidently not the only planet in the galaxy where
it appeared to be advisable for the casual visitor to wear a
good, thick hat.

Splash! Feliz snorted water out of his nose and shook
his head to clear it. His brain exploded in a piercing pain
that faded suddenly to a steady, heavy ache; he blinked his
eyes and looked around to discover that he was seated on a
hard chair in an ornate black-walled office, facing a desk
and a black-uniformed man behind it, flanked on both
sides by the boys with the nightsticks.

"All right, spy!" grated the man at the desk. "Talk!"

Feliz sat up in his chair. With a movement of theatrical
swiftness, the man whipped out a needle gun and pointed
its slim snout across the desk top at Feliz. "Sit still!" he
snapped. "Any tricks and you will be shot."

Feliz stared at him in bewilderment. All three of the men in black wore looks of suspicion upon their tight faces; but the one in the center, there was no doubt, seemed to carry his the most naturally. He was a tall, thin man, with a long, oval face. His nose was fleshy, his lips thick, and a little parted when he breathed. Dark eyes looked out from under untidy brows.

"I'm not a spy," growled Feliz, feeling his dander rising.

"You *are* a spy!" asserted the man at the desk. "Don't lie to me, spy. If you lie, you will be shot; I will give you three seconds to start telling the truth. One, two—"

"You tin-whistle idiot!" roared Feliz. "I'm a perfectly legitimate knowledge trader."

"Now we're getting someplace," snapped the needle-gunner. "You admit to being a knowledge trader."

"What d'you mean, admit—" Feliz was beginning, when the other interrupted.

"Violence does not impress me," he said. "You must prove yourself. For all I know, you may be lying when you say you are a knowledge trader. Prove yourself; explain to me what knowledge trading is."

"Oh," said Feliz, beginning to scent a rat in the woodpile. However, just to be on the safe side, he gave a straightforward description of his work.

"That is correct," said the man behind the desk, when he was finished. "You are exonerated on one count of spying. Now—"

But Feliz, in the process of explaining himself, had found time to think. And now he spoke up. "Listen," he interrupted. "Maybe your men didn't notice it when they picked me up, but I had just finished talking to your mayor—"

The slight good impression Feliz had seemed to have produced with the explanation of his work vanished immediately.

"Mayor!" shouted the central figure opposite him. "What is this nonsense? What lies are these? There is no mayor in this city. There is only the Controller—me—Taki Manoai. Talk to me of mayors and I'll have you shot."

"Well, he called himself a mayor," growled Feliz. "An old gink in a red kilt and tunic."

"Enough of such deviationist talk!" stormed the Controller. "Kilts are decadent; tunics are forbidden. The aberrant strain that pretended to see different shades in the One Color Black eradicated itself from this planet years ago."

"Look around you, Bub—" began Feliz; but that was as far as he got. Then Controller began to foam at the mouth; and nightsticks approached . . .

Feliz nursed his aching head and contemplated a bowl of synthetic gruel that sat before him. It was the first jail he had been in where a small bribe slipped to the jailer could not manage to arrange a few palatable additions to the ordinary diet. The turnkey in this case had merely looked blank when Feliz had mentioned protein steak.

"What kind of machine does that come out of?" he had inquired.

"The same machine as this," said Feliz.

"No it don't," said the guard. "I been watching that thing for years and the only thing that come out was gruel."

"You nitwit!" roared Feliz, "you've got to change the settings."

"Nunh-uh," said the guard, backing away. "You don't get me to commit no sabotage."

Now, for some hours, Feliz and his bowl of gruel had been left severely alone. He got up now from his cot and stepped over, with an intention of testing his strength against the bars that formed the front of his cell. He could handle most ordinary metal, provided it was not too thick—

but these upright shafts seemed to have a particularly tough core. They gave a little, but sprang back into shape. Through the high-barred window of his cell, he could see that night was drawing on. If he could find a soft spot in his cell, and vigilance was sufficiently relaxed during the dark hours, there was a chance he could break out of here. And then—head for the ship and wide open space.

The chances looked good. For a number of hours now, no jailer had approached him; and as far as he could see down the corridor both ways, the cells about him appeared to be deserted. In fact, as far as he had been able to discover, he was the only prisoner in the whole jail building. This situation, if true, was fantastic, but no more so than a host of other things that Feliz was learning to accept as the norm for this screwy world.

The daylight was dwindling and the lights (evidently thousand-year automatics) waxed into brightness to take its place. Feliz eyed the closest glowing spot and calculated whether a well-thrown shoe could put it out of commission.

III

A timid little voice said, "Pardon me. Are you really not a hallucination?"

Feliz Gebrod jumped like a startled elephant; he had been certain that he was alone in this part of the building. He jerked his head to the left, and saw, peering at him from the corridor around the wall that separated his cell from the one on its left, the face of the girl in the woods.

"You!" bellowed Feliz, bounding to his feet.

The face jerked back. Feliz rushed to the bars, and, craning his neck, stared down the corridor to his left. He was just able to make her out, shrinking against the bars of the cell next door.

"Come here," ordered Feliz, in the impatient tone of voice people use on a lost puppy when they want to look at the owner's name on its collar, and the pup, not understanding, is shy.

She shook her head.

"Damn it, come here!" said Feliz impatiently; "I won't bite you. Don't you know I can't get through these bars?" He shook them—but carefully—to emphasize his point.

Shyly, she approached.

"Are you sure you aren't a hallucination?"

"Do I look like one?" demanded Feliz, exasperated.

"Oh, yes," answered the girl. "You aren't wearing the right kind of clothes for a real person at all."

Feliz stared at her.

"And what kind of clothes would that be?" he asked at length.

"You know," said the girl.

"No, I *don't* know," gritted Feliz, maintaining a stranglehold on his temper by heroic effort.

"Why, the kind of clothes I'm wearing," said the girl. "Kilt and tunic. Of course, your things are brown instead of black; that's one of the reasons I came after you."

Feliz hung on the bars, helplessly. "Thank you," he said weakly. "And what're some of the other reasons?"

She blushed. "There's really only one," she said.

Feliz looked at her, puzzled.

"I'm ashamed to admit it," she squirmed. Feliz began to feel a little uncomfortable himself. "—But when I bit into it—"

"You *what?*" cried Feliz.

"Well, after all, there's nothin' more natural than that you would have a hallucination about something you want very much," said the girl, suddenly speaking very rapidly, "and if there was anything I badly wanted, it was something to eat. Who would have thought there was food of that shape and color and taste that you gave me? —I mean,

I didn't realize it was food at first; but after I ran away with you and found I still had it in my hands, I couldn't resist taking a bite because I was so hungry, and it tasted good and I ate it all—'' she ran down suddenly and went back to looking embarrassed again ''—and I'm not hungry any more.''

"Ye gods," said Feliz in a hopeless tone, collapsing on the cot in his cell.

"Oh, are you all right?" cried the girl, with a sudden rush of anxiousness.

"Superb," said Feliz, faintly. He breathed deeply for a couple of minutes, shook himself and stood up again. "Look, can you help me get out of here?"

She nodded.

"Go ahead, then," said Feliz. She moved up to the barred door of his cell and fiddled with it, apparently working some kind of combination from the outside. Eventually it swung open.

Feliz came out. "Fine," he said. "Thanks. Now let's go. It's a long way back to the ship." He started off down the corridor.

"No, it isn't," said the girl, half-running to keep up with his long strides.

"Hah!" said Feliz. "Don't tell me—I've been through those woods."

"Yes, but you went all crooked," said the girl. "I was watching you. Actually, if you go straight, it's not more than fifteen minutes from the city."

She was right, of course.

Feliz helped the girl through the hatch, and then entered himself. "Mother of Mephis! I could eat a horse and then sleep for a week."

"You could? What's a horse?" asked the girl. Feliz looked at her.

"Ever hear of an accelerated metabolism?" he said. She

shook her head. "Well, it's what I've got," said Feliz. "In other words, I need a lot of food and sleep."

"Oh," said the girl.

"Yes, oh," said Feliz, opening the food locker, extracting handfuls of comestibles and piling them on the control room table. He seated himself on a stool and sank his teeth into a three-inch hunk of precooked protein steak. "Help yourself," he mumbled.

The girl poked interestedly at the stuff on the table.

"What funny food," she marveled.

"Fummy?" echoed Feliz around a mouthful of steak. "What's fummy aboub it?" The girl did not answer. He swallowed convulsively. "What do you eat?"

"Natural things," she answered. "Nature's bounty. Fruits and nuts and roots. We find them in the woods."

"How come you were so hungry when I met you, then?" demanded Feliz. The girl hung her head.

"I didn't know where to look," she said; "the old people always did the food hunting."

"I see," said Feliz severely and was about to add to it by suggesting that she let that be a lesson to her when a certain native caution silenced him. It never does any harm in cases like this, he reflected sagely, to hold your tongue.

"You should have stolen some of that synthetic gunk they handed out to me in the jail," he said.

"Oh that." She shuddered. "That's what the hallucinations eat."

"Hallucinations!" barked Feliz—this was a sore spot with him. "Don't start that again!"

"Oh, I'm so mixed up," wailed the girl. She seemed to be on the verge of dissolving into tears again.

"Hold it—" said Feliz, hastily. "Hold it. Maybe I can help you. Suppose you fill me in on the whole business from the beginning."

The girl sniffed a few times, but willpower won out over waterpower.

"Well, I'm an artist," she said, and looked at Feliz as if that explained everything. Chewing an opportune mouthful, he waved at her to continue.

"—I mean we're all artists, of course, in the sense that we choose one means or another for creative self-expression. But I mean I'm a painter of the Neo-Classic school of expression." Feliz's eyebrows went up in a mute question. "Oh, that's right, you wouldn't know about that. The Neo-Classic school believes in Interpretative Representationalism."

Feliz's eyebrows remained up. "You know!" said the girl, exasperatedly. "Well, you know what representational painting is, anyway, don't you? When you see a house, you paint a house; it's like making a print of it. Well, Interpretative Representationalism is where you represent the house exactly as it is, but through the modified use of color, and the addition of detail, you interpret the essential personalo-creative essential and make it manifest."

Feliz's eyebrows came down, defeated. "Never mind," he groaned.

"But you don't understand," the girl rushed on, "it was all right for a while; but after a time I began painting in things that weren't there."

"The hallucinations, I suppose," said Feliz with heavy irony.

"Yes," she sighed. "And then, of course, I started seeing them." Her eyes clouded up again. "Oh, I knew it was an aberrant pattern; I knew my adjustment was slipping. But like a fool I closed my eyes to the facts. A fool!" The note of high tragedy in her voice rang a little tinny and practiced at the end, and she glanced sideways at Feliz to see how he was taking it. "Don't you think so?" she inquired.

"Damned if I know," said Feliz, unhelpfully. He loosened his belt and pushed the rest of the food away from him. "Now for a short session of sleep."

"But I'm not finished," she protested.

"Oh," yawned Feliz. Sleep was really overpowering him now, and he had to fight to keep his eyes open. "Go on."

"Well, sooner or later it was bound to slip," the girl went on. "Every day I expected to give myself away about what I was seeing. I remember one day I was talking to Esi Malto—she's a girl friend of mine—and she said to me, 'How's the painting coming?' and I said to her . . ." Feliz dozed off, hearing her voice fade into a drone and then into nothingness.

"—Bang! And so I was disintegrated!"

Feliz sat up with a jerk.

"What? Wh—" Abruptly he remembered what had been going on. He licked his lips and swallowed to clear his mouth, which seemed to be filled with the kind of fuzz that collects in corners and under beds. "I tell you what, kid; let me sleep on it." He shoved himself to his feet, staggered across the control room, into the cabin and fell on the lefthand bunk.

"Why don't you catch a few winks yourself?" he said; and tumbled off into the deep, deep, bottomless, all-obliterating well of slumber.

When he woke it was daylight again, with sunbeams coming in through the open hatch and casting their reflection through the cabin door, on the wall above his bunk. Filled with a sudden alarm at his carelessness, Feliz thrust himself from the bunk, stumbled to the controls and closed and locked the hatch; then, dropping into the control room pilot's chair with a heavy sigh, he sat back to give himself a chance to wake up. Out of sight behind him, he heard the girl, singing some local song full of odd tremolos and repetitions. He painfully craned his neck around and looked at her. She was drawing something in his logbook. Suddenly he remembered the shower off the cabin; getting up, he staggered back and fell into it.

After blasting himself first with hot water, then cold, he became sufficiently awake to feel comfortable again. He stepped out of the shower, dressed, and returned to the control room. The girl was still at it. From somewhere she had produced a stick of charcoal and was sketching the figure of a man. Feliz looked closer. It was himself, stretched out on the lefthand bunk and dead to the world. He opened his mouth to protest and then closed it again.

"How do you like it?" asked the girl, turning around.

"I'd like it better if it wasn't in my logbook." growled Feliz. And then, as the girl's face fell— "Never mind. I'm sure the port inspectors will understand." He rubbed his hands together. "Well! How about some breakfast."

"I ate last night," said the girl. "After you went to sleep. Are you hungry *again?*"

"Got to keep my strength up," said Feliz jovially; turning to the food locker, "we've got a long trip ahead of us to Congerman."

"To Congerman?" echoed the girl.

"Why, yes," replied Feliz, "you see, I figure—" he let go of the locker door handle suddenly and turned. He walked across to the controls, unlocked and opened the hatch. He started to walk toward the open hatch.

The girl stared at him. "Where are you going?"

"I don't know," yelled Feliz, climbing out the hatch. "Stop me!"

He reached the ground; and, turning his head toward the distant city, started to walk off. "Help!" he yelled.

The girl scrambled out of the hatch and hurried after him. "Are you under compulsion?" she asked anxiously.

"Yes!" roared Feliz. "Do something!"

The girl wrung her hands. "There isn't anything I can do," she said. "How did you ever get put under compulsion?"

"I met that old unmentionable that calls himself your mayor!" snarled Feliz, his face reddening from the fight he was putting up against the coercion that was being exercised upon him. "The misbegotten, unclean article of refuse did this to me once before."

"Oh, dear," said the girl, "El Hoska is awfully severe. He's the one who decided I had to be disintegrated."

Feliz turned his head sideways with an effort to look at her. "What's that?" he asked in sudden alarm.

The girl's lower lip began to quiver at the memory. "He said I had become so greatly maladjusted that there was no hope of correcting me; and that I was a danger to the community." She choked. "He said he'd have to disintegrate me. Then he snapped his fingers. And bang, just like that, I ceased to exist."

"What do you mean?" barked Feliz. "Ceased to exist? You're existing now, aren't you?"

"You're the only one who thinks so," said the girl; "nobody else can see or feel me. And maybe we're both hallucinations."

Feliz grunted in supreme scorn, but conserved his breath and put his mind to work on the situation he now found himself in.

They had been following almost a straight line through the woods. Now they came out near the stone wall where Feliz had met El Hoska before; and sure enough, here he was again, beaming all over his bony, ancient face.

"Good morning, good morning," he cried, as Feliz marched up to him. "I hope you had a pleasant night."

The compulsion ceased abruptly; Feliz, by a great effort of will, restrained his natural impulse to pick up the skinny mayor and break him in half. "Marvelous," he gritted from between clenched teeth. He looked from the mayor to the girl and back again. "You two know each other, I suppose?"

"I beg your pardon," said El Hoska, with a puzzled expression on his face.

"The girl here," roared Feliz, jerking a thumb at her. "The one you disintegrated, remember?"

"But there is nobody here but the two of us," said El Hoska; and the girl began to sob quietly. Suddenly the mayor's face saddened. "You wouldn't—" he began. "You haven't possibly heard of the girl named Kai Miri, who I was forced to disintegrate a few days ago? Would that be who you mean?"

"Well, for the love of Mephis!" cried Feliz. "She's standing right in front of you."

"Now, now," soothed the mayor, paying no attention to Kai Miri at all, "you are obviously a maladjusted young man. Look at the matter logically. When she was disintegrated, the atoms of which she was composed were scattered over a tremendous area, and the natural air-currents will have dispersed them further. Don't you see that it would be impossible to collect them all together again in one spot, even if by doing so you could put them back the way they were and restore her to life?"

Kai Miri began to sob even louder at the thought of the wide acres over which her atoms had been distributed by the natural air-currents.

"Never mind, never mind," condoled Feliz, reaching an awkward hand over to pat her shoulder comfortingly.

"Tch, tch," clicked the mayor, his eyes on Feliz's pawing hand. "You must let me give you some counselling, my boy; you have a bad hallucination there."

"I'm leaving," said Feliz.

"But you mustn't!" cried the mayor. "Really, we must insist that you stay. There's something we need badly that only you can do for us."

"What?" demanded Feliz, suspiciously.

The mayor folded his skinny hands complacently over the white sheaf of his beard. "As I told you previously," he began in a fond tone, "we have passed through and beyond the stage of a mechanical civilization, sloughing off those maladjusted minds which would have retarded our development some centuries back. We have little use for the city nowadays. Although some of us still sleep and gather in its quaint old halls—"

"Ever been in its quaint old jail?" inquired Feliz, nastily.

"Pardon?" said the mayor.

"Nothing—" said Feliz. "Go on."

"—But we do retain a fondness for one part of it—and that is the public square to which I led you yesterday. There, many of us still love to gather in the sun and hold intelligent conversations. Now—" he paused and squinted roguishly at Feliz, "after I left you yesterday, a thought struck me. The one thing needed to perfect the square for our purposes. The sun and the air—two of the three parts of nature are there—but where is the water? In short, what we need in the square is a pool with a tinkling fountain in its center."

"You do?" said Feliz, coldly.

"Exactly," answered the mayor with satisfaction. "And since all of us have passed beyond the knowledge of mechanical things, it occurred to me that you, being of a more primitive order, would be the very man to construct such a pool and fountain."

"Thanks," said Feliz.

"You're welcome," said El Hoska.

"But no thanks," said Feliz. "As I told you, I'm leaving."

"But we couldn't permit that," said the mayor, with a shake of his head, "no, we couldn't permit that at all."

"Gonna make me build you a fountain, huh?" growled Feliz, his ample jaw jutting dangerously.

"Certainly not!" Shocked horror showed on the old

man's face. "I know you will be glad to do this, if you only give yourself time to think it over. Merely let me insist that you be our guest until such time as you make up your mind."

"I've already made up my mind," said Feliz.

"No, no," corrected the old man. "You just *think* you've made up your mind." He relaxed, beaming. "But, enough of business for one day. Come with me to the square."

"Charmed," gritted Feliz, as his legs began, willy-nilly, to carry him down the slope alongside El Hoska.

Kai Miri timidly brought up the rear.

They halted on the edge of the square. "Within this city," said the mayor, "you will find inspiration."

"That's not all I'll find," said Feliz. Two of the black uniformed men crossing the area had just spotted him and were now approaching at a run. One was a tall, unhappy-looking man with a watery nose, which he wiped on his sleeve as he ran. The other was short and fat. Both drew their sidearms as they approached.

"True," replied El Hoska, obliviously. "The city will undoubtedly make its impact upon you in other ways."

"Halt, jailbreaker!" shouted the tall man with the runny nose as he skidded to a halt, covering Feliz with his weapon. "Make a move and you will be shot. Come with me."

"Us," said the short man.

"Us," agreed the tall one.

"I'd like to, boys," said Feliz, "but the old gent here has a mind clamp on me."

"What nonsense is this?" demanded the tall man. "Come at once!"

"Excuse me," said Feliz to El Hoska, "I've got to go."

"Go where?" asked the mayor.

"Wherever these ginks want to take me," said Feliz.

The mayor stared blankly at and through the two uniformed men.

"Young man," he said firmly, to Feliz, "you are obviously badly maladjusted. I would be remiss in my human duty if I did not begin counselling you at once with a view toward returning your mind to a better state of health. You are obviously seeing things. Sit down and relax, now, and let your mind go blank—"

Feliz tried with all his will to fight the compulsion as his knees folded beneath him and he sank to the ground.

"What obstructionist tactics are these?" shouted the tall man, wiping his nose. "Get up at once, fugitive, or you will be shot!"

"Kai!" called Feliz, desperately.

"Yes?" quavered the girl.

"Can you see these boys with the guns?"

"They were the first hallucinations to obsess me," she sighed.

"Well they're about to obsess me for keeps unless I go with them," yelped Feliz. "Will you kindly clunk the old man over the head with something so I can get loose."

Kai looked doubtful; but took off her right sandal. It had a thick wooden sole, which connected with the mayor's head with a satisfying noise. El Hoska sagged like an empty sack; Feliz, leaping to his feet, literally hurried his captors out of the square, leaving Kai looking down at El Hoska with an odd, pleased expression on her pretty face.

They whisked around a corner and into a building that Feliz did not remember having seen before. An escalator rose before them, but it did not seem to be moving; they went up its steps as if it had been an ordinary stair.

On the second floor was a long hallway. Some distance down this, the tall man and the short directed Feliz off to the right, into a smaller corridor, which led through a door into a lofty and somewhat over-furnished apartment. Stand-

ing by a table with a glass of purple liquid in his hand was
the man who called himself City Controller, Taki Manoai.

At the sight of Feliz, his face lit up. "Ah, so you've
recaptured him," he said to the two men. "Good."

He turned to Feliz. "What have you to say for yourself, spy?" he demanded. "You broke out of our jail.
Jailbreakers—"

"I know," interrupted Feliz, wearily, "jailbreakers are
shot. Never mind about that now. The important thing is
that at any moment now I may try to get away again; and
I'd appreciate it if you restrained me, firmly but—ah,
gently."

Taki Manoai scowled. "What is this farce?" he inquired. "If you do not wish to leave, why should you try
to leave? Besides, if you do we will shoot you."

"Look," said Feliz desperately, "you don't understand.
The man who calls himself the mayor of the people in
colored clothes—"

"Silence!" shrieked the Controller. "You are aberrant.
Mayors. People in colored clothes. There are no such
things; there is nobody here but us."

IV

Behind Feliz Gebrod, the door made an opening and
shutting noise; Kai Miri came into the room. None of the
three men paid the slighest attention to her.

"Oh, there you are," she said, to Feliz. "I was afraid I
wouldn't find you. El Hoska thinks he had a brain-stroke
and he's not going to try to locate you mentally until his
headache goes away. He's gone home to lie down and rest
his head. Some of the real people are looking for you
physically, though. But they went off toward your ship, so
you're all right for now."

"All right!" exploded Feliz. "All right—when these people here may blow my head off at any minute?"

Kai Miri looked doubtfully at the other three men. "I suppose they could, at that," she admitted slowly. "I'm so used to thinking of them as unreal, it's hard to take them seriously."

The Controller had been shouting at Feliz during this conversation. Now Feliz turned to him to see what it was he wanted.

"—and stop talking to empty air. I command you!" the Controller was thundering. "If I were a mentally weak person, it would be very disturbing. Stop it immediately; that's a direct order."

"All right," said Feliz, mildly.

The Controller stopped shouting and mopped his brow. "That's better," he said in a normal tone of voice. He gulped thirstily from the drink in his hand. "I'll teach you to obey orders. Now sit down; I want to talk to you."

Feliz took the indicated chair and the Controller flopped into one facing it. He set down his empty glass on the desk beside him.

"What about?" asked Feliz.

"Silence," barked the Controller. "I am not going to talk *with* you, I am going to talk *to* you. Your function is to listen and obey."

"Or else I get shot," said Feliz.

"Exactly," said the Controller. He blinked at Feliz; and then glared at him. "What do you mean by that?"

"Nothing," said Feliz, innocently. "It's the truth, isn't it?"

"Everything I say is the truth," snarled the Controller.

Kai Miri had disappeared through a door into the interior of the apartment. Now she returned, staggering slightly under the weight of a huge, ornate vase, with sharp, metallic corners.

"Shall I clunk him over the head with it?" she asked, taking up her station behind the Controller's chair.

"No!" shouted Feliz, casting a sudden apprehensive glance at the weapons which still covered him in the hands of the tall man and the short.

Disappointed, she lowered the vase to the floor and sat on it. The Controller waved his fist in front of Feliz's nose, foaming at the mouth.

"Do you dare to contradict me?" he shouted.

"Slip of the tongue," said Feliz, hastily.

"It better not slip again," said the Controller, ominously. "Listen and obey; you are full of knowledge about new inventions, aren't you?"

"More or less," said Feliz, cautiously.

"Well, I happen to need your abilities at the moment," said the Controller. "Only when everybody works for the good of all, can good for all be obtained. Since universal good is the universal desire of the general populace, it follows that everybody wants to work for the good of all at all times. But since the individual suffers from human weakness, it follows that a constant reminder of what is universal good would be a great help. Now I want you to build me a reminder which will keep everybody aware of what they ought to be doing at all times."

Feliz scratched his head. "Just what did you have in mind?" he asked.

"Oh, I'll leave the details up to you," said the Controller, waving his hand, airily. "Just don't take more than three days building it, or you will be shot."

"But," protested Feliz, "I've got to have a clearer picture of what you want."

"It should be obvious," glowered the Controller. "A job for everybody and everybody at his job—that's what I want."

"Tote that barge, lift that bale, eh?" said Feliz.

"What's that?" demanded the Controller sharply.

"Just something out of history," answered Feliz.

"It better be," said the Controller. "I don't like the

sound of it." He glared at Feliz. "I want something to
make people work."

"Sort of a compulsion gadget?"

"Exactly," said the Controller. "Build it immediately."

"There's only one drawback," said Feliz; "it may look
a little like a fountain in the city square when it's finished."

"Drawbacks are prohibited," snapped the Controller.
"Make it look like something else."

"If I do, it won't work," said Feliz. "But maybe it
wouldn't be such a drawback at that. Think of the advantages. Nobody would realize it was a compulsion unit;
they'd take it for a thing of beauty."

"I don't know if I approve of beauty," scowled the
Controller. "Sounds a little bit as if it might distract
people from their work. But, if it *has* to look like a
fountain, go ahead. Men—"

The tall and the short of it, who had been guarding Feliz
all this time with drawn guns, snapped to attention.

"—Take the spy out and shoo—I mean, give him every
facility he needs to complete his job," said the Controller.

They went out, Kai Miri following.

The man with the watery nose sniffled, "Well, spy,"
when they were once more outside the apartment building.
"What sort of stuff do you want to start work with?
Answer immediately."

"You go to hell," replied Feliz, gently. The man with
the watery nose stared at him. "Be nice to me," Feliz
went on, "or I'll report you to the Controller in there for
not cooperating." He leered at the two uniformed individuals. "Well, how about it?"

"Yes, sir," said the man with the watery nose, nervously; and a murmur from his short companion echoed
the sentiment.

"That's better," said Feliz. "Now, I'll tell you what
we're going to do. One of you is going to walk about ten

yards ahead of me and point out the way; the other is going to walk about ten yards behind and bring up the rear. You may hear me talking to myself from time to time, but don't let it disturb you; I'll just be working out my plans.''

Feliz glared at them to make sure that there was no opposition to this arrangement; but it seemed that his threat about the Controller had settled their relative positions once and for all. In fact, the two men seemed rather glad to be back in the normal position of taking orders, rather than giving them.

''Yes, sir, where to, sir?'' said the tall man, sniffling.

''To your power machine warehouse,'' replied Feliz. ''I've got to see what you've got in the way of equipment for this job.''

They led off.

As they went down the street, Feliz reached back for Kai Miri, who was lagging behind him, caught hold of a corner of her cloak and drew her up level with him. ''Now listen,'' he said tensely. ''It's high time you and I got down to some facts—''

''There's something you've got to tell me first,'' she interrupted.

''What?'' said Feliz, remembering at the last minute not to shout his exasperation.

''What's your name?'' she asked.

''I told you my name,'' he said.

''No, you didn't.''

''Yes, I did.''

''No, you didn't.''

''Didn't I?''

''No.''

''Well, for the sake of sweet Mephis! It's Feliz Gebrod; I don't know why you had to wait until just now, when time is short, to ask me that.''

''I like it.''

"Like what?"

"Your name."

"Ye Gods!" bellowed Feliz, raising his fists to the sky (his two man escort jumped and cringed). "Will you stop maundering on about my name? I'm trying to talk about something important." He took a deep breath. "Now tell me. How long have your bunch and this outfit in black been ignoring each other?"

"Names are important," said Kai. "Ignoring each other?"

"You know what I mean," Feliz said.

Kai sobered suddenly; and a little fear came creeping into her eyes. "Nobody's ever paid any attention to hallucinations," she said. "Nobody. Except—except," her voice stumbled, "maybe the children."

"The children?" demanded Feliz.

"When you're very young, you see hallucinations all the time," she answered. "But when you get older, they disappear." This reminded her of her own tragedy. "Except in my case," she quivered.

"How long have children been seeing them?" asked Feliz.

"Why," said Kai, "ever since the world began, I suppose. For thousands of years."

"Great Mother!" ejaculated Feliz, in astonishment, looking at her. "Don't you know your history only goes back about four hundred years?"

"Why, it does not!" cried Kai. "The world is millions of years old. If you knew any geology, you'd realize that, yourself." And she stamped on ahead, prettily angry.

Feliz took two long strides and caught up with her. "Sure," he said, "sure, about three billion years to be exact. But it wasn't colonized—none of the worlds in this sector of the galaxy was colonized by the human race until about five hundred years ago."

"Oh, don't be silly," said Kai, disgustedly. "How could we have reached such a high level of civilization in a thousand years? We're *much* more advanced than a mechanical savage like yourself.''

"Who in the name of all that's natural said you'd reached a high level of civilization?'' shouted Feliz. The guard behind stopped to fasten his bootstrap; the one ahead quickened his pace. Prudent men, both.

"Isn't it obvious?'' she said. "We have, unlike you, passed beyond the need for mechanical things. We have gone back to nature on a higher plane, where material elements are not necessary.''

"Oh no?'' snapped Feliz. He reached out and grabbed a handful of her cloak. "Look at this. Cast plastic. The same material my clothes are made of. The same material that goes into the uniforms these black-dressed monkeys wear.''

His last sentence drove all the color from her face. She swayed and would have fallen if he had not caught her.

"Here—'' said Feliz, overwhelmed. "What's the matter? Stand up.''

With an effort she regained her feet; but she walked beside him, trembling. "Don't ever say that,'' she whispered. "You make me go sick all over when you say that. Their clothes aren't like ours. They're nothing like us; they're hallucinations!''

"You know better than that,'' said Feliz, brutally, and she all but collapsed. "Sweet Mephis!'' said Feliz. "What gets into you when I point out similarities between you and them?''

"I don't know,'' she whimpered.

They walked along in silence for a while. Then something occurred to Feliz. He shouted to the tall man ahead to wait and caught up with him.

"What's your name?'' asked Feliz.

"Og Lokman, sir,'' sniffled the guard.

"Well, well, Og Lokman,'' said Feliz, with a side glance at Kai. "That's a fine old name.''

"Do you think so, sir?" said Og, doubtfully. "I invented it myself when name-choosing time came around."

"That so?" said Feliz, in quick recovery. "At what age do they choose names around here?"

(*"Do you choose names where you come from?"* asked Kai, looking at Feliz.)

(*"Certainly not,"* said Feliz. *"I'm just gaining his confidence."*)

"Beg pardon, sir?" said Og.

"I didn't hear your answer," said Feliz. Og cleared his throat and spoke forcefully, if somewhat adenoidally.

"I said—twelve years old, sir," he replied.

"Before that, I suppose you're in school, learning things," said Feliz.

"Oh, yes sir," said Og enthusiastically. "We sing—" and without further warning, he broke into a tune:

> *"All hail to the Controller*
> *Whoever he may be*
> *And hail to the beautiful black*
> *Only color I can see.*

"Little nonsense rhymes like that, sir," said Og, dropping suddenly back into prose. "A lot of them don't make any sense—I mean—since black's the only color, how could you see any other kind anyhow. But we play games and dance to them. It improves our coordination."

"But don't you have any history courses?" asked Feliz.

"Oh, yes, sir," said Og; and began to recite. "History began with the first Controller. His name was Upi Havo and he was a good man. He improved the lot of the people, and died full of years. The second Controller—"

"How long ago was this first Controller?" interrupted Feliz.

"Two hundred and thirty-eight years, sir," said Og; "before that was Chaos."

"Chaos?" echoed Feliz.

"Yessir," said Og. "The planet was colonized four hundred years ago, but the first two hundred years there was nothing but Chaos, because the world was full of aberrant people." He waved his thin hands in a wide arc. "All the city here was built during Chaos. A terrible time." He shuddered.

"Why?" asked Feliz.

Og looked puzzled. "Why?" he repeated. "I—er— couldn't tell you exactly. It just was. Everybody knows that."

"Tell me," said Feliz, drawing closer to the man confidentially. Og drew back in some apprehension; but Feliz clamped a powerful hand on his wrist and dragged him close. "Tell me, just between the two of us—do you ever *see* things?"

Beads of sweat burst out on Og's forehead and his knees buckled.

"No, no!" he cried, in a high-pitched, terrified voice. "I never see anything. Never! Never!"

"Come now," growled Feliz, shaking him annoyedly. "Tell the truth. I'm not like the rest of you, you know; I know you see things. I see things myself; that's why I know."

"No!" screamed Og. "I see nothing. Absolutely nothing. Even when I was a child, I didn't see people in impossible-colored clothes like the other children did. I never have glimpses of people; I don't ever feel anyone near me. I'm perfectly adjusted, I tell you. Perfectly!"

"All right," said Feliz, disgustedly. He let go of the man and Og staggered ahead, intent on putting as much space between them as Feliz's order had allowed.

"Well, what do you think of that?" asked Feliz, turning to Kai. "I—" he stopped. She was deathly pale.

"I don't know!" she cried, suddenly. "Leave me alone!" Abruptly she twisted away from him; and, running off, disappeared down one of the side streets. Feliz growled after her, wondering why all these people made such a fuss over admitting to the fact that what they thought were hallucinations were actually realities. Which led him, by a sort of reverse action, to speculate idly whether this whole planet might not be a hallucination of his own, a sort of feverish nightmare brought on by the fact that he was in delirium someplace—say in the wreck of his spaceship, which had cracked up on landing, after all. Abruptly he shivered; and began thereafter to think more sympathetically of Kai and the rest.

"Sir," said Og, reluctantly allowing him to approach. "Here is the power machine warehouse."

Feliz waited a moment for the short man behind to catch up and then they went in, all three of them.

V

The warehouse was a lofty building, well filled with rank on military rank of mobile construction equipment. Feliz Gebrod strolled down the center corridor, looking over the ranks like an inspecting general and debating which of the many machines available he could (a) use and (b) run. Then it struck him that undoubtedly there were skilled machine operators among the black-uniformed people. He turned and put the question to Og.

"Sir?" said Og, blankly.

"I said," said Feliz impatiently, "you have men who know how to run these things, don't you?"

"No, sir," said Og.

Feliz stared at him. "You don't?" he echoed incredulously. "Where are the machine operators, then?"

"There aren't any, sir," said Og, almost stuttering in his alarm at having to disappoint Feliz and probably therefore also the Controller. "We've just enough men to run the food plant and the clothing unit, sir. Nobody was ever trained on these machines, sir. Please, sir—"

"Oh, shut up!" said Feliz, disgruntled. He turned around and stumped back through the machines. Nobody to run their construction equipment. No wonder the city was running downhill. The mayor's people, those bright colored butterflies, would never consider anything so crude as running a machine; and these people didn't have the personnel—besides a social setup which, if he were any judge, would be sure death to initiative. If the whole planet was like this one city, the world of Dunroamin was going to hell in a hand-basket.

"How about other cities?" he asked. "Could they lend us some machine operators?"

"Sir?" said Og, astounded.

"You heard me," barked Feliz, impatiently.

"N-no sir. I'm sure not," stuttered Og. "They wouldn't have any, either; but anyway we don't have anything to do with each other, since right after the Great Purge."

"What great purge?" asked Feliz.

"Two hundred and thirty-eight years ago, sir. After Chaos. When they got rid of the Color People."

"Go on!" snapped Feliz.

"The Color People were evil," shuddered Og. "They wouldn't do any work; they just sat around in the sun doing immoral things, like talking and singing about things not connected with duty, and cutting pieces of wood and stone into shapes and making images on paper. So we had to purge them. And then, after they were gone, we discovered all the other cities had set up imposters as Controller; and we haven't had much to do with them since."

"Imposters?"

"Yes, sir. The only real Controller is here, sir."

"Hah!" said Feliz.

"Yes, sir," said Og.

Feliz looked back at the machines. His own knowledge was highly specialized, in the sense that it was concerned primarily with theoretic techniques. He could, he told himself, probably teach himself to manipulate the necessary equipment; but his nature revolted against the waste of time and the effort involved. Besides, if he could just avoid these guards of his and the mental lasso El Hoska seemed to be able to manipulate, he was going to take off. And that would be a lot easier to do, if he was busy in a supervisory capacity.

"What the hell," he said. "I suppose you have some men who can use a pick and shovel."

"No, sir," said Og.

"No?" repeated Feliz. He grinned to himself. "Well, don't let that worry you," he went on, patting the tall man on the shoulder, "I'll show your machine shop how to make some and—you *do* have a machine shop operating?"

"Oh, yes, sir," said Og.

"Why then, we're all set," said Feliz.

The mayor said, "Young man, your attitude concerns me."

"Swing those shovels faster!" yelled Feliz, looking down into the hole in the middle of the square where a number of the black-clad men were laboring. He wiped his forehead and turned back to the mayor. "What's that?" he asked.

El Hoska looked at him with benign sorrow. It was three days since Feliz's inspection of the machinery warehouse and his decision to use hand tools. That evening El Hoska and his group had caught up with him, and only some very fast talking on Feliz's part had prevented a reestablishment of the mind clamp. He had promised them immediate action on their fountain; and explained that he had run off to make some necessary arrangements preparatory to the actual work. The following day and the next, both the mayor and the Controller had come out to the job and breathed on his neck in relays. But on this day he had, so far, been left alone.

In fact, the only thing that wasn't running quite according to schedule was Kai Miri, who had not put in an appearance again since three days before—when she had run away from him down that side street. Feliz frowned unseeing at the black-clad pick-and-shovel workers. To his own constant annoyance, he found himself worrying more and more about her as one day followed another. After all, when he had first bumped into her, she had been headed, it seemed, for sure starvation, since she did not know how to find her ordinary food. He had occasional, infuriating visions of her collapsed in an alley somewhere from weakness, or injured as a result of some accident. But there was nothing he could do about it at present. Two sets of observers kept him quite effectively under surveillance.

"What's that?" he repeated, turning to El Hoska.

"I am concerned," said the mayor, "over this." He waved a hand to indicate the pit where the black-clad men were working.

"What about it?" asked Feliz, suspiciously.

"Come, come, my boy," said El Hoska, linking a skinny arm through Feliz's tree trunklike one. "This machinery you're using."

"Machinery?" Feliz blinked at the sweating laborers.

El Hoska chuckled and dug him in the ribs with a skinny thumb. "To be sure, the machinery," he said. "You didn't think I was to be fooled by the fact that it's of some kind of transparent plastic, do you? I admit I had a little trouble seeing it at first; but after all, a pool just doesn't excavate itself, does it? No, no. But that wasn't the aspect of it I wanted to discuss with you. It's your own moral attitude that bothers me."

"Uh—I see," said Feliz.

"But *do* you?" inquired El Hoska, drawing him cozily

aside. "The machinery probably does the work faster; but do you realize how you are inhibiting your natural and elemental self, blinding and blunting the sensitivity of your self-identification with Mother Earth by using it? How much better it would have been for you to have gotten down there and labored directly with your hands. Feel the good, rich soil crumble under your eager fingers, and the gratification of your straining muscles."

"Oh?" said Feliz. "If it's so blasted good, why don't you volunteer for the job yourself?"

"But my boy!" cried El Hoska. "I have spent my life becoming attuned to nature; I have *made* my identification. You are the one who needs help; and that is what has brought me to you. I really think we should start your counselling immediately."

Feliz looked at the old man. There was something hidden behind the faded old eyes; and he was not quite able to read it. He looked about him. The Controller was not in evidence, and the only people of the black clothes around was his laboring crew. This might be his chance.

"Carry on," he said abruptly to the crew; and, turning to El Hoska, went on, "There's something I have to get from my ship for the fountain. Why don't you walk out with me; and you can counsel on the way?"

"Excellent," glowed El Hoska. "The forest, the trees. Nature."

"Exactly," said Feliz. He looked about him. The square was still empty of free blacks.

"Let's go," he said.

Feliz could hardly believe his good luck. They had reached the edge of the woods without a single black-clad individual showing up in pursuit. A few strides further and the leafy branches hid them from view. Feliz let out a long-held breath and turned to El Hoska, who had been babbling steadily since they had left the square.

"—The monotheistic attitude of the divertant ego," the mayor was saying, "embranchiates and impalpitates the conscious mind."

"All right," said Feliz, turning to him. "You can turn it off now; we're alone."

The old man winked and chuckled. "Very well, my boy," he said. "Let's get down to plain language: frankly, you're a danger to the community."

"I'd say it was the other way around," commented Feliz. "But let's not worry about that. I've got a nice, simple solution. Just let me get in my ship and take on off out of here."

"Hum," said El Hoska. "Well, now, it isn't quite that easy. You see, you'll be landing on other worlds shortly, and you might mention us; I don't think that would be a good thing."

"Why not?" demanded Feliz bluntly.

"We have progressed a long way from the barbaric stage of life you represent," said El Hoska. "An influx of backward peoples is the last thing we want."

Feliz stared at him. "You don't really believe that guff about having progressed?" he said incredulously. "I gave you credit for more intelligence."

A thin film, like a nictating membrane, seemed to flicker down over the old man's eyes, turning their sunny emptiness suddenly cold and hostile. His voice when he spoke again, however, was still constrained to gentleness. "I believe you've had some little experience of how we've progressed," he murmured.

"The compulsion, eh?" said Feliz, grimly. "Look—all right, so you've got one psi faculty developed to a workable degree. Well, I've got news for you. There's a dozen other little independent human cultures that have done as well—though not necessarily in your direction. Believe it or not, we've all got the same level, more or less, of ability, psi-wise. It's an aspect of racial maturity, and we're getting to it—not through practice, but through evolution.''

"I don't believe you," said the old man. "Why can't you do the same if that's true?"

Feliz restrained an impulse to tear his hair. "Why can't I do stellar spectroanalysis?" he asked. "Why can't I design a spaceship? Because I've never had the inclination nor the training. Look, El Hoska; make an effort. This culture of yours is badly out of whack. Tell me honestly; don't you ever see people dressed in black?"

The mayor stiffened, his spare body like a dry reed leaning against the wind. "I," he said, spacing his words so that they dropped, individual and heavy, like single stones into a well, "see nothing but what is real."

Feliz threw up his hands. "I give up," he said.

They walked for some short distance in silence. Then Feliz felt the thistledown weight of the old man's hand on his shoulder, and turned to see the blue eyes on his own, deep with sincere sympathy. "You will feel better after we have reasoned with you," said El Hoska, gently; and Feliz felt a sudden cold shiver of apprehension that trickled icily down his spine.

They had traversed the green hush of the woods; and now they came out on the meadow. The ship stood as it had stood since the morning of its landing; the common-sense, down-to-earth reality of its appearance almost a shock (but a welcome one) to Feliz after the weirdness of his experiences during the last few days. At the hatch, El Hoska halted.

"I would not go any nearer to a machine than I can help," he said. "I'll wait for you out here." He turned a slightly troubled face toward Feliz. "You realize—if you try to get away, I can stop you."

Feliz nodded shortly, and climbed in through the hatch. After the bright sunlight of the meadow, the interior of the ship, illuminated only by what reflected light came through the hatch opening, seemed plunged in gloom. Even Feliz's excellent vision saw things only dimly. He sat down, therefore, on the chair before the control board and waited for his eyes to adjust.

As the room seemed to brighten about him, he began to notice differences about it. Here things had been slightly disarranged. Here they had been put back in an order different from the one he normally used. Feliz's eyes narrowed as it became apparent that someone, or more than one, had been here during his absence. He rose from the chair; his eyes, now fully adjusted, sweeping the room; and he stepped back into the cabin. Here, his searching eyes discovered further small evidence of trespassers. He turned back into the control room and yanked open the door of the food locker. Abruptly, his tension left him and he grinned. Some of the food was gone; but in addition to that, the charcoal sketch Kai Miri had made of him on a page of the logbook was lying there, only it had been added to in the form of a small devil with tail and horns who was tickling Feliz's unconscious feet with a large feather. So this was where the girl had been hiding out!

Feliz rubbed his nose, a trifle astonished at the relief that flooded over him at this realization. Abruptly he scowled. It was nothing to him what happened to the girl after she had run out that way. Still—it was good to feel that she was making out all right. He wondered where she was now.

He stepped back into the control room and looked out through the hatch. El Hoska was standing not ten feet away, his back to the hatch, apparently absorbed in his own thoughts.

Feliz's eyes narrowed. So he couldn't get away, huh? He remembered how he had broken free of the old man's control once before when Kai had hit El Hoska over the head with her sandal. He stepped over to a locker built in the control room wall and rummaged within it, coming out with a heavy metal object about eight inches in diameter. With this in his hand, he stepped once more to the hatch.

El Hoska was still with his back turned, still absorbed in contemplation.

Feliz weighed the thing he held grimly in his hand. A quick throw, and— He frowned suddenly. The thought of Kai Miri had just intruded itself on his mind. She could hardly live off the supplies of the space ship after the ship was gone. He remembered his original intention of carting her off with him to Congerman for treatment. She really should be looked at by a competent alienist, just to make sure there was nothing dangerous still buried in the back of her mind. Feliz cursed softly to himself. He stuck the gadget he held into his pocket and climbed out through the hatch.

"Let's go," he said to the mayor.

They walked in silence until they reached the edge of the woods. El Hoska seemed to be lost in his own thoughts still. Then, as they stepped into the shadows of the first trees, he sighed. "When you are old, and in a position of authority," he said, suddenly, with a note almost of wistfulness in his voice, "it is easy to be unfair."

Feliz looked at him sharply.

"It occurs to me," said El Hoska, turning his head to meet the younger man's eyes, "that I have not been exactly fair with you."

"What sort of new approach is this?" inquired Feliz, sourly.

"You don't trust me," sighed the mayor. "I don't blame you. You are full of suspicions, I wish I could make you see this world of ours as I see it."

"I don't doubt it," said Feliz, with grim humor.

"We have," said El Hoska, striding along beneath the trees, his spare body erect, "a good life here. Not a perfect life; and in many ways there are hardships. But there is a good core to it." He glanced at Feliz, sideways. "Would you like to hear our history?"

"I've heard some of it already," said Feliz, thinking of Kai Miri and Og.

"But probably not the full story," said El Hoska. "Few of us know that. It's not a happy story."

"Go ahead," said Feliz, genuinely interested.

"Most of our people don't know—I think they are better off without knowing—how we made the final break with mechanism. At one time what has become our way of life was—" El Hoska winced—"merely a political philosophy. You see," he went on, "I don't try to gloss the matter over. No, originally, we were merely a political party that advocated decentralization of government, and freedom of the individual. There was at that time another party, the Authoritarian Party, which believed in a strict regime and curtailment of individualism. The division was so sharp that, for a time, another people would have gone to war."

"Why didn't you?" asked Feliz.

"For a good reason," said the old man. "Our original colonists had done a wise thing in setting up the law that every child from birth must be hypnotically conditioned against mass violence. Not individual violence, mind you, for that would be an infringement and curtailment of individual rights, but mass or group violence. With this, of course, genocide became intolerable to the individual. Accordingly, we were faced with a split in political beliefs that seemed impossible to heal. So we took the only way out."

The old man turned a face toward Feliz on which pain was written with surprising clarity. "Recognizing that they were, in fact, insane," he said, "we sent all members of the opposing party to Coventry, as the old English expression used to go. In fact, we ignored them and their existence, and set to work to build a life of our own from which they were excluded."

"And what happened?" asked Feliz.

"They died," said the mayor, briefly.

"Died?" echoed Feliz, stopping in his tracks and staring at the old man.

"Of course," said El Hoska, calmly. "What else could they do? Adherents of an outmoded culture, they were not able to survive under our new conditions. Our people noticed them grow fewer and fewer, year by year; and eventually there came a time when no one was to be found anywhere."

"Were any bodies found?" demanded Feliz, bluntly.

"Oh, I imagine some must have been," said El Hoska. "Not many though. Most of them, I suppose, just went out and wandered the roads from town to town, looking for some place where the people would recognize them."

"You're sure of that?" said Feliz, looking hard at him.

"Oh—no," said El Hoska, slowly, "but I imagine that's what happened; something of that order must have taken place."

Feliz came to a decision. Halting, he swung the old man around to face him. "Look," he said. "Have you got an open mind?"

El Hoska smiled sweetly. "The most important aspect of our advanced culture is an open mind," he said.

"Are you willing to admit the *possibility* of something that would turn your whole system upside down?"

"Of course, my boy," said El Hoska. "After all what is real and what is not? No one can tell. I am perfectly ready to believe that I merely exist in your imagination, if you can prove it to me."

"Fine," said Feliz. "Then try this out. Those political opponents of yours didn't die off. They've gone on living side by side with you all these years, conditioning *their* children to ignore *you!*"

El Hoska neither laughed tolerantly, nor looked startled. The shadow of a sadness crossed his ancient face. "So you've been infected, too," he said, laying a hand sympathetically on Feliz's heavy sleeve. "Tell me—you've been seeing people in odd, stiff-cut black clothes, haven't you?"

"And feeling them—" began Feliz.

"Now, now, let's not embroider the tale," said the mayor, gently reproving, "such hallucinations are, unfortunately, common among my people. Many have come to me, to see if I can't help them cure themselves of such. However," he sighed, "there's really nothing I can do to help them. The hallucinations are the result of a racial guilt complex for what our ancestors did to the unfortunate ones many years ago. I am a little surprised that you have been affected, however; the group mind must be stronger than I realized."

"Group mind?" echoed Feliz, dumbfounded.

"Certainly," said the mayor. "The control I exercised over your physical body is merely a funneling and directing of the power of the group mind of my people. Is it surprising that a group mind that can do that should not also be able to impress you with its own hallucinations?"

"Oh, for the sake of my dear, deceased Aunt Hannah!" exploded Feliz. "How extensive a rationalization can you get? I tell you those people are alive and real!"

"Tch, tch," the mayor clicked his tongue, looking at Feliz sympathetically. "No, no, my boy. Take my word for it, these are all mere figments of your imagination. Just keep insisting to yourself firmly that they are not real and they will go away. This advice may seem a little like sophistry at first; but if you try it, I think you'll find it's good, down-to-earth common sense. You, especially, should be able to rid yourself of such fantasies."

"Why me?" asked Feliz.

"Because you come from off-world; and are a barbarian— now, don't be offended, young man—it is precisely because you are a barbarian unable to perceive greater truths that I am taking this much trouble with you. There *are* virtues which a primitive way of life instills in backward peoples—notably the ones of energy and a desire to build. And that, I will admit freely to you, is the one thing my people need. To be truthful with you—" the mayor lowered his voice shamefacedly—"there are only two others besides myself I can count on to do the necessary work in the plastic clothes casting works; and the younger generation will go to any lengths to avoid gathering their own nuts and berries. Even a bountiful nature is abused. Of course I could compel each, individually, by impressment of the community will through the direction of my mind—but that would be authoritarianism. Seriously, young man, someone like yourself would be a great help to us." And he stared into Feliz's face with a sort of wistful hope.

Feliz snorted in loud embarrassment.

"Well, think it over," said El Hoska. "I don't like the idea of coercing you; but in conscience I cannot, and I will not, let you go while there is still a chance of you fitting in here."

VI

On their reentry into the square, Feliz Gebrod found the black-dressed contingent in an uproar over his disappearance. Taking a polite leave of El Hoska, and giving some excuse, he allowed himself to be marched at gunpoint to that office where he had first made the acquaintance of Kai Manoai, the Controller.

"Saboteur! Traitor!" shrieked that individual, bouncing to his feet as Feliz entered. "I will deal with you personally! Out!" The last word was roared at the guards who had brought him in. They scuttled backward and escaped through the door. Feliz braced himself for violent eventualities; but no sooner had the door slammed than the

Controller sagged limply, mopped his brow with an elaborately embroidered black handkerchief and hastily produced a bottle and two glasses.

"Whew!" he breathed, filling the glasses from the bottle with a trembling hand. "You almost gave me a heart attack." He looked reproachfully at Feliz. "What possessed you to run off like that? I thought you were gone for good. Just walked off. What's the trouble?"

"What's the trouble?" echoed Feliz, staring.

"To be sure. I'm a reasonable man," said the Controller. "If you want your working conditions improved, I'll improve them. I need you. You've no idea what it's like around here."

"Oh, don't I?" growled Feliz.

"No, you don't," said the Controller, his face twisting tragically. "Nobody has any initiative!" He pounded the desk, causing the filled glasses to hop and slop their contents. "They're like cattle. Obey orders—yes, fine. But damn it! I can't issue *all* the orders! There's a limit to what flesh and blood can accomplish in any single twenty-four hour period. Look around you—"

Feliz stared, puzzled, about the ornate office.

"Looks like a soft job, doesn't it?" said the Controller bitterly. "Only, it just so happens that about forty crises a day go with it." He groaned. "I don't know why it should be that way. All I ask is unthinking obedience; is it too much to want them to use a little intelligence in the process? I ask you?"

Feliz made a non-committal noise.

" 'Sir, what do I do about this?' " mimicked the Controller in that unpleasant, weak type of voice that people nearly always seem to have used when someone else is reporting the conversation. " 'Please sir, what do I do about that?' 'Sir, may I blow my nose now?' —Next thing they'll want me to blow it for them. Now—" said the Controller, suddenly brightening up—"you're different."

"Me?" said Feliz, taken by surprise.

"Yes, you," said the Controller. "You argued with me the first minute you saw me. It didn't sink in at first; but when I had time to think it over, I realized how wonderful that was. Why, do you realize—" he leaned forward in his chair and tapped Feliz on one baggy knee—"that if two men could approach a problem from two different points of view, they could probably each see the mistakes that the other one was making? And not only that. If they were two men like us, they could just sit down, face to face, and come right out and tell each other where they were wrong Now, what do you think of that?"

Feliz goggled.

"Speechless, eh?" said the Controller, triumphantly. "I thought you would be." He poured his own glass full for the second time and added a drop to Feliz's almost untasted portion. "Well, I'm about to offer you a job."

Feliz growled.

"Now, don't jump before you're hit," went on the Controller, complacently. "I don't mean to put you to work working *for* me, but working *with* me. How'd you like to be Co-Controller, with all rights, privileges, and duties appertaining thereto? I'll be honest with you; there's more duties than rights or privileges at the present moment; but with the two of us working together, we should be able to improve that aspect of the situation."

Feliz found his voice.

"No thanks," he said.

"Now, don't be hasty," reproved the Controller. "I can't afford to have you running around loose. If you say no and mean no, I'll have to shoot you the minute this compulsion gadget of yours is finished. And I'm serious when I say there's a real need for you here. These people are so used to being ordered that they'd starve to death if there wasn't someone to command them to eat at regular intervals. Think it over.''

"All right," growled Feliz. "I'll think."

"That's being sensible," said the Controller. "You've got until the gadget is finished to make up your mind. By the way, when will it be finished?"

"We'll be flooding the pool with water tonight," said Feliz. "I should be able to turn it on early tomorrow."

"Good," said the Controller. "We'll hold a full scale assembly in the square tomorrow at noon, then, for the celebration of turning it on. I still don't understand, though," he added with a frown, "what you need all that water around it for. It seems to me—look here, what *do* you want a pool of water for?"

"Oh—well," said Feliz, "tell me, do you know very much about the calculus of non-existent integers?"

The Controller looked somewhat taken aback. "Do I?" he said.

"Yes," said Feliz. "Do you?"

"Well, as a matter of fact," said the Controller, "if you put it that way, no, I don't—any more."

"Oh," replied Feliz. "That makes it a little difficult then, you see. I don't know how I'd go about explaining why I need that water without using derivatives of the functions of non-existent integers."

"Er-yes," said the Controller. "I see the difficulty. Well, go ahead with the plans as they stand. But when you get around to taking me up on this offer of mine, we'll sit down some afternoon and you can bring me up to date on this. My calculers is a little rusty, I'm afraid. That's what you said, wasn't it—the calculers of non-existing tigers?"

"Correct," answered Feliz.

"I'll make a note of it," said the Controller, ushering Feliz to the door, "and remind you of it at the earliest possible opportunity."

*   *   *

That night Feliz lay in the bedroom of an apartment in the same building that housed the Controller. His door was locked, and an armed guard stood outside it. Nevertheless, at a few hours after midnight there was a small clicking sound and the door swung inward, revealing a glimpse of a small body which slipped through the opening; then immediately closed the door behind it. Lying sleepless on his bed, Feliz saw the sudden flicker of light and shadowy movement; and was on his feet in a minute, moving soundlessly over the thick carpeting, away from the bed.

"It's just me," said an apologetic little voice in the darkness.

Feliz stopped short. "Kai?"

"Yes," Kai's voice came back. "Don't turn the light on. I look awful. I've been crawling in all sorts of dirty, dusty places and I haven't had any chance to get clean clothes since I first saw you." She moved toward him through the darkness and her outstretched fingers brushed his bare arm. "Oh, you haven't any clothes on."

"I've got enough," said Feliz, shortly. He groped in the darkness, caught her wrist, and led her over to a couch on the far side of the room. "Sit down. Where've you been?"

"Back in the stacks," she answered.

"Stacks?" echoed Feliz. "What stacks?"

"The stacks in the city library—nobody ever goes there any more," she said. "Oh, Feliz, you were right. They aren't hallucinations, they're just as real as we are." Her voice shook in the blackness. "They're even some of them d-distant relatives."

Feliz made a clumsy effort to pat her unseen back reassuringly through the darkness. She crept into his arms like a lost puppy; and he felt her shivering. "Hold me," she said, like a very young child.

Feliz held her. After a while she stopped shaking and began to talk again.

"—After I left you I just ran and hid for a long time. I

just wanted to get away from everything; from my people, from the hallucinations, but mostly from you. I didn't care if I lived or died. I just wanted to crawl into a hole and never come out again.''

Feliz cleared his throat uncomfortably in the darkness.

"Oh, that's all right," she said, snuggling closer into his arms. "You were just trying to make me see things for my own good. Well, I found a hole finally—a building neither our people or they went into—and lay there for almost a day feeling sorry for myself. But finally I reached a stage where I had sort of cried myself out—you know? And I had to start being sensible. So I got up and went out again.''

She paused.

"Well, I was awfully hungry; and the only place I knew I could get food was on your ship—"

"I know," interrupted Feliz. There was a moment's embarrassed silence from the general region of his arms.

"Oh, you saw it?"

"The drawing?" said Feliz. "I certainly did."

He could almost feel the warmth of her unseen blush. "I'm sorry," she said, in a small voice.

"That's all right," replied Feliz.

"—But you have such big feet."

"Thanks," said Feliz.

"Well, anyway—" she said, taking a deep breath and plunging back into her narrative, "after I'd eaten, I felt so much better, I began to think over everything you'd said, without getting worked up about it. And the more I thought about it, the more determined I was to get it straight. So I decided I'd just go to the library and check up."

"Good for you," approved Feliz.

"Well, I thought it was high time somebody did." Self-satisfaction flowed in her voice. "But Feliz—it was awful. There's all sorts of creeping and crawling things back in there where nobody's been for a hundred years;

and dust so thick you can't breathe; and in lots of places the lights don't work; and several times I got l-lost—'' She was shaking again.

Feliz patted her, soothingly. "But you found what you went after," he prompted.

"Yes, I did," she said. "And it's all true. First we started not having anything to do with them; and then we began to act and dress differently; and then we began pretending they weren't there. And all the time they were doing the same thing. Feliz, you've got to let me stay with you always, from now on!''

"Well, I—" stammered Feliz.

"I don't have any people but you any more," she clutched at him fiercely. "Can't we go away from the city and live off by ourselves somewhere where they'll never find us? They wouldn't follow us far into the hills; I know they wouldn't.''

"Hush," said Feliz, "we'll get away. But I want you to tell me now as much as you can about what you learned about things.''

"What do you want to know that for?"

"There's an old saying to the effect that knowledge is power; and it's the truth," replied Feliz, gently. "The more you know about things or people, the easier it is to handle them. Now, tell me—did you ever see either the others or your own people in public without their own special kind of clothes on?''

"Oh, no!" Kai's gasp was scandalized.

"How about in private?"

"Any decent person," she replied primly, "wears clothes *all* the time."

"Night and day, you mean?" demanded Feliz. "Alone, as well as in company?''

"Well, even if you were alone, you could never be sure someone might not come in.''

"But nobody ever did, did they?"

"N-no," she admitted reluctantly.

"Then what were you really afraid of?" he asked.

"Well," she said. "There was . . ." her voice trailed off uncertainly. After a moment she said in an altered tone, "I see; you mean, one of *them* might see you."

"Uh-huh," confirmed Feliz, softly; "you couldn't be sure they were all as blind as you made yourself be."

He heard the sharp hiss of her indrawn breath in the darkness. "Of course," she said, in a tone mixing chagrin and surprise. "I saw them all the time."

"All the time?"

"All the time," she repeated sharply. "I saw them when I was a child, but people always hushed me and said they weren't really there. And then I got so I wouldn't see them; but I *did* see them—I mean—" she turned in his arms "—do you know what I mean?"

Feliz nodded, forgetting that she could not see him.

"It's known as mass autohypnosis," he explained. "Your mind had to pretend they weren't there; but it still had to remain aware enough of them so that you wouldn't bump into them in the streets, or sit down where one of them was sitting."

"Then everybody knows about them!" cried Kai. "And they know about us!"

"That's about it," said Feliz. "You just can't get anybody to admit it to themselves. Those who do get treated the way you did—if they belong to your people. Probably, on the other side, they get shot."

Abruptly, Kai gagged. "I don't want to talk about it any more," she said.

"But I've got to be sure what cues these self-induced reactions," insisted Feliz, quietly. "I still need to know as much as possible. Do you think you can talk about the history part of it—what you picked up in the library?"

Kai hesitated. "I suppose—yes I can!" she said finally, with a mighty effort.

"Good for you," said Feliz, patting her approvingly.
"Now start at the beginning and go over everything you
found out . . ."

VII

Feliz Gebrod squinted at the sun of Dunroamin, which
was almost at its zenith. He stood on a small circle of
foundation material, a tiny, artificial island from which
the narrow neck of the fountain protruded and which hid
the power pack he had buried at its base and connected to
the bulge of apparatus at its tip; and his stormy blue eyes
looked up and beyond the city to where the trees hid the
ship and—he fervently hoped—Kai within it.

There had been some small discussion in the early hours
of the morning before the guard had knocked on his door,
summoning him to leave the room and supervise the last of
the construction work in the square.

"—But how do I know you'll get away all right?" Kai
had kept insisting.

"You'll just have to take my word for it," Feliz had
repeated.

"But why can't you tell me how you're going to do it?"

"Because you've been subjected to the same kind of
conditioning the rest of them have; and I don't know how
you'd react to the knowledge," said Feliz, exasperated.
"If everything goes all right, I'll be back at the ship by
noon. If I don't make it—"

"I don't care what happens if you don't make it!" cried
Kai and, tearing herself away from him, she had hammered on the door until the guard outside opened it and
stood blinking foolishly at Feliz; while she ducked under
the black arm and ran off.

Now it was almost noon; and Feliz could only hope that

she had made it to the ship. Fervently he hoped that, wherever she was, she was not still in the city. From his little island he looked out on a square thronged with black-clad and color-clad people alike; men, women, and children, half of whom were ghosts and less than ghosts to the opposite half. Did they realize the multitude of each other's presences? Here—inches apart only, in some cases— the deeply implanted convictions that blinded them must be strained to the breaking point by the nearness and numbers of the people whose existence they did not wish to acknowledge. The black-clad men were drawn up in military order, rank on rank, with their women and children gathered apart. But the color-clad people circulated amongst and between the rows of the others, paying scant attention to the little speech that El Hoska was trying to give them—the tenor of which was that the labor of the hands could also be satisfying to the artistic mind.

The only exception to all this was the behavior of the children, both of the black-clad and the color-garbed variety. Universally, they sensed and were troubled by the gathering and hung back, wherever possible, near the outskirts of the square. Feliz found time and opportunity to feel glad about that.

On the far side of the square from El Hoska, in front of the ordered rows of black uniforms, the Controller was also speechifying. More noisy, less original, and infinitely less gentle, his speech hammered home ad nauseum the virtues of blind obedience. "Yours not to reason why, yours but to do or die," was the burden of his message and he missed no opportunity to ram it down his listeners' throats. They did not seem to mind.

Eventually, however, he managed to run out of wind, and brought his peroration to a close. Leaving his people, he turned and walked down to the edge of the pool, and looked across six feet of water at Feliz.

"Well," he said, surreptitiously wiping his brow. "What did you think of it?"

"Instructive," said Feliz.

"Do you think so?" beamed the Controller. "I never miss an opportunity to reiterate the principles that have made our society efficient." He looked across at the fountain and the apparatus bulge at the top of it. Fishing in his pocket, he produced a sealed plastic box Feliz had prepared for him and from which several impressive-looking wires protruded. "Ready?"

"Uh—not just yet," answered Feliz, looking over at El Hoska, who was still talking. "I have to hagliate the beltansprung."

"Well, get on with it," said the Controller. "By the way, what have you decided about that little offer of mine?"

"I'm still thinking it over," said Feliz.

"No rush," the Controller told him, equably. "But keep an eye on him there, you men."

"Yes, sir," replied one of the five guards who stood around the pool, guns at the ready and their eyes on Feliz.

El Hoska finished his speech and came down to the opposite poolside.

"I'm through," he announced. Feliz nodded.

"I have been looking forward to this," the old man went on. "These young people have never seen anything like this and they are bound to be greatly impressed when the fountain actually starts playing. I anticipate quite a reaction."

Feliz nodded, a trifle grimly, and looked about the square. Now that there was nothing else to occupy their attention, all eyes were on him; and both the Colors and the Blacks were clustering close about the pool. The black uniforms had not really broken ranks, but they had edged forward and the brilliant cloaks were among them.

"Ready," said Feliz to El Hoska and the Controller

alike. The Controller lifted his impressive-looking plastic box.

"Ah," he said, beaming at his own people about him, "in a minute you will all be reacting as extensions of my own personality—"

Feliz threw a switch handily placed on the long, upright metal tube of the fountain's mouth; and the sentence was never completed.

A Mark III plastic converter is a very handy little tool when operated on low power with caution and restraint. With its governor operating properly, it can be set to soften, weld, cut or shape cast plastic (of which clothes are made) with the greatest of ease. But with its power stepped up, its governor removed, and with a general broadcast head that allows it to radiate in all directions, what it does instead of casting plastic is practically what Kai believed had been done to her at one time. In short, and for all practical purposes—it disintegrates the cast plastic.

Therefore, at one moment in the square of the city there was a horde of dressed people standing staring at Feliz; and in the next, in fact in the merest fraction of a second, there was only a horde of people. For a moment they held their positions, like startled statues; then the realization of their nakedness struck home, with results that would have gratified Satan himself, let alone the barrel-chested stepson of his spirit who stood at that moment in awesome nudity beside the switch he had just pulled.

People who have grown up in a normal civilization can imagine the effect produced at any public gathering if all those present were suddenly stripped to the buff. For these inhabitants of Dunroamin, it was infinitely worse. During the last two hundred years they had been distinguishing carefully between those whose existence they admitted and those whose existence they did not, by the color and cut of the clothes each wore. The nakedness taboo was much more deeply implanted than in a normal society. But, in addition and worse than that, was the fact that now, with no means to distinguish, their conditioning began to break down; and the horrified onlooker in the square, a split-second after realizing his own nakedness, looked around to recognize the fact that he was not only surrounded by other naked people, *but there were twice as many of them as there had been the minute before*. And in the instant of this last and most horrible realization, the crowd in the square melted into a seething, howling riot of humanity all fighting to escape in different directions.

It was Feliz's moment. Naked as the rest, he was the one man there who had been prepared and had his purpose firmly in mind; and his short, enormously thick legs drove him in a dive off the platform and straight through the crowd toward the exit nearest the hills above the city. No ordinary man could have made it through that struggling, screaming mob; and, powerful as Feliz was, he was tossed first to this side and then that, of his line of escape, like a swimmer in heavy rapids. But three hundred pounds of more solid flesh and bone than the lighter stuff around him told their story; and in a matter of minutes, bruised and bleeding from innumerable scratches, but otherwise unharmed, he broke free into the least dense section of the crowd at the edge of the square and headed toward the hills.

The streets were filled with city inhabitants, fleeing for sanity's sake toward the safe darkness of their homes and the full closets they expected to find there, but which would, as a matter of fact, almost certainly be empty. For the vibrations of a Mark III converter are not stopped by ordinary substances; there had been power enough in that one brief burst that had burnt out the power-pack in the fountain base to blanket the whole city area and some distance beyond as well. These fugitives Feliz joined—and passed.

*   *   *

A half-breed Micturian can run very swiftly for a short
distance. Feliz passed the people of the city at about thirty
miles an hour; but by the time he had reached the outskirts
he was wheezing badly, and heaving lungs forced him to
slow to a jog trot. This, however, he grimly kept up, as he
breasted the slope beside the stone wall and fought his way
uphill until he reached the woods.

Here, indeed, he collapsed, crumpling to earth like a
broken pillar; and lay helpless for several minutes, while
his lungs fought to return a sufficiency of oxygen to his
starving body and remove the fatigue poisons from the
muscle tissues.

After a short interval, however, he began to recover; he
swiveled about on his stomach and stared back down the
way he had come. The route behind him lay bare of
pursuers; and, as he watched, no small, naked forms erupted
from the outskirts to head his way.

Thanking whatever gods there be, Feliz forced himself
to his feet and tottered on into the wood. He had marked
the direction in his memory as well as he was able from
the time in daylight that El Hoska had walked with him to
his ship. Now he followed what he believed was the
proper way; but his heart stayed inconveniently near his
mouth until, finally, the trees thinned ahead of him; and,
looking through them, he saw the welcoming gray bulk of
his ship, with the hatch open and waiting.

Feliz staggered to the hatch and crawled through, collapsing in the chair before the control board. Gradually,
the specks swimming in front of his eyes faded and disappeared, his breathing slowed and became more natural,
and he found himself able to think beyond the present
moment. He heaved a deep sigh and looked around the
control room. And suddenly his heart congealed as if his
chest cavity had abruptly become filled with liquid air.

For the ship appeared to be empty of any human life but his own.

Where was Kai?

"Kai!" he shouted, leaping to his feet. His voice thundered in the narrow metal confines of the ship; but there was no answer. "Hell's bloody buckets!" he raved in a frenzy. Ahead of him he could see through the narrow cabin entrance and to the arms locker in the other room where his guns hung. He took one plunging step cabinward; and was halted by a shriek.

"Don't you dare come in here!" cried the voice of Kai.

Feliz thrust out his hands to check himself on the doorposts and backed away.

"Are you in there?" he asked foolishly. "Where are you?"

"I'm behind the partition to one side of the door," came back a very irate voice. "And if you try to come in here I'll hit you over the head with a thing."

"What kind of a thing? What have you got in there?" called Feliz, worriedly thinking of the guns, which were always loaded and which might have their safeties off.

"Never mind," said Kai. "It's a round thing with edges so it holds things and a handle and it's heavy."

"Oh," said Feliz, relieved, recognizing, from this rather sketchy description, his only culinary utensil, an electronic cooker-pan. He reflected that a diet of raw nuts and fruits would be the probable reason she had not recognized it as a kitchen accessory and wondered what instinct had caused her to pick that out of all the mayhem-suitable tools in the cabin. He was about to return to the essential question of her reason for all this odd behavior, when a casual glance through the hatch revealed three very angry-looking and very unclothed men breaking forth from the edge of the wood with guns in their hands and heading for the ship. The distance was a little great but Feliz almost thought he recognized the Controller as one of them.

"Strap yourself into your bunk!" he yelled, in the general direction of the cabin; and jumped for the control board. The hatch slammed shut, the firing chambers rumbled, the power needle rose up the scale to *ready*, and he threw in the switch. The ship lifted and the planet fell away on the outside screen.

A tense half-hour later they were in space.

Feliz leaned back and wiped sweat from his forehead. Free at last to turn his attention to more personal things, he turned once more, toward the cabin.

"Did you get yourself strapped in all right?" he called.

"Yes," came the answer. "Why didn't you tell me you had clothes in a box-thing here?" And his spare trousers and tunic waddled into the control room with Kai's face looking absurdly small above them.

"You've got my clothes!" howled Feliz, as trousers, tunic and face, perceiving his unencumbered condition, retreated in some panic to the cabin.

"Don't come in here," ordered the once more invisible voice of Kai. "I'll hit you with my thing."

Feliz choked on the desire to tell her simultaneously that (a) it was an electronic cooker-pan (b) it was *his* electronic cooker-pan (c) that all this business of hitting him over the head was becoming somewhat repetitious and (d) *what was she doing in his clothes?*

He compromised on the last.

"What are you doing in my clothes?" he bellowed.

"What did you do to mine?" she retorted. A horrible realization suddenly dawned on Feliz. The effect of the Mark III converter must have been far-reaching enough to make itself felt even at the ship. The ship itself would damp out such radiation; so Kai must have been outside at the time he threw the switch. That would explain why his spare suit was all right, but her clothes were gone. Grinning a little, he gave her an account of what he had done; and the results thereof. He was still grinning when his memory reminded him, with a nasty jar, that there had been only one spare outfit in the locker.

"Listen," he called, nervously, "I've got to have my clothes."

"And leave me without any? No thank you," the invisible voice of Kai responded.

"But I can't land on the planet we're going to without clothes," he shouted.

"I can't either," she retorted.

"They're my clothes."

"Possession is nine points of the law."

"You give me those clothes!"

"I won't!"

"Then I'll come and get them myself."

"You step a foot a single inch through that door," said Kai, "and I'll hit you over the head with my thing."

It was an interesting situation.

Brotherhood, maturation, solidarity, and the irresistible power of indomitable will are themes that weave like shining threads through the fabric of Gordon Dickson's fiction. Strands first visible here in "Steel Brother" have since thickened and spread into the pattern of the Childe Cycle. Thomas Jordan and his memory bank are the earliest prototypes of Hal Mayne and his Final Encyclopedia. A twinned guardian who makes his rite of passage on behalf of the whole race is the classic Dickson hero.

Steel Brother

". . . Man that is born of woman hath but a short time to live and is full of misery. He cometh up and is cut down, like a flower; he fleeth as it were a shadow and never continueth in one stay—"

The voice of the chaplain was small and sharp in the thin air, intoning the words of the burial service above the temporary lectern set up just inside the transparent wall of the landing field dome. Through the double transparencies of the dome and the plastic cover of the burial rocket the black-clad ranks could see the body of the dead stationman, Ted Waskewicz, lying back comfortably at an angle of forty-five degrees, peaceful in death, waxily perfect from the hands of the embalmers, and immobile. The eyes were closed, the cheerful, heavy features still held their expression of thoughtless dominance, as though death had been a minor incident, easily shrugged off; and the battle star made a single blaze of color on the tunic of the black uniform.

"*Amen.*" The response was a deep bass utterance from the assembled men, like the single note of an organ. In the front rank of the Cadets, Thomas Jordan's lips moved stiffly with the others', his voice joining mechanically in their chorus. For this was the moment of his triumph, but in spite of it, the old, old fear had come back, the old sense of loneliness and loss and terror of his own inadequacy.

He stood at stiff attention, eyes to the front, trying to lose himself in the unanimity of his classmates, to shut out the voice of the chaplain and the memory it evoked of an alien raid on an undefended city and of home and parents swept away from him in a breath. He remembered the mass burial service read over the shattered ruin of the city; and the government agency that had taken him—a ten-year-old orphan—and given him care and training until this day, but could not give him what these others about him had by natural right—the courage of those who had matured in safety.

For he had been lonely and afraid since that day. Untouched by bomb or shell, he had yet been crippled deep inside of him. He had seen the enemy in his strength and run screaming from his spacesuited gangs. And what could give Thomas Jordan back his soul after that?

But still he stood rigidly at attention as a Guardsman should; for he was a soldier now, and this was part of his duty.

The chaplain's voice droned to a halt. He closed his prayerbook and stepped back from the lectern. The captain of the training ship took his place.

"In accordance with the conventions of the Frontier Force," he said, crisply, "I now commit the ashes of Station Commandant First Class, Theodore Waskewicz, to the keeping of time and space."

He pressed a button on the lectern. Beyond the dome, white fire blossomed out from the tail of the burial rocket, heating the asteroid rock to temporary incandescence. For a moment it hung there, spewing flame. Then it rose, at first slowly, then quickly, and was gone, sketching a fiery path out and away, until, at almost the limits of human sight, it vanished in a sudden, silent explosion of brilliant light.

Around Jordan, the black-clad ranks relaxed. Not by any physical movement, but with an indefinable breaking of nervous tension, they settled themselves for the more prosaic conclusion of the ceremony. The relaxation reached even to the captain, for he about-faced with a relieved snap and spoke to the ranks.

"Cadet Thomas Jordan. Front and center."

The command struck Jordan with an icy shock. As long as the burial service had been in progress, he had had the protection of anonymity among his classmates around him. Now, the captain's voice was a knife, cutting him off, finally and irrevocably, from the one security his life had known, leaving him naked and exposed. A despairing numbness seized him. His reflexes took over, moving his body like a robot. One step forward, a right face, down to the end of the row of silent men, a left face, three steps forward. Halt. Salute.

"Cadet Thomas Jordan reporting, sir."

"Cadet Thomas Jordan, I hereby invest you with command of this Frontier Station. You will hold it until relieved. Under no conditions will you enter into communications with an enemy nor allow any creature or vessel to pass through your sector of space from Outside."

"Yes, sir."

"In consideration of the duties and responsibilities requisite on assuming command of this Station, you are promoted to the rank and title of Station Commandant Third Class."

"Thank you, sir."

From the lectern the captain lifted a cap of silver wire mesh and placed it on his head. It clipped on to the electrodes already buried in his skull, with a snap that sent sound ringing through his skull. For a second, a sheet of lightning flashed in front of his eyes and he seemed to feel the weight of the memory bank already pressing on his mind. Then lightning and pressure vanished together to show him the captain offering his hand.

"My congratulations, commandant."

"Thank you, sir."

They shook hands, the captain's grip quick, nervous and perfunctory. He took one abrupt step backward and transferred his attention to his second in command.

"Lieutenant! Dismiss the formation!"

It was over. The new rank locked itself around Jordan, sealing up the fear and loneliness inside him. Without listening to the barked commands that no longer concerned him, he turned on his heel and strode over to take up his position by the sally port of the training ship. He stood formally at attention beside it, feeling the weight of his new authority like a heavy cloak on his thin shoulders. At one stroke he had become the ranking officer present. The officers—even the captain—were nominally under his authority, so long as their ship remained grounded at his Station. So rigidly he stood at attention that not even the slightest tremor of the trembling inside him escaped to quiver betrayingly in his body.

They came toward him in a loose, dark mass that resolved itself into a single file just beyond saluting distance. Singly, they went past him and up the ladder into the sally port, each saluting him as they passed. He returned the salutes stiffly, mechanically, walled off from these classmates of six years by the barrier of his new command. It was a moment when a smile or a casual handshake would have meant more than a little. But protocol had stripped him of the right to familiarity; and it was a line of black-uniformed strangers that now filed slowly past. His place was already established and theirs was yet to be. They had nothing in common any more.

The last of the men went past him up the ladder and were lost to view through the black circle of the sally port. The heavy steel plug swung slowly to, behind them. He turned and made his way to the unfamiliar but well-known field control panel in the main control room of the Station. A light glowed redly on the communications board. He thumbed a switch and spoke into a grill set in the panel.

"Station to Ship. Go ahead."

Overhead the loudspeaker answered.

"Ship to Station. Ready for take-off."

His fingers went swiftly over the panel. Outside, the atmosphere of the field was evacuated and the dome slid back. Tractor mechs scurried out from the pit, under remote control, clamped huge magnetic fists on the ship, swung it into launching position, then retreated.

Jordan spoke again into the grill.

"Station clear. Take-off at will."

"Thank you, Station." He recognized the captain's voice. "And good luck."

Outside, the ship lifted, at first slowly, then faster on its pillar of flame, and dwindled away into the darkness of space. Automatically, he closed the dome and pumped the air back in.

He was turning away from the control panel, bracing himself against the moment of finding himself completely isolated, when, with a sudden, curious shock, he noticed that there was another, smaller ship yet on the field.

For a moment he stared at it blankly, uncomprehendingly. Then memory returned and he realized that the ship was a small courier vessel from Intelligence, which had been hidden by the huge bulk of the training ship. Its officer would still be below, cutting a record tape of the

former commandant's last memories for the file at Headquarters. The memory lifted him momentarily from the
morass of his emotions to attention to duty. He turned
from the panel and went below.

In the triply-armored basement of the Station, the man
from Intelligence was half in and half out of the memory
bank when he arrived, having cut away a portion of the
steel casing around the bank so as to connect his recorder
direct to the cells. The sight of the heavy mount of steel
with the ragged incision in one side, squatting like a
wounded monster, struck Jordan unpleasantly; but he
smoothed the emotion from his face and walked firmly to
the bank. His footsteps rang on the metal floor; and the
man from Intelligence, hearing them, brought his head
momentarily outside the bank for a quick look.

"Hi!" he said, shortly, returning to his work. His voice
continued from the interior of the bank with a friendly,
hollow sound. "Congratulations, commandant."

"Thanks," answered Jordan, stiffly. He stood, somewhat ill at ease, uncertain of what was expected of him.
When he hesitated, the voice from the bank continued.

"How does the cap feel?"

Jordan's hands went up instinctively to the mesh of
silver wire on his head. It pushed back unyieldingly at his
fingers, held firmly on the electrodes.

"Tight," he said.

The Intelligence man came crawling out of the bank, his
recorder in one hand and thick loops of glassy tape in the
other.

"They all do at first," he said, squatting down and
feeding one end of the tape into a spring rewind spool. "In
a couple of days you won't even be able to feel it up
there."

"I suppose."

The Intelligence man looked up at him curiously.

"Nothing about it bothering you, is there?" he asked. "You look a little strained."

"Doesn't everybody when they first start out?"

"Sometimes," said the other, noncommittally. "Sometimes not. Don't hear a sort of humming, do you?"

"No."

"Feel any kind of pressure inside your head?"

"No."

"How about your eyes. See any spots or flashes in front of them?"

"No!" snapped Jordan.

"Take it easy," said the man from Intelligence. "This is my business."

"Sorry."

"That's all right. It's just that if there's anything wrong with you or the bank I want to know it." He rose from the rewind spool, which was now industriously gathering in the loose tape; and, unclipping a pressure-torch from his belt, began resealing the aperture. "It's just that occasionally new officers have been hearing too many stories about the banks in Training School, and they're inclined to be jumpy."

"Stories?" said Jordan.

"Haven't you heard them?" answered the Intelligence man. "Stories of memory domination—stationmen driven insane by the memories of the men who had the Station before them. Catatonics whose minds have got lost in the past history of the bank, or cases of memory replacement where the stationman has identified himself with the memories and personality of the man who preceded him."

"Oh, those," said Jordan. "I've heard them." He paused, and then, when the other did not go on: "What about them? Are they true?"

The Intelligence man turned from the half-resealed aperture and faced him squarely, torch in hand.

"Some," he said bluntly. "There's been a few cases

like that; although there didn't have to be. Nobody's trying to sugar-coat the facts. The memory bank's nothing but a storehouse connected to you through your silver cap—a gadget to enable you not only to remember everything you ever do at the Station, but also everything anybody else who ever ran the Station, did. But there've been a few impressionable stationmen who've let themselves get the notion that the memory bank's a sort of a coffin with living dead men crawling around inside it. When that happens, there's trouble."

He turned away from Jordan, back to his work.

"And that's what you thought was the trouble with me," said Jordan, speaking to his back.

The man from Intelligence chuckled—it was an amazingly human sound.

"In my line, fella," he said, "we check all possibilities." He finished his resealing and turned around.

"No hard feelings?" he said.

Jordan shook his head. "Of course not."

"Then I'll be getting along." He bent over and picked up the spool, which had by now neatly wound up all the tape, straightened up and headed for the ramp that led up from the basement to the landing field. Jordan fell into step beside him.

"You've nothing more to do, then?" he asked.

"Just my reports. But I can write those on the way back." They went up the ramp and out through the lock on to the field.

"They did a good job of repairing the battle damage," he went on, looking around the Station.

"I guess they did," said Jordan. The two men paced soberly to the sally port of the Intelligence ship. "Well, so long."

"So long," answered the man from Intelligence, activating the sally port mechanism. The outer lock swung open and he hopped the few feet up to the opening without waiting for the little ladder to wind itself out. "See you in six months."

He turned to Jordan and gave him a casual, offhand salute with the hand holding the wind-up spool. Jordan returned it with training school precision. The port swung closed.

He went back to the master control room and the ritual of seeing the ship off. He stood looking out for a long time after it had vanished, then turned from the panel with a sigh to find himself at last completely alone.

He looked about the Station. For the next six months this would be his home. Then, for another six months he would be free on leave while the Station was rotated out of the line in its regular order for repair, reconditioning, and improvements.

If he lived that long.

The fear, which had been driven a little distance away by his conversation with the man from Intelligence, came back.

If he lived that long. He stood, bemused.

Back to his mind with the letter-perfect recall of the memory bank came the words of the other. Catatonic— cases of memory replacement. Memory domination. Had those others, too, had more than they could bear of fear and anticipation?

And with that thought came a suggestion that coiled like a snake in his mind. That would be a way out. What if they came, the alien invaders, and Thomas Jordan was no longer here to meet them? What if only the catatonic hulk of a man was left? What if they came and a man was here, but that man called himself and knew himself only as—

Waskewicz!

"No!" the cry came involuntarily from his lips; and he came to himself with his face contorted and his hands half-extended in front of him in the attitude of one who wards off a ghost. He shook his head to shake the vile suggestion from his brain; and leaned back, panting, against the control panel.

Not that. Not ever that. He had surprised in himself a weakness that turned him sick with horror. Win or lose; live or die. But as Jordan—not as any other.

He lit a cigarette with trembling fingers. So—it was over now and he was safe. He had caught it in time. He had his warning. Unknown to him—all this time—the seeds of memory domination must have been lying waiting within him. But now he knew they were there, he knew what measures to take. The danger lay in Waskewicz's memories. He would shut his mind off from them—would fight the Station without the benefit of their experience. The first stationmen on the line had done without the aid of a memory bank and so could he.

So.

He had settled it. He flicked on the viewing screens and stood opposite them, very straight and correct in the middle of his Station, looking out at the dots that were his forty-five doggie mechs spread out on guard over a million kilometers of space, looking at the controls that would enable him to throw their blunt, terrible, mechanical bodies into battle with the enemy, looking and waiting, waiting, for the courage that comes from having faced squarely a situation, to rise within him and take possession of him, putting an end to all fears and doubtings.

And he waited so for a long time, but it did not come.

The weeks went swiftly by; and that was as it should be. He had been told what to expect, during training; and it was as it should be that these first months should be tense ones, with a part of him always stiff and waiting for the alarm bell that would mean a doggie signaling sight of an enemy. It was as it should be that he should pause, suddenly, in the midst of a meal with his fork halfway to his mouth, waiting and expecting momentarily to be summoned; that he should wake unexpectedly in the nighttime and lie rigid and tense, eyes fixed on the shadowy ceiling and listening. Later—they had said in training—after you have become used to the Station, this constant tension will relax and you will be left at ease, with only one little unobtrusive corner of your mind unnoticed but forever alert. This will come with time, they said.

So he waited for it, waited for the release of the coiled springs inside him and the time when the feel of the Station would be comfortable and friendly about him. When he had first been left alone, he had thought to himself that surely, in his case, the waiting would not be more than a matter of days; then, as the days went by and he still lived in a state of hair-trigger sensitivity, he had given himself, in his own mind, a couple of weeks—then a month.

But now a month and more than a month had gone without relaxation coming to him; and the strain was beginning to show in nervousness of his hands and the dark circles under his eyes. He found it impossible to sit still either to read, or to listen to the music that was available in the Station library. He roamed restlessly, endlessly checking and rechecking the empty space that his doggies' viewers revealed.

For the recollection of Waskewicz as he lay in the burial rocket would not go from him. And that was not as it should be.

He could, and did, refuse to recall the memories of Waskewicz that he had never experienced; but his own personal recollections were not easy to control and slipped into his mind when he was unaware. All else that he could do to lay the ghost, he had done. He had combed the Station carefully, seeking out the little adjustments and conveniences that a lonely man will make about his home, and removed them, even when the removal meant a loss of personal comfort. He had locked his mind securely to the storehouse of the memory bank, striving to hold himself isolated from the other's memories until familiarity and association should bring him to the point where he instinctively felt that the Station was *his* and not the other's. And, whenever thoughts of Waskewicz entered in spite of all these precautions, he had dismissed them sternly, telling himself that his predecessor was not worth the considering.

But the other's ghost remained, intangible and invulnerable, as if locked in the very metal of the walls and floor and ceiling of the Station; and rising to haunt him with the memories of the training school tales and the ominous words of the man from Intelligence. At such times, when the ghost had seized him, he would stand paralyzed, staring in hypnotic fascination at the screens with their silent mechanical sentinels, or at the cold steel of the memory bank, crouching like some brooding monster, fear feeding on his thoughts—until, with a sudden, wrenching effort of the will, he broke free of the mesmerism and flung himself frantically into the duties of the Station, checking and rechecking his instruments and the space they watched, doing anything and everything to drown his wild emotions in the necessity for attention to duty.

And eventually he found himself almost hoping for a raid, for the test that would prove him, would lay the ghost, one way or another, once and for all.

It came at last, as he had known it would, during one of the rare moments when he had forgotten the imminence of danger. He had awakened in his bunk, at the beginning of the arbitrary ten-hour day; and lay there drowsily, comfortably, his thoughts vague and formless, like shadows in the depths of a lazy whirlpool, turning slowly, going no place.

Then—*the alarm!*

Overhead the shouting bell burst into life, jerking him from his bed. Its metal clangor poured out on the air, tumbling from the loudspeakers in every room all over the

Station, strident with urgency, pregnant with disaster. It roared, it vibrated, it thundered, until the walls themselves threw it back, seeming to echo in sympathy, acquiring a voice of their own until the room rang—until the Station itself rang like one monster bell, calling him into battle.

He leaped to his feet and ran to the master control room. On the telltale high on the wall above the viewer screens, the red light of number thirty-eight doggie was flashing ominously. He threw himself into the operator's seat before it, slapping one palm hard down on the switch to disconnect the alarm.

The Station is in contact with the enemy.

The sudden silence slapped at him, taking his breath away. He gasped and shook his head like a man who has had a glassful of cold water thrown unexpectedly in his face; then plunged his fingers at the keys on the master control board in front of his seat—Up beams. Up detector screen, established now at forty thousand kilometers distance. Switch on communications to Sector Headquarters.

The transmitter purred. Overhead, the white light flashed as it began to tick off its automatic signal. "Alert! Alert! Further data follows. Will report."

Headquarters has been notified by Station.

Activate viewing screen on doggie number thirty-eight.

He looked into the activated screen, into the vast arena of space over which the mechanical vision of that doggie mech was ranging. Far and far away at top magnification were five small dots, coming in fast on a course leading ten points below and at an angle of thirty-two degrees to the Station.

He flicked a key, releasing thirty-eight on proximity fuse control and sending it plunging toward the dots. He scanned the Station area map for the positions of his other mechs. Thirty-nine was missing—in the Station for repair. The rest were available. He checked numbers forty through forty-five and thirty-seven through thirty to rendezvous on collision course with enemy at seventy-five thousand kilometers. Numbers twenty to thirty to rendezvous at fifty thousand kilometers.

Primary defense has been inaugurated.

He turned back to the screen. Number thirty-eight, expendable in the interests of gaining information, was plunging towards the ships at top acceleration under strains no living flesh would have been able to endure. But as yet the size and type of the invaders was still hidden by distance. A white light flashed abruptly from the communications panel, announcing that Sector Headquarters was alerted and ready to talk. He cut in audio.

"Contact. Go ahead, Station J-49C3."

"Five ships," he said. "Beyond identification range. Coming in through thirty-eight at ten point thirty-two."

"Acknowledge," the voice of Headquarters was level, precise, emotionless. "Five ships—thirty-eight—ten—thirty-two. Patrol Twenty, passing through your area at four hours distance, has been notified and will proceed to your Station at once, arriving in four hours, plus or minus twenty minutes. Further assistance follows. Will stand by here for your future messages."

The white light went out and he turned away from the communications panel. On the screen, the five ships had still not grown to identifiable proportions, but for all practical purposes, the preliminaries were over. He had some fifteen minutes now during which everything that could be done, had been done.

Primary defense has been completed.

He turned away from the controls and walked back to the bedroom, where he dressed slowly and meticulously in full black uniform. He straightened his tunic, looking in the mirror, and stood gazing at himself for a long moment. Then, hesitantly, almost as if against his will, he reached out with one hand to a small gray box on a shelf beside the mirror, opened it, and took out the silver battle star that the next few hours would entitle him to wear.

It lay in his palm, the bright metal winking softly up at him under the reflection of the room lights and the small movements of his hand. The little cluster of diamonds in its center sparked and ran the whole gamut of their flashing colors. For several minutes he stood looking at it; then slowly, gently, he shut it back up in its box and went out, back to the control room.

On the screen, the ships were now large enough to be identified. They were medium-sized vessels, Jordan noticed, of the type used most by the most common species of raiders—that same race which had orphaned him. There could be no doubt about their intentions, as there sometimes was when some odd stranger chanced upon the Frontier, to be regretfully destroyed by men whose orders were to take no chances. No, these were *the enemy*, the strange, suicidal life form that thrust thousands of attacks yearly against the little human empire, who blew themselves up when captured and wasted a hundred ships for every one that broke through the guarding stations to descend on some unprotected city of an inner planet and loot it of equipment and machinery that the aliens were either unwilling or unable to build for themselves—a contradictory, little understood and savage race. These five ships would make no attempt to parley.

But now, doggie number thirty-eight had been spotted and the white exhausts of guided missiles began to streak toward the viewing screen. For a few seconds, the little mech bucked and tossed, dodging, firing defensively, shooting down the missiles as they approached. But it was a hopeless fight against those odds and suddenly one of the streaks expanded to fill the screen with glaring light.

And the screen went blank. Thirty-eight was gone.

Suddenly realizing that he should have been covering with observation from one of the doggies further back,

Jordan jumped to fill his screens. He brought the view from forty in on the one that thirty-eight had vacated and filled the two flanking screens with the view from thirty-seven on his left and twenty on his right. They showed his first line of defense already gathered at the seventy-five kilometer rendezvous and the fifty thousand kilometer rendezvous still forming.

The raiders were decelerating now, and on the wall, the telltale for the enemy's detectors flushed a sudden deep and angry purple as their invisible beams reached out and were baffled by the detector screen he had erected at a distance of forty thousand kilometers in front of the Station. They continued to decelerate, but the blockage of their detector beams had given them the approximate area of his Station; and they corrected course, swinging in until they were no more than two points and ten degrees in error. Jordan, his nervous fingers trembling slightly on the keys, stretched thirty-seven through thirty out in depth and sent forty through forty-five forward on a five-degree sweep to attempt a circling movement.

The five dark ships of the raiders, recognizing his intention, fell out of their single file approach formation to spread out and take a formation in open echelon. They were already firing on the advancing doggies and tiny streaks of light tattooed the black of space around numbers forty through forty-five.

Jordan drew a deep and ragged breath and leaned back in his control seat. For the moment there was nothing for his busy fingers to do among the control keys. His thirties must wait until the enemy came to them; since, with modern automatic gunnery, the body at rest had an advantage over the body in motion. And it would be some minutes before the forties would be in attack position. He fumbled for a cigarette, keeping his eyes on the screens, remembering the caution in the training manuals against relaxation once contact with the enemy had been made.

But reaction was setting in.

From the first wild ringing command of the alarm until the present moment, he had reacted automatically, with perfection and precision, as the drills had schooled him, as the training manuals had impressed upon him. The enemy had appeared. He had taken measures for defense against them. All that could have been done had been done; and he knew he had done it properly. And the enemy had done what he had been told they would do.

He was struck, suddenly, with the deep quivering realization of the truth in the manual's predictions. It was so, then. These inimical others, these alien foes, were also bound by the physical laws. They, as well as he, could move only within the rules of time and space. They were shorn of their mystery and brought down to his level. Different and awful they might be, but their capabilities were limited, even as his; and in a combat such as the one now shaping up, their inhumanness was of no account, for the inflexible realities of the universe weighed impartially on him and them alike.

And with this realization, for the first time, the old remembered fear began to fall away like a discarded garment. A tingle ran through him and he found himself warming to the fight as his forefathers had warmed before him away back to the days when man was young and the tiger roared in the cool, damp jungle-dawn of long ago. The blood-instinct was in him; that and something of the fierce, vengeful joy with which a hunted creature turns at last on its pursuer. He would win. Of course he would win. And in winning he would at one stroke pay off the debt of blood and fear which the enemy had held against him these fifteen years.

Thinking in this way, he leaned back in his seat and the old memory of the shattered city and of himself running,

running, rose up again around him. But this time it was no longer a prelude to terror, but fuel for the kindling of his rage. *These are my fear*, he thought, gazing unseeingly at the five ships in the screens, *and I will destroy them*.

The phantasms of his memory faded like smoke around him. He dropped his cigarette into a disposal slot on the arm of his seat, and leaned forward to inspect the enemy positions.

They had spread out to force his forties to circle wide, and those doggies were now scattered, safe but ineffective, waiting further directions. What had been an open echelon formation of the raiders was now a ragged, widely dispersed line, with far too much space between ships to allow each to cover his neighbor.

For a moment Jordan was puzzled; and a tiny surge of fear of the unexplicable rippled across the calm surface of his mind. Then his brow smoothed out. There was no need to get panicky. The aliens' maneuver was not the mysterious tactic he had half-expected it to be; but just what it appeared, a rather obvious and somewhat stupid move to avoid the flanking movement he had been attempting with his forties. Stupid—because the foolish aliens had now rendered themselves vulnerable to interspersal by his thirties.

It was good news, rather than bad, and his spirits leaped another notch.

He ignored the baffled forties, circling automatically on safety control just beyond the ships' effective aiming range; and turned to the thirties, sending them plunging toward the empty areas between ships as you might interlace the fingers of one hand with another. Between any two ships there would be a dead spot—a position where a mech could not be fired on by either vessel without also aiming at its right- or left-hand companion. If two or more doggies could be brought safely to that spot, they could turn and pour down the open lanes on proximity control, their fuses primed, their bomb loads activated, blind bulldogs of destruction.

One third, at least, should in this way get through the defensive shelling of the ships and track their dodging prey to the atomic flare of a grim meeting.

Smiling now in confidence, Jordan watched his mechs approach the ships. There was nothing the enemy could do. They could not now tighten up their formation without merely making themselves a more attractive target; and to disperse still further would negate any chance in the future of regaining a semblance of formation.

Carefully, his fingers played over the keys, gentling his mechs into line so that they would come as close as possible to hitting their dead spots simultaneously. The ships came on.

Closer the raiders came, and closer. And then—bare seconds away from contact with the line of approaching doggies, white fire ravened in unison from their stern tubes, making each ship suddenly a black nugget in the center of a blossom of flame. In unison, they spurted forward, in sudden and unexpected movement, bringing their dead spots to and past the line of seeking doggies, leaving them behind.

Caught for a second in stunned surprise, Jordan sat dumb and motionless, staring at the screen. Then, swift in his anger, his hands flashed out over the keys, blasting his mechs to a cruel, shuddering halt, straining their metal sinews for the quickest and most abrupt about-face and return. This time he would catch them from behind. This time, going in the same direction as the ships, the mechs could not be dodged. For what living thing could endure equal strains with cold metal?

But there was no second attempt on the part of the thirties, for as each bucked to its savage halt, the rear weapons of the ships reached out in unison, and each of the blasting mechs, that had leaped forward so confidently, flared up and died like little candles in the dark.

*　　*　　*

Numb in the grip of icy failure, Jordan sat still, a ramrod figure staring at the two screens that spoke so eloquently of his disaster—and the one dead screen where the view from thirty-seven had been, that said nothing at all. Like a man in a dream, he reached out his right hand and cut in the final sentinel, the *watchdog,* that mech that circled closest to the Station. In one short breath his strong first line was gone, and the enemy rode, their strength undiminished, floating in toward his single line of twenties at fifty thousand with the defensive screen a mere ten thousand kilometers behind them.

Training was strong. Without hesitation his hands went out over the keys and the doggies of the twenties surged forward, trying for contact with the enemy in an area as far from the screen as possible. But, because they were moving in on an opponent relatively at rest, their courses were the more predictable on the enemy's calculators and the disadvantage was theirs. So it was that forty minutes later three ships of the alien rode clear and unthreatened in an area where two of their mates, the forties and all of the thirties were gone.

The ships were, at this moment, fifteen thousand kilometers from the detector screen.

Jordan looked at his handiwork. The situation was obvious and the alternatives undeniable. He had twenty doggies remaining, but he had neither the time to move them up beyond the screen, nor the room to maneuver them in front of it. The only answer was to pull his screen back. But to pull the screen back would be to indicate, by its shrinkage and the direction of its withdrawal, the position of his Station clearly enough for the guided missiles of the enemy to seek him out; and once the Station was knocked out, the doggies were directionless, impotent.

Yet, if he did nothing, in a few minutes the ships would touch and penetrate the detector screen and his Station, the nerve center the aliens were seeking, would lie naked and revealed in their detectors.

He had lost. The alternatives totaled to the same answer, to defeat. In the inattention of a moment, in the smoke of a cigarette, the first blind surge of self-confidence and the thoughtless halting of his by-passed doggies that had allowed the ships' calculators to find them stationary for a second in a predictable area, he had failed. He had given away, in the error of his pride, the initial advantage. He had lost. Speak it softly, speak it gently, for his fault was the fault of one young and untried. He was defeated.

And in the case of defeat, the actions prescribed by the manual were stern and clear. The memory of the instructions tolled in his mind like the unvarying notes of a funeral bell.

"When, in any conflict, the forces of the enemy have obtained a position of advantage such that it is no longer possible to maintain the anonymity of the Station's position, the commandant of the Station is required to perform one final duty. Knowing that the Station will shortly be destroyed and that this will render all remaining mechs innocuous to enemy forces, the commandant is commanded to relinquish control of these mechs, and to place them with fuses primed on proximity control, in order that, even without the Station, they may be enabled to automatically pursue and attempt to destroy those forces of the enemy that approach within critical range of their proximity fuse."

Jordan looked at his screens. Out at forty thousand kilometers, the detector screen was beginning to luminesce slightly as the detectors of the ships probed it at shorter range. To make the manual's order effective, it would have to be pulled back to at least half that distance; and there, while it would still hide the Station, it would give the enemy his approximate location. They would then fire blindly, but with cunning and increasing knowledge and it would be only a matter of time before they hit. After that—only the blind doggies, quivering, turning and trembling through all points of the stellar compass in their thoughtless hunger for prey. One or two of these might gain a revenge as the ships tried to slip past them and over the Line; but Jordan would not be there to know it.

But there was no alternative—even if duty had left him one. Like strangers, his hands rose from the board and stretched out over the keys that would turn the doggies loose. His fingers dropped and rested upon them—light touch on smooth polished coolness

But he could not press them down.

He sat with his arms outstretched, as if in supplication, like one of his primitive forebears before some ancient altar of death. For his will had failed him and there was no denying now his guilt and his failure. For the battle had turned in his short few moments of inattention, and his underestimation of the enemy that had seduced him into halting his thirties without thinking. He knew; and through the memory bank—if that survived—the Force would know. In his neglect, in his refusal to avail himself of the experience of his predecessors, he was guilty.

And yet, he could not press the keys. He could not die properly—*in the execution of his duty*—the cold, correct phrase of the official reports. For a wild rebellion surged through his young body, an instinctive denial of the end that stared him so undeniably in the face. Through vein and sinew and nerve, it raced, opposing and blocking the dictates of training, the logical orders of his upper mind. It was too soon, it was not fair, he had not been given his chance to profit by experience. One more opportunity was all he needed, one more try to redeem himself.

But the rebellion passed and left him shaken, weak. There was no denying reality. And now, a new shame came to press upon him, for he thought of the three alien vessels breaking through, of another city in flaming ruins, and another child that would run screaming from his destroyers. The thought rose up in him, and he writhed internally, torn by his own indecisions. Why couldn't he act? It made no difference to him. What would justification and the redeeming of error mean to him after he was dead?

And he moaned a little, softly to himself, holding his hands outstretched above the keys, but could not press them down.

And then hope came. For suddenly, rising up out of the rubble of his mind, came the memory of the Intelligence man's words once again, and his own near-pursuit of insanity. He, Jordan, could not bring himself to expose himself to the enemy, not even if the method of exposure meant possible protection for the Inner Worlds. But the man who had held this Station before him, who had died as he was about to die, must have been faced with the same necessity for self-sacrifice. And those last-minute memories of his decision would be in the memory bank, waiting for the evocation of Jordan's mind.

Here was hope at last. He would remember, would embrace the insanity he had shrunk from. He would remember and be Waskewicz, not Jordan. He would be Waskewicz and unafraid; though it was a shameful thing to do. Had there been one person, one memory among all living humans, whose image he could have evoked to place in opposition to the images of the three dark ships, he might have managed by himself. But there had been no one close to him since the day of the city raid.

His mind reached back into the memory bank, reached back to the last of Waskewicz's memories. He remembered.

Of the ten ships attacking, six were down. Their ashes strewed the void and the remaining four rode warily, spread widely apart for maximum safety, sure of victory, but wary of this hornet's nest which might still have some strings yet unexpended. But the detector screen was back to its minimum distance for effective concealment and only five doggies remained poised like blunt arrows behind it. He—Waskewicz—sat hunched before the control board, his thick and hairy hands lying softly on the proximity keys.

"Drift in," he said, speaking to the ships, which were cautiously approaching the screen. "Drift in, you. Drift!"

His lips were skinned back over his teeth in a grin—but he did not mean it. It was an automatic grimace, reflex to the tenseness of his waiting. He would lure them on until the last moment, draw them as close as possible to the automatic pursuit mechanisms of the remaining doggies, before pulling back the screen.

"Drift in," he said.

They drifted in. Behind the screen he aimed his doggies, pointing each one of four at a ship and the remaining one generally at them all. They drifted in.

They touched.

His fingers slapped the keys. The screen snapped back until it barely covered the waiting doggies. And the doggies stirred, on proximity, their pursuit mechs activated, now blind and terrible fully armed, ready to attack in senseless directness anything that came close enough.

And the first shells from the advancing ships began to probe the general area of the Station asteroid.

Waskewicz sighed, pushed himself back from the controls and stood up, turning away from the screens. It was over. Done. All finished. For a moment he stood irresolute; then, walking over to the dispenser on the wall, dialed for coffee and drew it, hot, into a disposable cup. He lit a cigarette and stood waiting, smoking and drinking the coffee.

The Station rocked suddenly to the impact of a glancing hit on the asteroid. He staggered and slopped some coffee on his boots, but kept his feet. He took another gulp from the cup, another drag on the cigarette. The Station shook again, and the lights dimmed. He crumpled the cup and dropped it in the disposal slot. He dropped the cigarette on the steel floor, ground it beneath his boot sole; and walked back to the screen and leaned over it for a final look.

The lights went out. And memory ended.

The present returned to Jordan and he stared about him a trifle wildly. Then he felt hardness beneath his fingers and forced himself to look down.

The keys were depressed. The screen was black. The doggies were on proximity. He stared at his hand as if he had never known it before, shocked at its thinness and the lack of soft down on its back. Then, slowly, fighting reluctant neck muscles, he forced himself to look up and into the viewing screen.

And the ships were there, but the ships were drawing away.

He stared; unable to believe his eyes, and half-ready to believe anything else. For the invaders had turned and the flames from their tails made it evident that they were making away into outer space at their maximum bearable acceleration, leaving him alone and unharmed. He shook his head to clear away the false vision from the screen before him, but it remained, denying its falseness. The miracle for which his instincts had held him in check had come—in the moment in which he had borrowed strength to deny it.

His eyes searched the screens in wonder. And then, far down in one corner of the watch dog's screen and so distant still that they showed only as pips on the wide expanse, he saw the shape of his miracle. Coming up from inside of the Line under maximum bearable acceleration were six gleaming fish-shapes that would dwarf his doggies to minnows—the battleships of Patrol Twenty. And he realized, with the dawning wonder of the reprieved, that the conflict, which had seemed so momentary while he was fighting it had actually lasted the four hours necessary to bring the Patrol up to his aid.

The realization that he was now safe washed over him like a wave and he was conscious of a deep thankfulness swelling up within him. It swelled up and out, pushing aside the lonely fear and desperation of his last few minutes, filling him instead with a relief so all-encompassing and profound that there was no anger left in him and no hate—not even for the enemy. It was like being born again.

Above him on the communications panel, the white message light was blinking. He cut in on the speaker with a steady hand and the dispassionate, official voice of the Patrol sounded over his head.

"Patrol Twenty to Station. Twenty to Station. Come in Station. Are you all right?"

He pressed the transmitter key.

"Station to Twenty. Station to Twenty. No damage to report. The Station is unharmed."

"Glad to hear it, Station. We will not pursue. We are decelerating now and will drop all ships on your field in half an hour. That is all."

"Thank you, Twenty. The field will be clear and ready for you. Land at will. That is all."

His hand fell away from the key and the message light winked out. In unconscious imitation of Waskewicz's memory he pushed himself back from the controls, stood up, turned and walked to the dispenser in the wall, where he dialed for and received a cup of coffee. He lit a cigarette and stood as the other had stood, smoking and drinking. He had won.

And reality came back to him with a rush.

For he looked down at his hand and saw the cup of coffee. He drew in on the cigarette and felt the hot smoothness of it deep in his lungs. And terror took him twisting by the throat.

He had won? He had done nothing. The enemy ships had fled not from him, but from the Patrol; and it was Waskewicz, *Waskewicz*, who had taken the controls from his hands at the crucial moment. It was Waskewicz who had saved the day, not he. It was the memory bank. The memory bank and Waskewicz!

The control room rocked about him. He had been betrayed. Nothing was won. Nothing was conquered. It was no friend that had broken at last through his lonely shell to save him, but the mind-sucking figment of memory-domination sanity. The memory bank and Waskewicz had seized him in their grasp.

He threw the coffee container from him and made himself stand upright. He threw the cigarette down and ground it beneath his boot. White-hot, from the very depths of his being, a wild anger blazed and consumed him. *Puppet*, said the mocking voice of his conscience, whispering in his ear. *Puppet!*

Dance, Puppet! Dance to the tune of the twitching strings!

"No!" he yelled. And, borne on the white-hot tide of his rage, the all-consuming rage that burnt the last trace of fear from his heart like dross from the molten steel, he turned to face his tormentor, hurling his mind backward, back into the life of Waskewicz, prisoned in the memory bank.

Back through the swirling tide of memories he raced, hunting a point of contact, wanting only to come to grips with his predecessor, to stand face to face with Waskewicz. Surely, in all his years at the Station, the other must sometime have devoted a thought to the man who must come after him. Let Jordan just find that point, there where the influence was strongest, and settle the matter, for sanity or insanity, for shame or pride, once and for all.

"Hi, Brother!"

The friendly words splashed like cool water on the white

blaze of his anger. He—Waskewicz—stood in front of the bedroom mirror and his face looked out at the man who was himself, and who yet was also Jordan.

"Hi, Brother!" he said. "Whoever and wherever you may be. Hi!"

Jordan looked out through the eyes of Waskewicz, at the reflected face of Waskewicz; and it was a friendly face, the face of a man like himself.

"This is what they don't tell you," said Waskewicz. "This is what they don't teach in training—the message that, sooner or later, every stationman leaves for the guy who comes after him.

"This is the creed of the Station. *You are not alone.* No matter what happens, *you are not alone.* Out on the rim of the empire, facing the unknown races and the endless depths of the universe, this is the one thing that will keep you from all harm. As long as you remember it, nothing can affect you, neither attack, nor defeat, nor death. Light a screen on your outermost doggie and turn the magnification up as far as it will go. Away out at the limits of your vision you can see the doggie of another Station, of another man who holds the Line beside you. All along the Frontier, the Outpost Stations stand, forming a link of steel to guard the Inner Worlds and the little people there. They have their lives and you have yours; and yours is to stand on guard.

"It is not easy to stand on guard; and no man can face the universe alone. But—*you are not alone!* All those who at this moment keep the Line, are with you; and all that have ever kept the Line, as well. For this is our new immortality, we who guard the Frontier, that we do not stop with our deaths, but live on in the Station we have kept. We are in its screens, its controls, in its memory bank, in the very bone and sinew of its steel body. *We are the station,* your steel brother that fights and lives and dies with you and welcomes you at last to our kinship when for your personal self the light has gone out forever, and what was individual of you is nothing any more but cold ashes drifting in the eternity of space. *We are with you and of you, and you are not alone.* I, who was once Waskewicz, and am now part of the Station, leave this message for you, as it was left to me by the man who kept this guard before me, and as you will leave it in your turn to the man who follows you, and so on down the centuries until we have become an elder race and no longer need our shield of brains and steel.

"Hi, Brother! You are not alone!"

And so, when the six ships of Patrol Twenty came drifting in to their landing at the Station, the man who waited to greet them had more than the battle star on his chest to show he was a veteran. For he had done more than win a battle. He had found his soul.

In 1505, when zesty young Michelangelo undertook the commission to carve Pope Julius II's tomb, he expected to finish the colossal structure within five years. Forty frustrating years later, the work was still incomplete. Another vastly ambitious project is Gordon Dickson's three million-word-long Childe Cycle. Here its creator briefly lays mallet and chisel aside to take stock of his creative progress over the past quarter century.

The Childe Cycle Status Report

The first line of the Childe Cycle to be written was the first line of the novel *Dorsai!*, set down in 1958. But the final concept of the Cycle itself took form in one asthmatic night at the Milford Science Fiction Conference more than a year and a half later; and its roots are so intimately connected with my own life that some biographical information is necessary to an understanding of what it is, where it is at the present moment, and where I plan it to be as a finished piece.

I was one of those individuals who teaches himself to read when he is four years old. I had at least one tremendous advantage aiding me to do this. My mother was in love with both poetry and prose; and my father was a mining engineer who was necessarily away from home for extended intervals in my early years. As a result, I had the ideal situation of any young child—my own private adult, full time, to play with.

My mother not only read to me a great deal, she recited endless stories and poems; and my learning to read began with my holding a book and pretending to read, while reciting from memory the words I had heard when it had been read to me. From this to actually associating the words on the page with the words I was speaking was a natural evolution. By the time I was six years old, I was making up my own stories and announcing that I intended to write books. No one told me at that time that this was anything but a good idea. The result was that by the accident of sheer luck, I was unconsciously starting to plan my life by the time I entered first grade.

Two years later, in Ladner, British Columbia, Canada, I was reading adult fiction from the local library; and this turned out to be my launching ramp. On a couple of occasions during the three years we lived in Ladner, I had a poem of mine published in the local paper. Then there followed five years in a private school in Vancouver, British Columbia, where I absorbed a little Latin, a little French, a world of English literature, and all the other, unusual items in the curriculum of grades five through ten. Between the ages of nine and twelve I first began writing prose seriously—things I called books, although they were at most no more than fifteen or twenty thousand words. These were written in longhand in ruled notebooks; and I threw them away after I finished them, because at that time, all the fun was in making them. It was just that writing them down made the stories more real. It literally did not occur to me then to keep them—something I am sorry about now. I would like to see them today and find out if there is still anything in them of the overwhelming excitement and satisfaction I remember feeling when I first scribbled the words down.

Time moved on. My father died when I was thirteen and my mother brought my younger brother and me back down to Minneapolis, Minnesota, where her family lived. In 1939 I graduated from high school at fifteen, went all through a long summer of hunting a job with no luck, and ended up applying for entrance to the University of Minnesota. The university was not happy. As a diplomaed graduate of a high school accredited by the state, it was impossible for them to turn me away, in spite of my age.

The admitting authorities, however, insisted on running me through their Testing Bureau—and as a result of that testing, I was steered to a major in creative writing, put in three years and a bit, left to go in the army for World War II, spent three years in the army and another year getting back to Minnesota, re-entered the university, got my B.A. degree and—momentarily brainwashed by the superhardheaded attitude of the postwar years—got sidetracked into graduate school with the down-to-earth idea of getting my doctorate, and writing only as a sideline to teaching. As a result, I spent a year as a graduate student before coming to my senses, cutting loose from school, and diving into a full-time effort to support myself by writing.

In all this time, from the age of six years on, I had been thinking of what I wanted to do with the books I was hoping to write. I had had a dream of breaking new ground, exploring new literary territory; and as the years went by, the way I hoped I might do this dream had begun to take some shape. I had, by the time I was in graduate school, reluctantly put aside my early dreams of doing long narrative poems like Tennyson's *Idylls of the King*, facing the fact that I was not in an age when such poetry had a readership; and I had finally settled on the idea of novels—probably historical novels.

These novels, as I imagined them, would be made out of the simplest and most easily understood materials. The plain and direct stories they embodied would be drawn in the bright, primary colors and strong action of those books I had lost my heart to in the Ladner library, between the ages of six and nine. Their language would also be simple and familiar. In short, they would be as readable as possible, as unpretentious as possible. Only the concept, the reach of them, would try to do the different thing I wanted to do—but had actually not yet defined. This last was something that in 1948 I could feel strongly, but not quite bring into focus. It was a little like having a head filled with all possible colors without being able to conceive of a rainbow.

Nonetheless, all this time I had been learning, and working my way into an understanding of story structure—though it was some years still before I realized that without knowing it, I had already recognized the separate idea of craft as a necessary part of what I wanted to do. In fact, this recognition had probably helped to bring me through more than five years of academic writing classes without turning me into a word-player and a talker-about-writing, rather than a working writer.

There were things to be learned; and, in fact, the writing classes themselves had some good people among those teaching them—Anna von Helmholtz Phelan, Sinclair Lewis, Robert Penn Warren, and Alan Tate (in chronological order). Of these, far and away the most useful was Robert Penn Warren, who could both use and teach the craft of writing. But, all had things to tell me, in one way or another; and I gradually began to focus in on the image of what I was reaching for.

I knew even by 1948, for example, that it was the concept behind the action of the story that I wanted to control—what I was later to label the thematic argument; and in 1948, in this time when I was playing with the idea of teaching for a living and letting the teaching pay for the writing, I was working on a novel laid in fifteenth-century Italy and with the primary purpose of examining a type of character I then conceived to be purely a Renaissance product but have since discovered rather to be a medieval one. This was a nobleman of one of the city-states in Italy who showed, on one hand, a disconcertingly modern intellectual sensitivity; and on the other a completely conscienceless, almost Stone-Age, barbarism and brutality—all without the society of his time considering him (as our present society would) to be a form of psychotic. I was fascinated not so much by the man himself, as by the society that could find hard and real reasons for enduring such an individual, and the interplay that must have taken place between such an individual and his society.

To demonstrate this man and society, I planned to show them through the eyes of a young Swiss foreign to them both, one member of a levy of pikemen who had been, in effect, sold south to the mercenary, inter-city Italian wars of the time in order to swell the cantonal coffers. The novel was to be called "The Pikeman."

When, in 1950, I renounced my only source of fixed income, the G.I. bill which had been paying me subsistence as a full-time student, I also put on the shelf the manuscript of "The Pikeman." I saw no way at that time to support myself for the time it would take me to do a full novel. So I concentrated on short stories—mainly for the SF magazines, but actually for any magazine market to which I thought I could sell the sort of story I wanted to write.

I survived, partly through luck, partly through an already established ability to sit at the typewriter, and partly as a result of having unconsciously studied the hard bones of story-making all those years since I had first been impressed with their existence. Finally, I did do a novel that ended up in an Ace double, then another.

By this time—1957—I had just about forgotten "The Pikeman," when I found myself getting interested in the notion of an individual who could bypass the ordinary slow patterns of logic. At first this character was simply floating around loose in my mind, and I had no clear image of what I wanted him to do. Then, from the deep wells at the back of the head where ideas lay soaking, came a number of stored ideas including the concept of a theorist surrounded by pragmatists, which had fascinated me when I encountered it in the fictional pattern Rafael Sabatini had used in his novel *Bellarion.*

I already had stored away the idea of a science-fiction novel about a world of professional soldiers, built roughly to the plan of the fifteenth-century Swiss cantons. The idea had emerged, as I thought then, out of a single character referred to as a Dorsai, in a story called "Lulungomeena," which I had written sometime earlier and published in *Galaxy* for January 1954. The character in question was the narrator of "Lulungomeena," a battle-scarred veteran from a group of worlds called the Dorsai Planets. Perking away in the back of my head, the Dorsai Planets became a single world, engaged in the production and export of highly trained professional soldiers. From these diverse elements, in time, came *Dorsai!*, a novel which was originally serialized in *Astounding* at its full written length of 80,000 words and later appeared, cut by about one-third, as the larger half of an Ace double novel, the other half being an expanded novelette of mine.

Dorsai! grew enormously in concept during its writing, so much so that at its final length of 80,000 words, it was actually in a very lean form indeed of what I would have liked to make of it, but did not dare since I did not think there was a chance of anyone buying it at over that length. Such self-limiting decisions are always frustrating; and even after I mailed *Dorsai!* off, it continued to resonate in the back of my mind and grow. It did not merely multiply, it extended in depth; as I began to realize consciously where all its bits and pieces had come from.

What I had done was zero in once more on my groping

toward a novel of thematic argument; and as soon as I recognized this, I began to see how I had unconsciously mined "The Pikeman" for much of what I had done in *Dorsai!* Of course, matters like the necessary figuring to give me some idea of the time it would take the lead character, Donal Graeme, to get from a world around one star to a world around another had no parallel in the notes for the historical novel. But many other elements were remarkably parallel.

Once I realized consciously and fully the connection between *Dorsai!* and "The Pikeman," I began to think seriously about either an expanded version of the later novel, or—more sensibly—a sequel of some sort in which all the extra ideas and material locked out of the original could be used. The notes I worked on at that time have since been lost, but I remember counting them at one time and finding I had a hundred and eighty-three pages, about half the number of the typewritten pages in the final version of *Dorsai!* itself.

The June following the publication of that book as a serial in *Astounding*, I was at the Milford Science Fiction Conference. Milford was then held in Milford, Pennsylvania, a resort/rural area that effectively guaranteed to trigger my allergies to various grasses and pollens into an asthmatic attack if I went up there. But I went anyway, every year, because of the deep and abiding hunger to have some other writers to talk with.

This summer, also, the usual happened. I was short of breath the first day, wheezy the next, and by the third day well on my way to a steady-state attack. Along toward the end of the week, I had reached that stage where the asthmatic goes to bed, thinking—"Maybe I'll sleep through . . ." and falls off into slumber which lasts possibly an hour and a half before being succeeded by a deep attack which puts an end to any thought of sleep, and any position except an upright one.

I came to, accordingly, sitting up in bed, breathing by spoonfuls of air at a time and facing another five hours or so of being just like this until dawn, when such attacks have a tendency to slack off. Those who have not had asthma or known asthmatics may not be aware that it is not an inability to get air into the lungs that is the problem in an attack, it is the inability to get air out. The chest effectively gets pumped up with unexpelled air; there is no room for fresh, oxygen-laden air to get in; and the chest muscles, after a time, effectively go into cramp.

The effect is like that of being slowly suffocated; and the result is that, physically, the asthmatic is totally immobilized. At the same time, his body adrenaline climbs off the map in an attempt to combat the situation—adrenaline being not only what your body chemistry supplies, but what a physician will give you to fight this type of attack—and the practical result of all these factors is that the asthmatic finds himself with a body effectively incapable of moving, but with a mind spinning at ninety miles an hour.

I had five hours to wait, a body that was out of control, and a mind galloping madly away. In those five hours, the complete pattern of the Childe Cycle worked its way out in detail in my head; and the next morning, as soon as the attack let up and people were awake, I went over to the cottage occupied by Richard and Eva McKenna and got the whole project organized in words by telling Mac all about it. It took me about three hours to lay the whole thing out for him.

At the time I thought I had merely come up with a plan on which I could build in time to come. Curiously, however, the original form of the Cycle as conceived then has resisted any change. There was a time in the mid-1960's when I made up my mind to change it whether it wanted to be changed, or not. But I had to admit defeat. It simply would not work properly in any but its original pattern of conception.

This may be the result of its complexity. The Cycle embodies nearly a dozen diverse literary and narrative elements that have been fascinations of mine for a long time; and any change that would improve the situation for one of the elements would almost inevitably worsen it for at least one of the others, in the tight pattern of the original concept. Whatever the reasons, however, the Cycle has resisted any real change from the beginning and I no longer expect any to occur as the later books are written.

The Cycle's main purpose in being is to present, as a literary argument, the thesis that an evolution of the human race may presently be going on under our noses, unrecognized; that perhaps it has in fact been going on for some time. It is an evolution that is neither physical nor mental, but—for want of a better word—ethical; and it is an evolution that is occurring in response to human apprehension at seeing great tool-using powers becoming available to individuals who possibly are not to be trusted to use those powers wisely enough not to put the rest of us in danger.

The argument treats the human race as if it was an anthill or beehive insofar as its unconscious racial wants and desires are concerned. It postulates, in fact, a form of racial id embodied in each living individual of the race, but reacting in the race mass in very primitive fashion. This racial id, from the Cycle's point of view, is occupied by one particular long-standing bit of internal dissension, the struggle between the instinctive urge toward conservatism and safety, on one hand, and the opposing urge toward adventure and possible danger—the same views which some millions of years ago debated the safety of the tidal pool against the possible discomforts and gains inherent in an attempt to crawl out of the water and try being an amphibian, and which now in the twentieth century debate the possible dangers of space exploration as opposed to its possible benefits. The Cycle's argument views all the past development of the human race, prehistoric as well as historic, in the context of that id-argument.

My fictional premise is that this controversy reached an active stage at some time in the past; and is soon to enter its last act, in which it will choose up sides among the individuals of the race and enter a stage of final struggle in which the decision will be made once and for all whether the undying, self-renewing animal which is the race is to be ruled by a decision to adventure and change no further, or whether it will face up to adaptation and growth as a continuing way of racial life. Being of the optimistic persuasion, I am, of course, opting for the choice of adventure and change, and the Cycle works itself out to that end, accordingly.

This thesis, by itself, could have given me simply a large propagandistic novel told in a projected twelve volumes, or acts. However, since my early dream was to plow new literary territory, what the twelve books are aimed toward doing at the same time is to showcase a literary form which I hoped will be one step forward from the propagandistic novel. This is a form on which I have pinned the label of the "consciously thematic" story, or novel. The name, of course, is only a tag. It attempts to describe what I am working with; but since what I am working with is something that did not exist until now, any present label must necessarily fall short of adequately defining it. The full definition of the consciously thematic novel can only be found in the completed Cycle as a whole, if and when all twelve volumes are done to a point of satisfaction; and the decision as to whether I really have come up with a new useful literary form will be made by library readers a hundred years from now, if all or any part of the Cycle is then still being shelved in libraries and read by their frequenters. If it is not, then the work will have represented only a personally satisfying experiment. But if it is, then perhaps I will actually have pioneered a new form and opened up new literary territory.

The argument of the Cycle is designed to be stated thematically, only. The individual novels of the Cycle are organized so that they may be read individually, without the need to relate them to their fellow novels—unless the reader so wishes—and as straightforward literary entertainments. The difference between the consciously thematic novel and its propagandistic ancestor is that the propagandistic novel forces the reader to choose sides—either for or against the situation demonstrated in the pages of the novel. But the consciously thematic novel supplies the reader with realistic elements only, and leaves it to the reader whether he or she wishes to pick these up and fit them together to imply a certain general conclusion.

In the Cycle, this thematic burden is carried primarily by the events chosen, but also by the overall multi-novel pattern of the Cycle itself. Each book of the Cycle showcases one of three archetypes—the Philosopher, the Warrior, or the Faith-Holder. The Philosopher and the Warrior are single-faced, the Faith-Holder is Janus-faced, one face being that of (there is no good word for it in present vocabulary; ''Saint'' falls short and does not fit the literary situations set up) the true Faith-Holder, and the other face is that of the Fanatic.

The Cycle was originally planned to consist of nine novels: three historical, three laid in the twentieth century, and three in the future. Within twenty-four hours after the Cycle's conception, however, a little thought convinced me that at that time in the late fifties no editor in his right mind was likely to be talked into buying a 150,000-word science-fiction novel; and the future three became the future six.

The Cycle itself was planned to cover a period from the fourteenth century and the early years of the Renaissance, to the twenty-fourth century. It would follow the pattern of a science-fiction story, in that the thematic argument would be authenticated by the established facts of the three early historical novels, covering the years from 1400 to 1900, and by those of the three novels laid in the twentieth century, all of which would work within the confines of known history; and the future leg would be extrapolated as rigorously as possible from the line of logical development laid down by these first six novels. The end result of this fictional argument was to be what I had come to label the Responsible Individual—which would be a status achieved by Hal Mayne at the end of the final novel, "Childe."

The first novel according to the internal chronology of the Cycle is one based on what is known of the life of Sir John Hawkwood, who was born in the 1320's in Sibil Hedingham, England, and died in Florence, Italy, in 1394. He has been referred to as "the first of the modern generals" and was involved in the early events of the Hundred Years War of England with France. He became one of the first of the *condottieri* in Italy during the years following the Peace of Bretigny, which concluded the victory won by the Black Prince at the Battle of Poitiers; and later he became captain general of the Florentian forces. As such, he was responsible later for frustrating Giangalleazo Visconti when that Milanese ruler threatened to take control of all Italy; a move that, for reasons discussed in the Cycle, could have stifled the Renaissance at its birth.

The second novel showcases the poet John Milton (Faith-Holder/Friendly) during the years in which he effectively was a propagandist for the Cromwellian government. Milton is ideal for the Cycle's purpose in this period, since he embodies both of the Janus-faces of the Faith-Holder: his poetry reflecting his attitude as True Faith-Holder, and his pamphlets reflecting his role as Fanatic.

The third historical novel makes use of Robert Browning, as a Philosopher whose poetry is a vehicle for his philosophy. This heavy use of poets, by the way, is not unintentional. At the very end of the Cycle, in "Childe" and "The Final Encyclopedia," the showcased character, Hal Mayne, finally makes use of poetry as a creative lever to put the matter-energy device called the Final Encyclopedia to its proper use.

The first of the twentieth-century novels will draw on the life and character of Georges Santayana to showcase a Philosopher.

The second of the twentieth-century novels will be laid in the years of World War II, with a Warrior showcased, and the protagonist will be no single historical character, but draw on several actual historical characters.

The final novel of the twentieth century will showcase a Faith-Holder, probably in the person of a woman and in the time of the 1980's. I can speak of setting this book's story in the 1980's since it will be the last book to be written, which means that I will almost certainly be writing it in the decade of the 1990's. At best estimate, there will be at least another seventeen years of writing required to finish the Cycle, and somewhere along the way the first four novels already published were expanded to their natural length.

Chronologically, the first of the novels of the future leg is *Necromancer*, showcasing the Philosopher, which is laid in the later half of the twenty-first century.

Tactics of Mistake, showcasing the Warrior, is laid in the twenty-second century.

Dorsai! (Warrior) is laid in the twenty-third century. It is contemporaneous with *Soldier, Ask Not* (Faith-Holder: Jamethon Black). In fact, one scene overlaps in both books— the same scene from two different points of view—following Donal's victory over Newton.

The Final Encylopedia, the long novel which I have just published, is laid in the twenty-fourth century, as are *Chantry Guild* and *Childe*, the last novel of the cycle. *The*

Final Encyclopedia and the other two books are prequel and sequels. That is, together . . . they make up a single story; and Hal Mayne, the third appearance of the Donal Graeme identity, is the point-of-view character in both of them. Hal Mayne is the first Responsible and embodies all three archetypes.

At this point enters one of the complications of the Cycle. While the chronological order is as laid out above, there is another—a story order—which in the future leg begins with Donal Graeme in the opening of *Dorsai!* Donal Graeme alone, of all the characters from the beginning to the end of the Cycle, is something more than an ordinary human being—or rather he is an ordinary human being in the process of becoming the first of the Responsible Individuals.

His basic identity goes through three growth stages and four novels in this process. He is born and grows up to what would be the equivalent of a late teenager in *Dorsai!*—in terms of his individual development. In chronological terms, of course, he is in his late twenties at the end of that book.

In *Dorsai!*, he effectively tries to remake the race using brute force—which is what his ability of intuitional logic effectively amounts to. With it, he forces the people of the various worlds into a single political unit; and at the end, with the maturity he has acquired in the process of doing this, he faces the fact that this, alone, is not the answer. The answer will require abilities which are not yet developed in him, and upon a different effect and control within his race.

Effectively, he must make changes without forcing them. One of the strictures that had to be laid upon the Cycle was that physical time travel was not possible. Aside from the fact that this would be unrealistic, the reason for such is obvious. If time travel was possible, so that even one person could go back and change the root values of history to a different purpose, then there would never have been a problem—in short, permitting time travel would make the whole racial problem imaged in the Cycle a paper dragon.

However, since Donal needs changes, he must find another way to make them. His solution is to go back in time—not physically, but in identity—and not to make physical changes, which are impossible, but to alter the implications of what has already happened, so that these will have a different effect in the future at a time after the point at which he had sent his identity back.

Accordingly, he sends his identity back and enters on his second growth process, by re-animating the drowned body of Paul Formain, a mining engineer of the twenty-first century, in *Necromancer*. As Formain, he becomes involved with the root elements of twenty-first century society that will eventually become the operating social elements of later times—with the Chantry Guild, which is to become the Exotic society, and with the proto-members of the other splinter cultures, including his own Dorsai, and the Friendlies.

As in each of his stages of development, he starts out without knowledge of his former existence. He is, exclusively, Paul Formain as the book opens; and only gradually does he come to realize that he is also Donal and what his reasons are for being there in Formain's body. He is there primarily to accomplish two things. One is to achieve the second stage of his development. In *Dorsai!*, he had showcased the role of the Warrior. Now, in *Necromancer*, he steps into the role of Philosopher/Exotic, in which he must achieve the operative ability and function of an empath. The other accomplishment is the task he has to perform with regard to the race as a whole.

This is to achieve the necessary splitting of the racial id, so that the conflict between its conservative and adventurous parts can be fought out in the open, with human champions on both sides—whereas, in the past, through all the books of the Cycle until now, the battle has been fought within each living individual of the race.

It is this part of *Necromancer* that makes the book in certain sections read like fantasy rather than science fiction. The reason for this is that the stage on which the final battle will be fought, in *The Final Encyclopedia* and *Childe*, is what I have ended up calling the Alternate Universe. This is the universe in which whatever you can imagine becomes real, the only requirement being that if you wish to imagine, say, a castle, you can only bring it into reality if you understand what makes up a castle, right down to its most sub-submicroscopic component . . . and that requires a knowledge of architecture, history, and even of the minds of the people who built the original castles from which your knowledge is derived.

The tool to do this is already under construction in Donal's twenty-third century, but the tool alone is not the complete answer. It requires someone with the ability to use that tool—which is why Donal is back living and learning through a second existence as Paul Formain. However, it should be noted that, because of the creative nature of that tool, the fantasy-note that seems to echo in *Necromancer* will also seem to echo in *Childe*, the final novel of the Cycle.

The third stage of Donal's development is to take place in the twenty-fourth century in which he grows up as Hal Mayne. Hal Mayne is found as a very young child—a baby—drifting in a small interstellar courier-class spaceship, near Earth. The ship and its contents sell for enough to set up a trust to raise and educate the boy, who is raised by three tutors: one Exotic, one Dorsai, and one Friendly, until he is about sixteen—when his home is taken over by the heads of the self-named Other People.

These are cross-breeds from the now-disintegrating splinter cultures. The political organization Donal had set up a hundred years earlier to weld the human-occupied worlds into one unit has spelled the beginning of the end for the diversity that permitted the splinter cultures to exist and develop. The cross-breeds have much of the abilities of the cultures from which they derive, plus the vigor of the hybrid. With their most effective people, this becomes a charismatic power that allows them to easily make adherents of most men and women. But their numbers are relatively few, and the control they desire is one that requires the least effort from them as individuals. They have therefore, in effect, evolved a loose, mutually-supportive organization rather like a super-Mafia, which has as its aim the control of existing governments, rather than the usurpation of their powers. They represent, in other words, the ultimate product of the conservative part of the racial id, in its now-separated state; as Hal Mayne is to represent the ultimate product of its adventurous part.

The Others do not trust even each other; and they will feel secure only when all the peoples on all the inhabited worlds are effectively under their control. Some of these peoples, however, have a natural resistance to this charisma of theirs; and the result is that, while they control most worlds completely, a few are still in dispute and a few resist them utterly.

Those in dispute include the two Friendly Worlds, in which groups and individuals have literally chosen up sides for and against the forces controlled by the Others (effectively, for and against the opposing id-parts) and bitter, civil-type war is in progress; and the Exotics, who as a culture and two worlds are untouched by the Others directly, but who, by virtue of their own choice of social weapons, are surrounded and as a whole at the mercy of the economic power that the Others do control.

Absolutely uncontrolled, but slowly being starved to death by the deliberate intent of the Others (who control the job market in which the Dorsai people have traditionally gone off-planet to make their living), is the Dorsai world. The only other world which is absolutely free of Other control is—curiously enough—Earth; which is both self-supporting, and has a people who, to the Others' puzzlement, are generally immune to the charismatic power of the hybrids. It was to be expected that the Dorsai and the Exotics, along with the true Faith-Holders of the Friendlies, would be resistant. But why the Earth-born should also be so is something that, in the beginning of *The Final Encyclopedia* in particular, the Others would give a great deal to learn. Earth does not lack individual people who will respond to the Others, but they are a handful compared to the general population.

In the beginning of *The Final Encyclopedia*, the Others take over the Hal Mayne estate, not realizing the potential danger of Hal to them; and the three tutors give their lives to give Hal a chance to run, undiscovered. He does run; and on Coby, then on Harmony, then on the Dorsai world, he grows up to the knowledge of what his purpose is. He ends up coming home, in effect, to the Final Encyclopedia, from which the last battle will emerge— the battle chronicled in *Childe*, in which the adventurous part of the id finally wins its ascendency over the conservative part, and the human identity is made whole again.

As things now stand, I have completed *The Final Encyclopedia*. As I may have said earlier, the demonstration of the consciously thematic novel will lie only in the completed Cycle itself. This is also true of all the other elements I mention. It would be possible to go on almost indefinitely, discussing the Cycle, but that would be an unsatisfying process. Barring interruptions, the rest of the books in the Cycle should from now on come out at a fairly steady rate at more or less two-year intervals, beginning with *Chantry Guild* (after *The Final Encyclopedia*); then will follow *Childe*, and Hawkwood, Milton, and

Browning; and in historically chronological order, the books of the twentieth century.

With luck, then, and an allowance for interruptions, the Cycle should be finished in another seventeen years. It has already taken twenty-seven, so that gives a total time from first book to last of forty-four years. That period has, of course, been extended by the fact that other things have had to be written, in between the Cycle books, to produce the income that makes work on the Cycle possible. Those of you who know me know that I see no reason why publishers should be alone in being hard-headed about bookkeeping. Not merely the cost of employees, of research, of equipment and travel, etc., need to be figured into the cost of doing a large piece of writing like this, but the working time of the author is a hard and figurable expense, a depreciable asset. By the time I finish each book of the Cycle, nearly two years of working time and costs will have gone into it. It follows then that it will be a long time before any of the novels of the Cycle pay their way. But the satisfaction in doing them is immeasurable.

Journalists interview; friends converse. Gordon Dickson and Sandra Miesel have taken their friendly conversations off the long-distance telephone lines and onto the programs of science fiction conventions across the country. Novelist and critic Miesel has been studying the Childe Cycle for more than a decade and is attempting to apply its literary principles in her own fiction. She is Dickson's research consultant in her areas of expertise (history, mythology, art) while he in turn has given her invaluable advice on developing her professional career.

A Conversation With Gordon R. Dickson

by
Sandra Miesel

DICKSON: We have to start with the fact that I've always been a writer, always intended to write. When you're very young people tell you, "Fine, go ahead." Nobody ever told me not to until later on, by which time it was too late. So after World War II, I was unduly sensible and said I will sit down and teach but write in my spare time—I was doing the abnormal thing. For me, the writing is what I want to do. The teaching is merely pleasant.

*   *   *

MIESEL: You started college majoring in creative writing. What turned you permanently toward a professional writing career despite your obvious natural gift for teaching?

DICKSON: But all writers are natural teachers. Once they're good writers, fine teaching comes automatically to them as breathing because essentially in their stories—if their stories are good—they're telling people things. Teaching goes to the same creative well as writing. There's a great deal of satisfaction in teaching which is why most people don't seem to be able to write and teach at the same time. And when you look right at it, you're talking to a much larger audience, much more effectively through the blinking books anyway. You just don't get the feedback.

MIESEL: You're one of the few people in SF who's been a full-time writer from the beginning of your career.

DICKSON: The more I look at it, the more convinced I become that I was a fully-formed writer long before I got my degree which is the reason the writing courses didn't scuttle me the way they often do people. In other words, I had enough mass and momentum along the road I wanted to travel so that I couldn't be jolted off. I've literally been a writer all my life, as far back as I can remember.

MIESEL: What have you done outside the SF field?

DICKSON: Well, in the beginning I did anything that would bring money in—I was just a free-lance writer. It's surprising even then how little I wrote that wasn't science fiction. But clear up to 1960, if you had asked me if I was a real science fiction writer, I would have said no. I had this historical novel *The Pikeman* that I was just waiting to get at. It was only later that I came to see that there was more freedom to move around in SF.

MIESEL: You had a long association with editor John Campbell of *Astounding/Analog*. Do you think your interaction with him was different because you didn't have the hard-science orientation his "school" of writers had?

DICKSON: No, as I said, it's amazing how little or how much of these thing you use. John, in spite of his own degree in physics, wasn't a hard-science writer either. What John really loved wasn't science fiction but idea-fiction and that's my territory.

MIESEL: Have you ever felt an impulse to write non-fiction popular history, or anything like that?

DICKSON: Yes, I've thought of things I'd like to do but they're so far down the list of wants. Let me mention something I'd enjoy and will get around to doing. I promise that certain things are going to happen by the turn of the century. One is the Neo-Puritan revolution. Another is long narrative poetry and the essay coming back. I very much love the elegance of the classical essay, the nineteenth century essay, people like Carlyle and Ruskin—particularly Ruskin—beautiful. It's an elegant way of making a point and I can have a lot of fun with that.

MIESEL: So could I. I have a personal interest in nonfiction because I've come into SF through the non-fiction end. Everything I do now really grows out of learning to write history research papers. It's made my style unusually formal.

DICKSON: You can't see your own style. If you can shift gears in your head for a moment, look at your pages not as words but as ideas in a package. The classical essay has the same strictures on it as good fiction—essentially you should become transparent and people end up reading it not so much for the words as for the ideas.

Everyone has unique powers, and if you exercise them, sooner or later the fabric of human society becomes aware that that individual is a source from which they can get something they can't get anywhere else.

The thing to do is just keep getting the stuff out. Go ahead making axeheads until they say: "My God, your axeheads throw like nobody else's." Say: "Yes, that's the way I designed it." And the word spreads around the world: you have a magic gift for making axeheads that throw.

MIESEL: Axeheads? What I want are more outlets for writing essays.

DICKSON: They aren't quite back yet but they will come. You have to have people who can appreciate the elegance before it can happen. It's just that positioned as you are in the universe, you can't see this happening. Your progress at present is imperceptible, just like my progress with the Childe Cycle was imperceptible in the early '60s.

MIESEL: Since we're going to be talking about the Childe Cycle, would you state briefly what it is and where it's going in terms of structure?

DICKSON: The Childe Cycle basically is one large novel consisting of twelve smaller novels. As one large novel, it is what I call a "consciously thematic novel." It is also a novel built on the pattern of a science fiction story in which we first establish the real-life basis on which the possible future is going to be laid and extrapolate rigorously from it. In this case, I'm going to be extrapolating from the three historical novels and the three contemporary novels into the six science fiction novels. Of the twelve, four on the science fiction end have been published: *Necromancer*, *The Tactics of Mistake*, *Dorsai!*, and *Soldier, Ask Not*. The fifth one was published in hardcover in October, 1984—that's *The Final Encyclopedia*. *The Final Encyclopedia*, *Chantry Guild*, and *Childe* are actually prequel and sequels, in other words, they make up one big novel by themselves.

MIESEL: Let's not forget the illuminations—"Warrior," "Brothers," "Amanda Morgan," and "Lost Dorsai." So the Cycle has been a deeply important part of your career for more than twenty years.

DICKSON: It's my showpiece for the consciously-thematic novel.

MIESEL: It's also a vehicle for the philosophy you were talking about even before you had the idea for the Cycle—the evolutionary philosophy. It even shows up in such early books as *Time to Teleport* in 1955 and *Mankind on the Run* in 1956. Many of the same ideas, such as man taking a role in his own evolution and the need for reconciliation between different aspects of the human personality—the conscious/progressive and the unconscious/conservative halves—are in *Space Swimmers* and *The Pritcher Mass*. So even when you are not working within the Cycle, you are still exploring the same themes.

DICKSON: Essentially, yes.

MIESEL: Therefore, one concludes that these themes are personally quite important to you.

DICKSON: Absolutely. I am a galloping optimist. It's an

argument for the fact that man's future is onward and upward.

MIESEL: I think I myself would choose to be the unconscious/conservative half of the debate.

DICKSON: How can you argue with two million well-reasoned words, which is what we're going to have at the end of it.

MIESEL: However, philosophy delivered in the form of adventure novels may not be recognized as such without additional cueing. When you eventually rewrite it in its polished, perfected form, I assume this is going to be made a little more explicit.

DICKSON: I'm at the curious necessity of having to rough-draft large sections of a two-million-word novel. Only after I've rough-drafted will I know exactly what I've got. Then I can go back and sharpen it up. Now again, because of the exigencies of time, space . . .

MIESEL: and publishers' schedules . . .

DICKSON: . . . and finances, I am rough-drafting it in sections and not even chronological sections. Each one of these sections has to fulfill two very strong strictures. One is that they be adequate entertainments apart from their place in the Cycle. The second is that they are consciously thematic novels, that their message is not an accidental or blurred thing but a clear statement for those who will look for it.

MIESEL: Ah, that's the key word, for those who are willing to *look* for it. Don't you have a problem of an awful lot of people only reading them as space operas?

This fills me with messianic zeal. I want to collar people and tell them the Truth.

DICKSON: Right! Pick them up by the ears and shake them.

MIESEL: And I can do it, too. How could anybody say that *Soldier, Ask Not* is a space opera! That is such a finely crafted work.

DICKSON: They certainly said it about *Dorsai!* One of the things that led them astray was that it appeared as an Ace Doublebook which meant strictly adventure science fiction.

MIESEL: Samuel R. Delany and other acclaimed authors first appeared in an Ace Double, too.

DICKSON: Depends on where you put your philosophy—on top or underneath.

MIESEL: I had been reading your stories since I was thirteen and enjoyed them, but until I actually read *Dorsai!* in 1973, the full emotional impact did not hit me. It was rather like the experience C.S. Lewis records in his autobiography about the first time he encountered Norse mythology. He was suddenly aware of something "cold, pale, remote, and immense." And that is exactly how *Dorsai!* hit me: these huge, pale, cloudless skies with rocky cliffs and mountains against them. Once having recognized it, I was eager to read the Cycle in correct order and to study it as I have continued to do for the past decade.

Since you had the basic ideas for the Cycle and produced the first installment, *Dorsai!*, before you had the full structure in mind, how did you come to devise it?

DICKSON: I wanted to do two things. What every writer wants to do is write the books that he would like to read himself. I wanted to write things that were enjoyable to read—great, powerful, actionful things. At the same time, I wanted to do something more, I wanted to plow new ground, open up new territory. Now, I was unconsciously searching for a way to do it in the '40s and I had a novel called *The Pikeman* started. Then I came to my senses, realized I didn't want to teach—I was in graduate school at the time—broke out and went into writing science fiction, which was magazine fiction, just to stay alive. And for some time I didn't think of a novel because I thought I would starve to death during the investment of time. However, I ended up writing a few of these earlier Ace books. Then I got around to writing *Dorsai!*

After I'd written it—only after I'd written it—did I realize I'd used a lot of the material, the idea, the thematic content that would have gone into *Pikeman*. What was behind *The Pikeman* was literally a thematic novel. I wanted to show a particular type of Renaissance character, a completely unempathic intellectual, through the clean eyes of a young Swiss pikeman, one of the levies hired south in the fifteenth century. And so the concept of the adventure story that was done for a purpose was already there. Then when I discovered I'd done it—and essentially done it successfully in *Dorsai!*—it began to cook.

So it had been brewing for more than a year before I got to the 1960 Milford Conference. While I was up there, I couldn't sleep that one night and went, Eureka! I had it! Got up the next morning trying to tell Richard McKenna about it which was actually a process by which I sorted it out in my own mind. The essential structure was born full-blown in that moment and has stayed the same.

MIESEL: It's interesting that it was McKenna you talked to. Was that an accident?

DICKSON: No, Mac was the one person there whom I could conceivably bounce this off of for a number of reasons. In the first place, he was also a thematic writer, although not a conscious one—in the particular, specialized sense in which I'm using that word. Secondly, and most importantly, he was a storyteller. We were both strongly derivative of Kipling, as a lot of people in the science fiction field are. In fact, it's freakish to see how much the hand of Kipling has influenced generations of science fiction writers at first, second, or even third hand. But also, he had done—or was doing?—*The Sand Pebbles*. It, too, was a big project and essentially revealed history through the medium of characters in action affected by that history.

And he did what a good pro writer does, he bounced things back off me without either trying to grasp it too quickly—that is, he waited to get the whole thing—and without trying to turn it into his story, rather than mine. It is an instinct when one carpenter speaks to another to say, "Well, the trouble with your adze is . . ." and talks about the way *he* would use an adze. It's quite all right to do it as long as you understand, as most professionals do, that your suggestions are never going to be used. Their purpose is merely to give the questioning writer something to work off of.

MIESEL: In this moment of inspiration, it's quite extraordinary that you hit upon basic and universal symbols so that you could continue to use them unaltered afterwards.

DICKSON: I think the symbols were there originally.

MIESEL: They give you a way to reach readers who only think they are reading an adventure story. They don't have to know anything about mythology to get the benefit of the symbols. They're responding to these symbols on a subconscious, emotional level.

DICKSON: The whole point about the new ground I want to plow in literature is to move one step closer to having the reader experience it for himself. Now bear in mind I was not deliberately charting those symbols. I was, however, conscious that I was writing philosophy. Or rather, rendering philosophy. And in the attempt to render philosophy, you invariably go to symbol-resonant materials. Since then, I've been waiting for somebody to notice what I was doing.

MIESEL: I'm trying! I'm trying!

DICKSON: No, you came along just in time. But I wanted this to work way down underground on the subconscious level. For one thing, I wanted to write something that wasn't teachable *per se*. It would be very hard to have a literature course in which you study the Cycle—they can hardly pound it into the heads of tenth graders.

MIESEL: The structure and the meaning of the Cycle are so tightly organized and skillfully intertwined that explicating the background is not an empty exercise. The form carries the function. The symbols and allusions are never merely decorative. They push the story forward.

DICKSON: Something important: you see, I'm not really writing for the person who will dig in and find these things out. I am writing something that I hope the average, wanting-to-be-entertained reader will pick up and absorb. That's the whole point of the consciously-thematic novel. It's a way of making a philosophical statement that the reader sort of swallows without having realized that they've swallowed it and only later realizes it's in there. The propagandistic novel gives you no chance but to accept or reject the statement. The consciously-thematic novel makes the statement available to you but does not require you to do either one. You can simply ignore it.

MIESEL: Are your readers going to be upset when you start explaining the Cycle?

DICKSON: Not if I've done my job well. Let me give you an example. Every so often I would go over and over something that fascinated me without being able to grasp it. In other words, while attempting to study it, I would be drawn into the action. Kipling is a very good example of this. Bob Heinlein's another. Try to read Heinlein and *study* what he does. You can't, 'cause you get caught up in the story. It's very hard to watch the machinery by which he is creating the illusion of reality. In the process of looking at the machinery you get caught up in it.

MIESEL: It's a basic psychological principle that you cannot both experience something and think about your experience at the same time. But at least theoretically, explanation of the theme and the symbols and the techniques ought to aid appreciation.

DICKSON: Where I expect the reader to get it is after the Cycle is done. Somebody who reads them all will see resonances and repetitions so he will do the work of looking at this slew of evidence I've laid out and will on his own come to the conclusion I'd like him to come to— ideally! You see, this is precisely the point of the consciously-thematic novel as opposed to the propaganda novel.

MIESEL: Would it be going too far to say that if you complete the Cycle the way you envision it and everything goes well, you will in a very small way have contributed to the actualization of the developments you're talking about in your fiction?

DICKSON: That essentially is the aim. I'm literally saying we've got to move forward and this would be a good direction to go in and I recommend it highly. It's amazing, the feedback I've gotten. There are individuals who come up to me and say: "Wouldn't it be nice if the future held worlds like this?"

MIESEL: If we look far enough into the future, who knows? Maybe the Childe Cycle will turn up on some thirtieth century list of Ten Books That Changed the Universe.

DICKSON: And what are the other nine? An artist has to have two things: he has to have, somewhere tucked away, a tremendous ego, the feeling that he is the best painter or writer that ever came down the pike, never in the history of the world, never before and never again. . . . On the other hand, he has to have a secret little gnawing, wizened doubt that comes out and bites him on the heel and says: "But did you do it right? Is it really art?" and so forth. The reason he has to have these two things is, when the world's brass bands march around him or her and banners are hung from the wall, to keep him or her from becoming a victim of adulation, this little doubt will creep out and say: "But, ah, yes, we know, don't we? You're a fake." And consequently, at the other end of the spectrum, when the world says it's absolutely no good, this "best thing that ever came down the pike" attitude keeps him or her alive and working. So you bobble back and forth between Scylla and Charybdis.

MIESEL: You have collaborated several times withother writers. What were those experiences like?

DICKSON: It's just that I never intended to do any of them. My theory was that I wouldn't write under a pseudonym and that I wouldn't collaborate. On the other hand, I'd already collaborated with Poul Anderson—only they weren't really collaborations, he'd done all the writing. We'd simply talked the thing over and the Hokas were a natural.

MIESEL: It must have been easy writing the Hoka stories—being a Hoka yourself.

DICKSON: Quite right! That's what people say. In the Hoka stories, I do the first draft, Poul does the second. In the case of the collaboration with Ben Bova, *Gremlins, Go Home*, we were supposed to do alternate chapters. He ended up doing about ten and I did two. In the case of *Lifeship*, Harry Harrison did a 30,000 word piece, sort of a strange bastardly cross between a novelette and an extended outline, and I took it from there. Really, it isn't a good way to write. I know of no instance of a collaboration being superior to solo work—no, maybe Nordoff and Hall is an exception—but they're a case of collaborators who never wrote anything much alone.

MIESEL: But what about Frederick Pohl and C.M. Kornbluth?

DICKSON: Possibly. Maybe that's right. Kornbluth was a marvelous idea man and Pohl was the worker, in truth.

MIESEL: Readers might guess some of your own personal interests from things that keep showing up in your stories: history, traditional literature, fine arts, military science, and so forth. Are you interested in behavioral psychology, too? You do such clever things with animal psychology and alien cultures extrapolated from animal behavior such as in *The Alien Way* and *None But Man*.

DICKSON: I tend to gestalt things, you know. I see humans and animals illuminating one another by what they do and also humans and animals illuminating aliens—and vice versa.

MIESEL: You're the only writer I can think of in SF who provides the journal article reference for source materials so that the reader could conceivably look it up for himself if his interests lay in that direction.

DICKSON: That's the doggone thematic thing. I'm kind of hoping they *will* go look it up.

MIESEL: But back to your sometime writing partner Poul Anderson. It annoys me no end to hear you two regarded as members of the same school when you are as unlike as any pair of people in the field.

DICKSON: Hear! Hear!

MIESEL: The fact that you came in with the Hoka stories and are known to be friends is coloring this judgment, but philosophically and in terms of content, you're so different. The only thing that you intersect on is the theme of individual responsibility. But you're Pelagian and he's Augustinian: the perfectibility of man versus the imperfectibility. And different attitudes toward the material universe, toward human beings, and quite a different style.

DICKSON: Quite right.

MIESEL: It seems to me that the grand underlying theme in all your works is the indomitable will. It is as though you turn the famous lines from *The Battle of Maldon* around so that "hearts will be bolder, wills will be stronger as our strength *waxes*." Now Poul Anderson has always taken them in the straight sense so he has this terrible sense of the northern heroic spirit confronting ultimate doom courageously. He's much concerned with the reactions of people in situations where they must eventually perish, yet they mean to endure until they're extinguished. Your characters are more concerned with ultimate triumph. We're in a depressed, doom-ridden period in cultural history when few people are concerned with victory or think that the future is a good thing to hope for.

DICKSON: Well, I see the human being as certainly improvable, if not perfectible. Perfectible is a little too good to be true. Improvable, tremendously improvable. And by his or her own strength.

MIESEL: Your characters are going to remake heaven and earth by force of will. It's very fashionable to accuse you of being a radical individualist and yet you have many occasions where the hero is the symbol of a larger group and it's really a corporate enterprise with everybody contributing something. Once you have the indomitable will operating, it will feed on its own energy, synergizing itself—a breeder reactor of the spirit, as it were. The Exotics, Friendlies, and Dorsai in the Childe Cycle are more distinguished by the way they use their wills than their intellects. The purely intellectual people on the scientific and technical worlds are more or less negatively characterized. That's not the future, you seem to be saying. Intellect for its own sake is not important. Salvation is integration.

DICKSON: What I see in this is essentially what the Childe Cycle says. You look at human beings from a completely non-partisan point of view and you see that they really aren't very good, but on the other hand, they come up with all these great things. And how do you explain this? They are by definition wildly egocentric with all the sins and failings, individually egocentric and mutually antagonistic, yet they flock together in groups and do violence to their own instinctive reactions in order to get along together. Really, the human animal is a fascinating contradiction all the way along the line.

MIESEL: As C. S. Lewis put it, "Akin on the one hand to angels and on the other to tomcats."

DICKSON: Right. The only key I've found to it is in the creative area. I've hypothesized that there's a great deal of creativity locked up, either culturally or simply because we haven't evolved far enough.

MIESEL: Creativity—building things—is the proper work of human beings. This is the most advanced, most liberating thing they can do. Your stories also dramatize the ability of human beings to act out of free will—an unfashionable idea these days. You have people triumphing over various biological and cultural imperatives. For instance, it seems to me that it was harder for Jamethon Black in *Soldier, Ask Not* to be a saint than for most people precisely because his culture was so religious.

DICKSON: Jamethon Black, he's the saint side of the Janus face. I'd already shown the fanatic side which is much easier to get across. Jamethon can only be what he is by acting as an individual in a highly non-individualistic culture and this is his real triumph.

MIESEL: The Cycle as a whole—and really, this could be stretched to apply to your other novels—has a pronounced epic structure. If one looks at them as epics they become much more coherent than if one tries to analyze them by the same criteria as contemporary mainstream novels. Consider the following quote: "He celebrates the exploits of men, the action is man to man, the thought is of men about men; men are raised to the level of supermen." This is not from a review of one of your books. It's a comment about the Persian epic the *Shahnameh*. These titanic struggles in your fiction, whether physical or metaphysical, are between men (or between men and other kinds of sentient beings) and not the more usual Western romantic conflict between man and nature.

DICKSON: Very interesting.

MIESEL: At the conclusion of the Childe Cycle, humanity will be breaking through the current level of existence and if that's where they're going, the exact lineaments of the present level are trivial. Your environments have always seemed to me to be extremely austere places colored in clean, cold pastels or monochrome hues.

Nor the schematic structures and the recapitulation, the macrouniverse against the microuniverse, your habit of turning every detail toward the principal theme, gives your work an architectonic quality that is most impressive. One is always aware that every story is a "made thing."

DICKSON: Aware? Uncomfortably aware?

MIESEL: No, just that you do bring the reader to understand that this is not naturalistic fiction. Eventually, I assume that the finished science fictional leg of the Cycle will have not a wheel out of place, not a gear unmeshed.

DICKSON: Hopefully. That's a lot to ask. That's going to be three-quarters of a million words long.

MIESEL: I have faith in you. But by leaving out spontaneity and randomness, you achieve a feeling of terrible relentlessness.

DICKSON: I'm glad to hear that.

MIESEL: This is probably more evident in your short fiction than in your novels. You have fate and destiny making evolutionary progress across human history, like very cold mountain streams racing through deep channels.

DICKSON: That's the kind of sentence you could put in a popular statement on the Cycle. The readers can follow metaphor and on the basis of that metaphor, they'll take your word for everything else.

MIESEL: On another topic, it is very interesting that your heroes, however much alienated by circumstances and set apart from other people by their special talents, still feel a solidarity with the rest of the human race—for which I applaud you. I hate to see that quality overlooked.

DICKSON: It doesn't matter.

MIESEL: But it's the truth.

DICKSON: In the end it'll all come out.

MIESEL: "Error has no right to exist." That's the motto of the Inquisition.

DICKSON: That's right: "Off with his head!"

MIESEL: Take the last scene in *The Pritcher Mass* where all living beings are awakening, all their powers are uniting, and the clouds roll back—what a lovely image of the corporate nature of life! You are not a radical individualist even though you deal with rather superhuman leading characters who are embodiments of forces, principles incarnate. They really do need other people's help to accomplish their mission. The highest does not stand without the lowest. Every part contributes to the final victory over evil. It is also remarkable throughout your work (particularly in *Soldier, Ask Not*), that you insist on the moral use of talent, that power alone without character is inevitably corrupted. Heinlein says if it prevails, it is right. You say that if it is right, it will, even *must* prevail.

But your use of mythology is an instinctive thing, obviously derived from an enormous background in reading the literary products of mythology. You are extracting by art the same patterns the professional mythologist extracts by his science. It behooves us to draw you to the attention of the professional mythologists so that you can be trotted out like a tame Trobriand Islander at their meetings and asked about your myths of kinship groupings.

DICKSON: Actually, I would like that. I hope it works out so as to direct their attention to the Cycle. My personal love, of course, is with the actual philosophical argument itself.

MIESEL: Why have you so consistently put down science in the Cycle, at least relative to the three major Splinter Cultures, the Dorsai, Friendlies, and Exotics?

DICKSON: The trouble with science in the Cycle is two things: first, I wanted to get away from using science in the foreground.

MIESEL: You're reversing one of the great SF myths— the old, old notion of the infinite perfection of science. But I don't think you give the scientists enough credit for creativity and, as for cerebral activity, it's made to appear a defect in their case.

DICKSON: Another problem is that scientific creativity doesn't render for my purposes. I was spotlighting human evolution and giving the human animal more and better tools begs the question of what I was after.

MIESEL: That's an answer. It also happens to reflect that you weren't scientifically trained.

DICKSON: Yes.

MIESEL: Because you're multi-talented, you can appreciate other kinds of creativity besides writing. But you have not experienced scientific creativity or developed enough of a feel for the mental language of science.

DICKSON: But I don't know if I made my point. Science doesn't "play" in the sense that an actor will say, "This line doesn't read." I mean it would "play" in a different literary vehicle but in the vehicle I've set up in the Cycle, it can be there but it isn't dramatic. Also, to a certain extent, I'm concerned with breaking away from something we still have—a worship of science.

Look on all of history of science as being the equivalent of science fiction from the '30s until now with the recent period in which science has been so damned useful as the equivalent of New Wave SF. There never was a New Wave in the sense of something standing alone. But what came of it—a small bit of metal was in the ore—it did direct attention of a lot of writers to the fact that we weren't paying enough attention to certain areas as we should. But it's back where it always was in the first place, which is a concern with literature as storytelling, the way literature has always been expressed.

In the same way, the scientific explosion—I'm talking about the hard science explosion—was an exercise or an adventure that (unlike the New Wave) actually did turn up a lot of things. But now they're being integrated back in, so hopefully in a hundred years or even less, there won't be the sharp divisions between the scientist and the humanist.

MIESEL: The human race has been through this once before. Mircea Eliade has a book called *The Forge and the Crucible* which is about myths of technology, having to do with the transition from Paleolithic to Neolithic and the discovery of metals, elaborations of metal-working myths, and the uses of tools. Some cultures went one way and said the smith was a supremely gifted man. You get this in Finnish and Central Asian mythology.

DICKSON: Oh yes, Väinomöinen.

MIESEL: The Wondersmith. They said the smith had magic powers and mastery over fire and tied him into shamanism. Other cultures said the smith is a dangerous man, we must lame him lest he do evil or run away. And you have Wayland and Volund and Hephaestus and so forth. It's a very interesting book because it implies that the modern age is going to have to work out myths of modern technology, particularly communications technology, and come to terms with it symbolically before we can fully use it.

DICKSON: That's exactly right. Hopefully, the rewrite of the total Cycle—Good Lord, I haven't even finished it and here I'm talking about the rewrite! It's way down the pike, ten or twelve years away. By that time I may be able to get a statement in on that end of it.

MIESEL: You know, it might have been easier if you had attempted a pop psychology best-seller?

DICKSON: I probably would have made more money that way and had more time to do other things.

MIESEL: And become an overnight sensation.

DICKSON: The trouble is, if I'd done something like that . . .

MIESEL: It would have been a misuse of your talent.

DICKSON: Yes. If you want to train yourself to throw *shurikin* Zen style where you think them into the targets and you take the time off to do it in a side show where you deliberately miss to build up the expectation of the audience, when you go back to thinking at the targets you find you'll have a hell of a time. And this is truer than a lot of creative writers and others think. A painter who grinds out illustrations without doing his best on them, a hack who cranks out things, spend the rest of their lives getting over it.

MIESEL: That's like the theory of magic. If you misuse the Power the Power will desert you.

DICKSON: I think that theory of magic came out of actual human experience.

MIESEL: But isn't it terribly arrogant to do exactly what one wishes and expect to be rewarded for it?

DICKSON: I've spent my whole life operating on the principle that exactly that should happen.

MIESEL: But it doesn't happen.

DICKSON: Oh yes it does. Keep going and it happens. Let's use the Cycle as a horrible example. Here I started out writing something that nobody understood and largely misunderstood and was consequently put down as a writer totally unlike what I actually am. And what is the end result, ten or twenty years later? I'm surrounded by friends, people are starting to pick it up, life is good, you know, the future is bright, and so forth. How did I get there? Just by simply going ahead anyway and lo and behold . . . Try it!

GORDON R. DICKSON